# FINDING

# REBECCA

# FINDING REBECCA

## EOIN DEMPSEY

LAKE UNION
PUBLISHING

Text copyright © 2014 Eoin Dempsey
All rights reserved.

Published by Lake Union Publishing, Seattle

www.apub.com

Amazon, the Amazon logo, and Lake Union Publishing are trademarks of Amazon.com, Inc., or its affiliates.

ISBN-13: 9781477826102
ISBN-10: 1477826106

Cover design by *theBookDesigners*
Library of Congress Control Number: 2014941172

Printed in the United States of America

*This book is for my wife, Jill*

# GERMAN MILITARY RANKS
## *and* DEFINITIONS

**Führer:** Adolf Hitler, the leader of the German Reich (Empire)

**Hauptsturmführer:** the SS equivalent of a captain

**Kapo:** a privileged prisoner who served as a barracks supervisor or led work details in a Nazi concentration camp

**Lagerführer:** SS officer responsible for discipline in the camp

**Lagerkommandant:** the head of a particular concentration camp—in Auschwitz, Rudolf Höss (1940–1943), Arthur Liebehenschel (1943–1944), and Richard Baer (1944–1945)

**Obersturmführer:** the equivalent of a first lieutenant in the US army

**Rapportführer:** a mid-level officer specific to the concentration-camp system, whose job was to oversee the officers below him who had more direct contact with the prisoners

**Reich:** the German Empire, specifically the Third Reich, which existed under the Nazis from 1933 to 1945

**Reichsführer:** Heinrich Himmler, the leader of the SS and Hitler's second-in-command

**Sonderkommando:** a work unit of Nazi concentration camp prisoners, composed almost entirely of Jews, forced under threat of death to aid with the disposal of victims of the gas chambers

**SS:** an elite military unit of the Nazi Party, which, after being founded as a guard for the Nazi Party itself, grew into an army of more than a million highly trained soldiers who were solely responsible for the guarding of the concentration camps

**Standartenführer:** the equivalent of a colonel in the US army

**Sturmmann:** a storm trooper, the equivalent of a regular enlisted soldier

**Untersturmführer:** the equivalent of a second lieutenant in the US army

**Wehrmacht:** the regular German armed forces, not involved in the running of the concentration camps

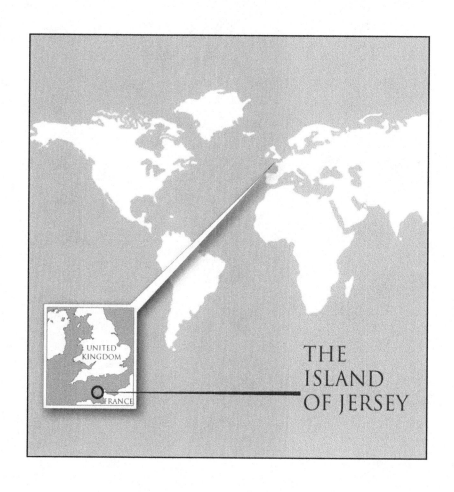

THE
ISLAND
OF JERSEY

# CHAPTER

---

## 1

*Auschwitz-Birkenau, September 1943*

The car pulled up outside a line of thirty warehouses in three rows of ten, each about forty feet wide and two hundred feet long. The driver opened the door for Rapportführer Friedrich, and Christopher got out after him.

"This is where you will be doing the majority of your work," Friedrich said. He took the ledger out from under his arm and lifted a piece of paper on top, looking underneath. "I see you've been selected for this position as a result of your background in accounting."

Christopher nodded. The barbed wire stood taut at the end of the rows of warehouses and behind. "I'm glad to see we have a professional to help out. I was a lawyer back in Frankfurt before the war myself. It says here you're a German but came to us from the occupied territories."

"Yes, I was living in Jersey before it was liberated."

"A blessed day I'm sure." Friedrich dropped the piece of paper back down onto the ledger, which he handed to his driver. "As an

SS officer, I'm sure you're more than aware of the importance of the job we have here."

"Of course, Herr Rapportführer."

"Such a strange accent."

It was a warm September day and Christopher felt a bead of sweat run down his back. His new uniform was painfully tight around his shoulders. Somewhere there was a band playing. He could hear the strains of Pachelbel's Canon in D, faint on the wind.

"There are too many tribes in Europe, too many differences, too much potential for conflict and war. You only need to look at the history of Europe to see the effect that this has had. Do you study history? Of course you do. I'm sure that was why you asked to be stationed here, to be at the hub of history? I feel the same way myself. We have much in common."

"Yes, Herr Friedrich."

"And the worst among these tribes has always been the Jews. They're responsible for this war. Facilities such as this one are in place to make sure that wars like this one never happen again. You understand that, don't you, Herr Seeler?"

"Yes, Herr Rapportführer, of course." A large concrete building stood four hundred feet away, its massive chimney extending twenty feet into the air, spewing out thick black smoke. Friedrich was speaking again.

"The point I'm trying to make is that we must be hard as granite. This is something I tell all my new officers. The work we do here is too important to be stained by any form of sympathy or compassion for the prisoners," he spat. "Any form of weakness, particularly toward the prisoners themselves, will not be tolerated. I need only hardened, passionately committed SS men. Do you understand me, Herr Obersturmführer?"

"Of course, Herr Rapportführer, I understand very well."

"Like all vermin, the Jew has learned to adapt, and with magnificent success. They know how to read our emotions, to tap into our fears. That is why this is the work that only a strong man could do, a man not susceptible to the vile efforts of the Jew to undermine all that is good in the world. You must know that any order given is for the good of the Reich and thus you must never question any order that you receive."

"I welcome the task, Herr Rapportführer."

"Good, good, I thought you'd say that. Yours is a very important task. With the expansion of our activities here, we have the need of a dedicated officer in charge of the redistribution of funds back to the Reich." They walked along the line of warehouses. The door to the warehouse in front of them was open. Inside there were perhaps twenty relatively healthy-looking women, sorting through suitcases with chalk markings scrawled on the outside. None looked up as they approached the door. Every few seconds one of them would step forward to pitch an armful of clothing into a massive pile or to dispatch jewelry onto a long desk overseen by armed SS guards.

"You will oversee the Sonderkommandos, the Jewish workforce we have here, in their duties of sorting through the goods and valuables that we are able to reclaim. You will then sort and dispatch them back to the Reich. Their safe passage will be your responsibility. I appreciate that it might take time to come up with a system, but please be expedient. The needs of the camp are too great to put up with any kind of laziness or inefficiency."

Friedrich motioned for Christopher to follow him, and they both took a few steps back. "You will be in charge of these." Friedrich pointed in the general direction of the warehouses in front of them. "Now, needless to say, corruption is not tolerated here. Be watchful both of yourself and others. The Political Department is always watching. As you know, they have the power to search anyone at any time, and are also constantly on the lookout for any unauthorized contact with the prisoners. If you are caught stealing, or embezzling as you accountants like to say, the punishment will be swift and harsh, but I'm sure there'll be no need for anything like that."

"Of course not, Herr Rapportführer."

"I'm curious, Herr Seeler; you've risen through the ranks quickly. It's most unusual for a new recruit to come in as an Obersturmführer."

"I'm an accountant, Herr Rapportführer. That rank was conferred upon me so the other bookkeepers will accept my authority."

"Even with that, I was under the impression your role would be filled by a wounded veteran. It's hard to believe that a young, able-bodied man from the United Kingdom was able to join the SS and secure a position here so quickly."

"The losses that our brave soldiers have endured has made it easier for someone like me who lived in a foreign country to join the SS. Now everyone has a chance to serve in Hitler's elite, native Germans and foreigners alike. It was a relief that I was able to fulfill my dream of becoming an SS soldier. After all, I was born in Berlin, Herr Friedrich."

Christopher didn't mention the enormous bribes his uncle had given to secure his position in the camp or, of course, his true reason for being there. The lies came easier with practice and Friedrich seemed happy with Christopher's answer.

"Walk with me." Friedrich went between two warehouses, and Christopher scuttled to catch up with him. It was strangely quiet. Christopher wondered where all the prisoners were. He had heard that there were thousands of them. "So, had you heard of our facility before you were stationed here?"

"I had. My uncle told me about it. He is an officer in the Wehrmacht, stationed on the Eastern Front."

"And how did he hear of the camp?"

"My uncle knew of my desires to serve the Reich and researched where I might be stationed."

"Our work here, although of vital importance, cannot be spoken of. I have no need to remind you of the oath of loyalty you took."

"I remind myself of it every day, Herr Rapportführer."

"Good to hear, young Herr Seeler. With men like you here, we will make the Führer proud." They emerged from the third row of warehouses in front of a large brick building. It looked like a massive farmhouse, stretching several hundred feet in length. "These buildings are new, only constructed two months ago. This is where you will be gathering the goods and belongings. This is a good time. It's always better to show new people around when it's empty. When we get a shipment in, things can get a little hectic."

Friedrich led him toward the entrance to the building and past several prisoners. They looked fit and seemed well fed. Each prisoner was carrying a tool of some sort, or pushing an empty cart. They walked through a small anteroom, which led straight into a large changing room lined with benches along the walls and up the middle. There were hooks every few feet along the benches. Each hook was numbered. The room was completely empty, windowless, and the air inside was thick. Christopher wanted to leave as soon as he walked in.

"You will organize the collection of the clothes and valuables of the undesirables liquidated here." The word "liquidated" reverberated through him, and he thought of Rebecca. He felt his legs weaken beneath him and immediately sat down on the closest bench. "This is no time to be taking a rest. There is much work to be done." He followed Friedrich back out through the anteroom, past the massive steel door with the peephole and the sign that read: "Harmful Gas! Entering Endangers Your Life."

Christopher sucked the air outside deep into his chest. Friedrich was already walking ahead. Christopher jogged to catch up with him, trying to slow down his breathing, trying to control his pulse. "I'm sure you can see the nature of our work here and why it is so sensitive."

Christopher didn't answer for a few seconds but then caught himself. "Yes, Herr Rapportführer, sensitive and important in equal measure."

"Yes, that is it. That is one of the crematoria you will be drawing the repatriated goods from. There are three others; soon there will likely be more. It seems that our work is never done here." Friedrich led Christopher back toward the car. "Your office is last along this row, but that also may change over time." The driver saluted as Friedrich approached, and held the door open for the two men. Christopher saw his hands were shaking and thrust them into his pockets. His heart was hammering in his chest, and he struck his head on the roof of the car as he got in. Friedrich seemed not to notice. The drive to the end of the row of warehouses took only a few seconds with Friedrich talking all the way—something about responsibilities and honor—but Christopher wasn't listening anymore.

The car pulled up at the end of the line of warehouses. It might have been quicker to walk. Friedrich strode ahead, still talking as he went, to a wooden door with a large glass window. Christopher opened it to let him walk inside. There were three other men in the room, who looked up as they entered. Friedrich led him through the room to a door to a private office. Bookshelves filled with files and ledgers lined the walls, and a window looked out onto a bleak yard outside. A wooden desk, clean except for a telephone and a stack of papers in the corner, sat with a large safe behind it. "This will be your office, although I expect you will spend much of your time in the warehouses and crematoria." They walked back out to where the other men were sitting. "Let me introduce you to your support staff." The other three men stood up. "Firstly this is

Karl Flick." A portly man with glasses stepped forward and shook Christopher's hand with a cold, wet palm. "This is Wolfgang Breitner." Breitner stepped forward, a small man with a large nose, who smiled as he greeted Christopher. "And this is Toni Müller." A tall, serious-looking man shook his hand.

"Welcome, Herr Obersturmführer. We look forward to working with you," Müller said. "I'm sure you have many great ideas for the reorganization of the accounting processes here."

"Yes, I do," Christopher replied, relieved to hear no trace of a tremor in his voice. "It seems a quiet day today, so we will need to prepare for the next shipment coming in. When is that due, Herr Rapportführer?"

"Tomorrow, I believe," Friedrich said, looking at his watch. "I should be leaving now. The men will show you to your quarters when the workday is over. Welcome to Auschwitz, Herr Seeler."

Friedrich closed the door behind him, and Christopher looked over at his new colleagues, his subordinates. Each had already sat back down at his desk and was poring over papers and ledgers. Christopher excused himself, walked to the bathroom at the end of the hall, and locked himself inside the farthest stall. He sat on the seat of the toilet for as long as he dared, clutching his knees close into his chest.

He counted down ten minutes before returning to his office. He shuffled the papers in the corner of the desk and laid them out to read. The accounts showed the enormous numbers of people coming through the camp. Many thousands were coming in every week, but only thirty thousand or so workers were required to work in the local factories. The huts in the main camp couldn't house any more than a few thousand workers. He couldn't make sense of it. The numbers didn't add up. In the desk, there were ledgers of the amounts "repatriated" back to the Reich from the prisoners, ledgers of reichsmarks, dollars, pounds, lire, pesetas, francs, Russian rubles, and every currency that he had ever heard of. There was a river of money running through the camp, a river whose course he was to control.

His colleagues led him down to the mess hall after work. The portions were large, and unlike at the SS training camp, the food was actually quite good. He was to share quarters with another young officer from the camp guard itself, Franz Lahm, a friendly young Untersturmführer from Regensburg. Lahm tried to get him to come out, to meet the other SS men, to see the cinema, the theater, or even the brothel available to the guards.

"Oh, come on. Come drink with us. If you go to bed early every time there's a new shipment, you'll never stay up with us."

"You go ahead. It's just that it's my first day. I'll meet everyone tomorrow night, I promise."

Lahm came in at three a.m., tripped on the table in the middle of the room, and fell asleep where he'd fallen. Within a few seconds the sound of his snoring filled the room. Christopher didn't react; he had been awake, alone in the dark, wondering how he would ever find Rebecca in all this mess of chaos and death.

# CHAPTER

## 2

"Herr Seeler, time to wake up. The shipment is coming in soon. We need to be down at the railway station in half an hour," Flick said.

Christopher's eyes were heavy from lack of sleep. Lahm was already gone, his spare uniform hanging on the closet door. There were tiny bloodstains on the cuffs. Christopher immediately recoiled but felt Flick watching him. He got up and changed into his uniform. He looked at himself in the mirror and took a deep breath, watching his chest expand and contract. He fixed his collar and walked out into the hallway. Flick was waiting and nodded before leading him into the dull morning sun. He handed Christopher a ledger. On the top sheet the numbers for the day were written in black. There was a shipment coming in from Lodz. The number on the ledger said 1200.

"Poles," Flick said. "They should be in pretty good condition. It's only a short journey. Have you been at a selection before?"

"Not as such, no."

"We just stand at the back and make sure that the luggage is taken care of. The Sonderkommandos will be there to do the lifting work. It's easy." Flick looked at Christopher through thick glasses. "Don't worry. They know it's your first day here. This will be very simple. Our work comes later."

"Thank you, but I'm sure I'll be able to handle this." He held his hands behind his back, after handing the ledger to Flick.

The train station looked like almost any other, with signs and a timetable pinned to the wall above the platform. The station house was dark inside and the door was locked. Other SS men gathered past the platform, including several in white coats. Emaciated prisoners, much thinner and sicker than the ones he'd seen the previous day, were running around, pushing ramps and pulling carts into place. One man slumped so much his chest almost touched the cart as he pushed it. Christopher couldn't believe that the half-starved figures of the prisoners could move as fast as they did. SS men were everywhere. Most of the SS were screaming at the prisoners, their own cacophony mixing with that of the dogs who struggled against the leashes that barely held them back. The train arrived. It moved past the platform. Christopher counted the carriages. The numbers were wrong. *How can twelve hundred people fit into a train that small, built for cattle transport?* When the train came to a halt, the doors slid back, and immediately the shouts of the SS men intensified, drowning out all but the sounds of the dogs snarling and barking. The Jewish prisoners ran to the open cattle truck and helped the people off the train. Bewildered men and women climbed out, looking around before running to one side or the other. Their faces were lined and thin, their mouths clamped shut. The SS men were on them immediately. Children and the elderly piled off onto the gravel of the train station. One old man had to be carried out. Several of the women held babies in their arms. The people were hustled into separate lines as soon as they clambered off the railroad cars, men in one line, women and children in the other.

The cars disgorged their human cargo within a few minutes. It was impossible to ignore the cries of the women as they were wrenched apart from their children; the fearful sounds of the dogs and the incessant shouting of the SS men in both German and Polish. Christopher took a deep breath, resisting the temptation to draw his hands up to his face. Flick stood still beside him. He seemed bored. The SS went into the train, guns drawn. Dead bodies were thrown out of the rail cars. They landed on the ground like loose sacks of sticks, the bones cracking as they fell, the blood from their wounds draining into the brown dirt on the ground. Another shot rang out, and the body of a young girl was thrown out onto the dirt. Christopher's blood was ice in his veins, and a helpless panic ran through him. The SS guards were still screaming at the lines of people, though the selection was now over. There were two new lines, one of younger, fitter-looking people, and then the rest, the older people and the children. The line of younger adults was maybe one or two hundred at the most, and they were marched off, back up toward Auschwitz. The rest of the people huddled together, easily a thousand strong, and the shouting of the SS began to die down.

Christopher turned to Flick. "How often do transports like this one arrive?"

"That depends. Sometimes we get several in one week, sometimes, several in one day. That's when the real work begins. One time . . ."

Christopher was not listening anymore. He couldn't fix on any one person in the crowd. He walked closer, completely ignoring Flick, completely ignoring everything except the mass of people, packed together, waiting to be taken away. He saw a middle-aged woman with a bright blue headscarf that seemed to have no business in a place like this. She held her baby tight to her chest. She was crying, but the baby was quiet. Breitner and Müller were looking through some of the suitcases left behind as the prisoners loaded them from their carts onto trucks. He motioned to Flick before walking toward Müller and Breitner. The SS men were noticeably calmer as they stood alongside the column of people waiting to be moved along. The terror in the eyes of the people had not changed, however, and the dogs still surged forward if any stepped out of line. The column of people began marching up toward Birkenau.

Another shot rang out from behind him and he swiveled around. Several SS men were poring over the piles of clothing left behind. "Ah, here we are, there's always at least one," a soldier said as he turned a coat over to reveal the shuddering form of a small boy crying for his mother. Christopher started toward him to bring him into the line. The SS man raised his rifle and shot the child in the face. Christopher stood frozen. The SS man shouldered his rifle and dragged the boy by the foot out of the pile of clothes and dumped his limp body in front of the railroad cars with the others. Christopher looked around at the other guards, wide-eyed, expecting something. They all carried on as normal. He turned around to walk toward Müller and Breitner. He stood back, about ten feet from them, a safe distance where they couldn't see the feelings coursing through him, in his eyes. They greeted him with a glance as he walked over.

*They are expecting an order,* he said to himself, *so give them one.* "I want all these cases loaded away within ten minutes, and all of these clothes. Is all this in order? Will the rest of the prisoners be keeping their belongings with them on their journey to the labor camp?"

Müller looked out of the side of his eyes at Breitner and then back at Christopher. "No, all the suitcases are still here; we will collect the rest of the prisoners' belongings once they get changed for their disinfection procedures." Christopher tried to slow his heart, to calm himself. The last of the prisoners were leaving. "Herr Obersturmführer, you should probably go up to the changing rooms. They're in number three, I believe," Müller said.

"Yes, of course. Herr Breitner, come along with me, please. I trust I can leave the procurement and cleanup of all that remains here to you, Herr Müller."

"Yes, Herr Obersturmführer, it will be done within the hour." Christopher didn't answer. Breitner motioned toward a waiting car. Christopher sat in the passenger seat, with Breitner driving. Breitner followed the column of people as they made their way up into the camp at Birkenau. Christopher saw the woman with the blue headscarf again for a brief second before she blended back into the crowd.

The SS guards were waiting with the Sonderkommandos, who were all prisoners themselves and were lined up at the side of the yard. The building that Friedrich had shown him the day before loomed behind the crowd. The SS men all carried truncheons. Behind them, lurking in the background, were the officers, including Friedrich. The people arrived onto the hard ground of the yard. They mostly wore dark clothes, and all carried the yellow Star of David insignia. The guards in the towers overlooking the yard were training their machine guns on the crowd.

"Herr Obersturmführer, you should meet the leader of the Sonderkommandos. They will be carrying out your orders." Christopher followed Breitner across the yard where the crowd of people had gathered in a huge group speaking Polish and Yiddish. The mood of the people had been lightened considerably by the behavior of the SS men, who had been polite and calm with them as they arrived in the yard, greeting them with smiling faces and even chatting and laughing with some of them. They directed the people like traffic policemen, evenly across the yard. One SS man patted an elderly man on the back, and helped him along. The people murmured among themselves. They still seemed nervous and suspicious. Friedrich and the other officers had disappeared. Breitner led him over to where the dozen or so Sonderkommandos were lined up. A tall, handsome man stood at the head of the line.

"This is Jan Schultz, head of the Sonderkommando unit working in the crematoria," Breitner explained. Christopher remembered not to proffer a handshake. "These men will go through the belongings the prisoners leave behind before turning them over to us."

"Very good," Christopher said, inspecting the line of men who stared straight ahead. Most had bruising on their faces. "Work hard, men, and you will be rewarded," he added.

Someone had begun to address the people behind him. The crowd fell silent. All eyes were on Friedrich who, with the other two officers, was now standing on the back of the flat end of a truck. "You have come here, to Auschwitz-Birkenau, as a vital cog in the war machinery of the Reich," Friedrich began. "You have come here to work. Your job is almost as important as those brave soldiers risking their lives every day on the front. All those willing to work will be safe and well fed." Friedrich addressed the crowd in German and, while most seemed to understand, there was a Sonderkommando below who was translating into Polish as he spoke.

The officer on Friedrich's left took over. "You have arrived here after a somewhat arduous journey. You are valuable to this camp and the Reich. First and foremost, we want to make sure that you are healthy and willing to work. For this purpose we will require that you shower and be disinfected. This is very important for the sake of your own ongoing health and well-being. We cannot tolerate any infections to spread among our workers." People in the crowd were smiling and hugging their children tighter, moving from foot to foot. Life came back to their faces; suspicion eroded by the light of hope. The officer continued. "Once you have your showers there will be a hot bowl of soup waiting for you."

The third officer stepped forward to speak. He pointed down at a man at the front of the crowd. "You there, yes, you, what is your trade?" The man was a carpenter. "Oh, very good, we have need for those," the officer replied. "You will be very useful to the cause. And you, what about you?"

"I am a doctor," the man replied.

"Excellent, we have urgent need for doctors in our camp hospital." He paused to look out over the crowd. "If there are any more doctors or nurses here, please make sure to report to me after your shower, and I will make sure you are stationed where your skills are most urgently needed."

Friedrich stepped forward once more. "We have need for doctors, dentists, nurses, mechanics, plumbers, electricians, and craftsmen of all kinds. But we will also need unskilled workers as well. All will be given well-paid work. All are important to the Reich and our fight against the threat of Bolshevism. Now please make your way down to the entrance to the changing room as the guards are directing you. Once inside, make sure to hang your clothes on the clearly numbered hooks and to make sure to remember these numbers for later. We only have one changing facility, which must be shared by both sexes—my apologies for this situation, which we are in the process of having amended." It was with smiling, reassured faces that the people herded through the entrance to the flat-roofed building and into the changing room. Christopher saw the woman with the blue headscarf again. Her face was doleful, resigned, different from the others.

Once they were all inside, the Sonderkommandos followed them and Christopher with them. The people changed and folded their clothes into neat piles below their coats, which hung from the numbered hooks. The Sonderkommandos repeated the instructions that the officers had given the crowd from the roof, this time in their native tongue. The people complied without any struggle or argument. He walked along the rows of people changing. He left and walked outside, not wanting to add to the prisoners' embarrassment at changing in front of other people. Relief coursed through his system. *The selection was a nightmare, the murder of the people at the train an indescribable horror, but at least that's over,* he thought to himself as he walked out into the now mainly empty yard.

Christopher stood alone in the yard and exhaled. Then he noticed the SS men on the flat roof of the building. The officers had gone. The remaining SS men carried metal canisters and wore gas masks. His blood froze. *They can't be doing this, not now, not after what they said.* He fought the urge to run back inside, to warn the prisoners. There was nothing he could do now. There was no way to change what was about to happen. Horror overtook him. He looked around the yard to make sure that no one was watching him. The SS men continued their practiced movements, looking almost insectoid in their gas masks, buzzing about the roof with drone-like efficiency. They removed covers from narrow metallic chimneys on top of the crematorium and poured the contents of the canisters down. Then the screaming began—hundreds of voices in concert but distinctly separate—unmitigated by the layers of brick and concrete. Trucks backed into the yard. The drivers fired their engines, revving them in an attempt to drown out the cries coming from inside. He could still hear them.

An SS man walking past cut a smile. "The water in those showers must be too hot," he observed. "The Jews don't like it."

The SS man walked on, and it was all Christopher could do to remain standing. The effort of not breaking down was numbing his entire body. He felt his uniform as a second skin and ran each open palm along the sleeves. His cap fell off as he bent his head down to his chest. Still the screaming went on, dulling now. He tried to think of Jersey, of Rebecca, of when they'd met, of anything but this. He wondered if he was too late, if she had succumbed as these people had this day. If she had died, what was there left for him now, in this place?

# CHAPTER

---

## 3

*The island of Jersey, June 1924*

It might have been his first week or first day living on the island when he met her. Christopher left his father in the house with Uncle Uli, who had come over with them from Germany to help them move. Alexandra was asleep upstairs. Christopher pushed the front door open and ran down the dirt track, which sprawled five hundred yards down to the beach and the sea. He picked up a smooth gray stone and hurled it as far as he could out into the blue water, then picked up another and ran down toward the seagulls resting on the shore. He threw the stone out toward them as they took off and watched them soar into the sky. He sat down on the rock where the birds had been, passing pebbles from one hand to another, listening to the sound they made as they clashed. The sun was hot again that day, and his green flannel shorts were heavy on his legs. His shoes and socks slipped off easily, and he walked out into the thin water a few feet from the shore. His father had forbidden him to go swimming on his own, and even though he could think of nothing more wonderful than to run out into the sea, Christopher obeyed. He watched his toes through the surf and felt the cool water lapping at his ankles. The huge expanse of land across the blue waters was France, less than twenty miles away. His father had told him so.

He wasn't sure what the noise was at first—it seemed to be coming from a fence just across the road that ran alongside the beach. He pulled his socks onto his wet feet and stepped into his shoes. He ran across the beach toward the sound of the wailing. As he drew closer, he became more convinced that it was a kitten and wondered if Father would let him keep it. The gray road that stretched along the shore was rough and unkempt. There was a small hedge running parallel to the road. Christopher looked both ways and made sure there were no cars coming. He waited a few seconds to be sure and then scuttled across, following the wail along the hedgerow. He called out in German and then remembered himself. Father had told him to speak in English, the language of his mother, who had grown up here. The first words he called out were a whisper that he hardly even heard himself. The wailing stopped. He called out again and heard a rustling through the bush directly in front of him. The bush was too high to see over. He struggled up and over it, and fell onto the grass below.

It wasn't a kitten. A girl was crying, her head bobbing up and down between her arms. She had a wide bruise spilling across her cheek. He stood in silence for a few seconds, not confident enough to speak in English, but eventually he began.

"Why are you crying?" She pushed her head back down between her knees. He thought the words through in his head, hearing his mother's voice. "My name is Christopher. I am six. What age are you?"

"I'm six too," came the tiny voice up through the folded arms and the dark blond hair. "My name is Rebecca."

"Why are you down here alone?"

"Will you run away with me?"

"I'm not sure. Perhaps . . ."

That was seemingly enough for her, and Rebecca stood up and took his hand. There was a small house about a hundred yards away. She took a few steps back toward it and stopped.

"Where should we go?" she asked. Christopher tried to think of somewhere, while he looked back at her looking at him. He didn't know anywhere except his own house and the beach. He led Rebecca through a gap in the hedgerow and across the road, making sure that there was no one around. They ran down toward the sea. She asked where they were going. He didn't answer; he just ran, clutching on to Rebecca's hand as they went. They arrived down at the water's edge and he turned to her.

"What happened to your face?" he asked. She didn't answer. She picked up a stone and hurled it into the sea. He began to look for stones to skim, just as Uncle Uli had taught him. He picked up a few flat stones, ran his fingers over them, imagined them skipping across the sea.

"Have you ever skimmed stones?"

"No. I don't think so."

"Here," he said, placing the stone into her hand, parallel to the water in front of them. "Try to throw it onto the water so it will make them skip along."

Rebecca drew her arm back. The stone flew about three feet, barely landing in the white ruffles of surf lapping against the shore. He placed another flat stone into her palm. She threw it again and the same thing happened. Unperturbed, he gave her another stone, and then another and then went to look for more until she had thrown about thirty stones into the surf at their feet. "Isn't this fun?" she said.

They played on the beach for an hour or so before he heard his father. He told her to hide; that he would come back down for her in a few minutes, and she scuttled behind a rock and stayed there. The voice came closer, and his father's familiar silhouette appeared.

His father called him for dinner and turned immediately to walk back. Once, he might have chased him down the beach and carried him, laughing, above his head back to the house, but he never did anything like that anymore, not since Christopher's mother died. Rebecca looked over at Christopher from her hiding place. He followed behind his father, losing ground with every step. Once his father was far enough ahead, he sprinted back to Rebecca.

"Come with me." He extended his hand to her. "Don't worry, you'll be safe."

Dinner was on the table when he arrived back. Uncle Uli picked him up and sat him down at the dinner table in between himself and Alexandra. His father didn't look at him, just at the plate of food in front of him. They spoke German at dinner, even though Father wanted them to start speaking English all the time.

"So how was your day down at the beach?" Uncle Uli asked. "You were gone for quite a while."

"It was fine."

"We had a very productive day painting the house, didn't we, Stefan?"

"Yes, we did," Christopher's father answered. Uncle Uli reached across to Alexandra and pinched her cheek, but no one spoke. They ate in silence for a few seconds before the crash came from upstairs.

"What was that?" Christopher's father said. "Do you know what that was, Christopher?"

"I don't know." He shrugged, his head in his plate. Another thump, followed by gentle footsteps, came through the floorboards above their heads.

"Christopher, have you something to tell us?" Uncle Uli asked. "Did you bring a cat home? Your father made it clear last time you did this."

"No, no. There's nothing there. It must have been the wind."

"We'll see," his father said, forcing his chair backward. "Come on.

You had better hope it was the wind, after all the trouble you've given me lately."

"No, Father, no. There's nothing up there. Can't we finish dinner?"

Christopher's father grabbed him by the arm and dragged him off the chair. Uli said something, but his brother ignored him. Alexandra followed them out of the kitchen and past the bare floors and onto the freshly sanded staircase. Another crash sounded upstairs and Alexandra laughed. Christopher tried to wriggle free, but his father's grip was too tight. His father forced him up the stairs and straight for the door to his room, which he threw open with a loud crack.

She was sitting in the middle of the floor, Christopher's mother's pearls hanging around her neck and one of her hats almost covering her eyes completely. Christopher grimaced as he saw her. He had told her to stay in the closet until he came back up. But she had come out and knocked over a carafe of water on the bedside table. Uncle Uli was laughing behind them, but his father certainly wasn't.

"Who is this, Christopher?" he said in English.

"It's my friend Rebecca."

"And where does Rebecca live?"

"I don't know."

Christopher's father let go of his son's arm and bent down to the little girl sitting on the floor in his dead wife's hat and pearls. "Did you hurt yourself?" he said, reaching down toward the puce-shaded bruise on the side of her face. She didn't speak. "Where do you live, Rebecca?" She took the hat off and pointed out the window.

Christopher's father took the hat into his hand and helped her take the pearls off from around her neck. "You live over there, do you? Is it far?" The little girl shook her head slowly and stood up. "Do your parents know you're here?" Again the girl shook her head. "Well, don't you think they will be worried?"

"No."

"Of course they will be," Christopher's father said, running his hand through his hair, but she got up and walked over toward the window. Christopher knew he wasn't getting away with this, no matter how cute the little girl happened to be. "Are you hungry?" he asked after a few seconds. "Would you like some food?"

Rebecca nodded, a sad expression on her face.

*Why couldn't she have stayed in the closet? It was no good being sorry now. So much for her plans to run away from home.*

Uncle Uli led everyone back downstairs. Christopher's father was trying to see where she lived and who was there, but she wasn't talking. He set up a chair for her at the table, and they all sat down to dinner again.

Uncle Uli was first to speak, smiling again. "Christopher, where did you meet your new friend? What brings her here to visit us?"

Christopher prodded at the potatoes on his plate. How could he tell them that Rebecca had tried to run away, and that he was only trying to help her? "I met her near the beach. She was crying, so I thought she needed some help."

"Bringing her back to the house and sticking her in your wardrobe isn't going to help her," Christopher's father said. Uncle Uli was laughing again. "Uli, please, I'm talking to my son here." He glared at his younger brother. Uli was still laughing but moved his hand up to cover his mouth. Christopher's father shook his head and moved his attention back to his son, who seemed to be trying to slide underneath the table. "Where does this little girl live? What happened to her face?"

"I don't know. I heard her crying in a field near the beach. I thought she could stay here for a while." He hoped that Rebecca didn't speak German and couldn't understand.

"Oh, did you? You were going to hide her in your room, were you? How long were you going to keep her there for?"

Christopher looked at his plate, at eye level now. "I don't know, I hadn't thought about that."

"There's a shock," his father said. "You never think, do you?" Rebecca had stopped eating.

Although the sun was still high in the summer sky, it was seven o'clock and time for Alexandra to go to bed. She couldn't stay up as late as Christopher as she was two years younger, not even four yet. Uli picked her up and brought her over to kiss her father. Christopher's father kissed her on the cheek. Alexandra waved down toward Rebecca, who managed a smile back. Uli took her upstairs, still laughing as he went.

"Rebecca," Christopher's father said in a low voice, "you need to tell us where you live. I know that if Christopher or Alexandra were out at this time of the evening, I would be very worried. Now, you don't want anyone to be worried about you, do you?"

Rebecca shook her head. Christopher's father had opened his mouth to speak again when she answered. "I live two houses away. I spilled my tea and Mother hit me. She fell down and I ran out."

His father stood up from the table. "I think I need to see your parents now, Rebecca. It's time to take you home." When she tried to squirm away from him, he picked her up and headed for the front door. "Uli, I'm taking her home," he shouted over his shoulder. Christopher ran out behind his father. "It would be good for you to see Rebecca's parents," his father remarked upon noticing him. "They're probably half-sick with worry." He put Rebecca down as they reached the road. "Now promise to be good and hold my hand." Rebecca gave Christopher a pleading look, but did as she was told. They set off down the road, with him lagging a few feet behind. "This is some way to meet the neighbors," his father muttered.

They shuffled along the road for a few moments in silence before Rebecca spoke. "That one's mine." She pointed to a small house just off the road, unkempt and weather-beaten, much like their own before they had arrived and started painting it. Rebecca was slowing now with each step and Christopher's father almost had to drag her into the driveway. Christopher ran to catch up with them and took Rebecca's free hand as they walked up to the house. Silent tears dripped down her reddened cheeks. Christopher's father walked up to the door, peeled and flaking brown flecks of varnish. The window by the door was gray and unwashed with a layer of spiderwebs visible through it. *Can't we just go home?* Christopher thought. There was no sound from inside. Christopher's father looked down at Rebecca as he knocked once more.

"Your parents must be asleep," he said, more to himself than to Rebecca. "Do you have any brothers or sisters?"

"No, I don't."

He knocked harder this time and the door came ajar. "Is there anyone there? Hello?" No answer came and he pushed back the door to walk inside.

The house was musty and old. They entered into a hallway with the kitchen on their left. The carpet was worn and threadbare and Christopher felt a nail jabbing into the bottom of his shoe, but he didn't speak. No one did. A shaft of light from an open window led them through the end of the hallway and into a living room with paintings of local scenery on the walls. There was a broken bottle on the floor, but there was no one there. Then they heard the voice from behind them, cracked and rough, uneven.

"Where the hell have you been?" They all turned around, and Rebecca hid behind Christopher's father's leg. A man in a faded suit stood in the doorway. He looked older than Christopher's father, but Christopher couldn't guess by how much—his brown hair suggested a much younger man than the lines on his face. His dark eyes darted back and forth. "Who are you? What are you doing in my house? Why is my daughter with you?"

Christopher's father stepped forward and proffered his hand. The man shook it, saying nothing. "My name is Stefan Seeler," his father said. His words were slow and deliberate. "My son found Rebecca on the beach earlier today. It seems she was in some distress." The man's face changed upon hearing his father's heavy German accent. His eyes bulged.

"You are German." The man's accent was French. Christopher's father nodded. The man continued. "She's always getting into some kind of trouble, clumsy . . . You know children these days." The man rocked backward slightly as he spoke. Christopher watched his father as he listened, saw his jaw tighten.

"Christopher, could you take Rebecca outside for a moment, please?"

"That won't be necessary. Thank you for bringing back my daughter, but now you must leave, before my wife comes home."

Christopher's father looked down at the little girl clinging tight to his trouser leg, and then down at his own son. "Come on, Christopher, let's go." He bent down to Rebecca. "We have to leave now, but you know you can always . . ."

"Goodbye, Mr. Seeler." Rebecca's father walked over, grabbing Rebecca by the arm. He walked her into a back room, and Christopher and his father were alone.

# CHAPTER

---

4

Rebecca came to the house again the next morning. She was sitting in the tree house that Uncle Uli had made for them in the back garden. She smiled as Christopher ran down toward her. Alex came out of the house and ran down too.

"Rebecca. You came back." She only nodded.

"How did you know about the tree house?"

"I found it." She had brought an old doll with her and, although it had an eye missing and was scratched and worn, its hair was perfectly combed. She held the doll close to her chest. "This is Susan."

"Alexandra has dolls too, don't you, Alex?" he asked as his father arrived too.

"Children, I'd like to speak to Rebecca for a moment."

"Hello, Mr. Seeler."

"Hello there, pretty one." He smiled. "Rebecca, did you ask your parents if you could come over here and play?"

She went back to playing with her doll without answering the question.

"Do they even know where you are?"

"They were still in bed."

"They were still in bed when you left this morning? Don't you think you should have told them where you were going?"

"I don't know. They were up very late last night. I could hear them talking."

"Do you miss your parents when they're not around?"

She shrugged.

"Can Rebecca stay here with us, Father?" Christopher asked. The look his father gave him silenced him immediately. He reached over and took Rebecca's hand and felt her fingers clasp around his.

"All right, you can stay here for a few hours, Rebecca. Uncle Uli is going to look after you. I will be back soon, and we'll see about you coming over to play."

They played in the tree house for a while and then Uli took them down to the rock pools and they waded through the cool water with their shoes and socks in their hands and the sun warm on their faces. They wanted to go swimming but had forgotten their swimsuits. They stayed at the rock pools and threw stones instead. Uli taught them how to throw them so that they flew faster, and they watched the ripples in the water as the stones plinked in. They stayed down there all morning. When Uli brought them back up to the house, Christopher's father was waiting for them.

"Hello, children, did you have a nice time down at the beach with Uncle Uli?" They all nodded in unison. "Uli, can you take Alexandra down to the tree house for a moment?"

"Of course, come on, little sunshine." Uli picked her up and brought her out to the garden.

"Sit down at the table, children," Christopher's father began. "Rebecca, you like coming here, don't you?"

"Yes, I wish I could stay here all the time." Christopher felt his heart jump as she answered.

"I spoke to your parents, both your parents." Rebecca's face froze. "After I saw your parents, I went down to the police station and I spoke to that nice policeman, Sergeant Higgins. He really knows everyone around here. I must tell you, Rebecca, that your father does not want you to come here and play. He doesn't want you to play in the tree house or with Christopher and Alexandra at all."

"But, Father . . ."

"Be quiet, Christopher. Let me finish." Christopher had never seen him quite like this before. "But I spoke to your mother and I've decided to let you play here."

Rebecca gasped. Christopher jumped up and down on the spot, clapping his hands.

"I thought long and hard about it and I really did not want to go against your father's wishes, but I think that it is for the best."

"Oh, thank you, Mr. Seeler."

"But if you get into any trouble, I will go straight down to your mother and tell her, and you'll never be able to come up to this house again. Do you understand?"

"Oh yes, of course. I will be really good."

Rebecca stayed that afternoon. Christopher's father let her stay for dinner too. She came again the next day and every day for the rest of that summer. They decorated the tree house with pictures they drew and laid out a tablecloth on the shelf. Every day was fun. There was always something new. Christopher had had friends before but never like Rebecca. He had never known someone who made everything into an adventure, who seemed to find joy in even the most mundane things.

Uli went home at the end of the summer. Christopher, Alex, and Rebecca wanted him to stay forever, but he couldn't. The children cried when they saw him off at the ferry in Saint Helier. Christopher's father hugged him so roughly that Christopher thought he was trying to smother him.

School started again. Rebecca went to an all-girls school in Les Croix, but it barely mattered that they were in different schools because Rebecca still came to visit almost every day. Her mother rarely cooked and when she did, Rebecca said she could hardly touch it. So she began to stay with them for dinner too. She would usually ask if she could stay the night, but Christopher's father would never allow that. Christopher would walk her home each night, down the road to where the bush bent around and Rebecca's house came into view.

As they grew older, the letters they wrote became their way of arranging to see each other, a way that her father would never understand because the language was their own. They were surrounded by language. By the time Christopher was twelve, he was fluent in German and English and could understand whole conversations in French and even Jèrriais. What Rebecca lacked in German she made up for in French. But their language was different from any of them. *Gunde de viznay bin Lion's Mane reiv* would mean that they would meet at the Lion's Mane at four, the number on the end being the German but backward. It was a language only they knew and, apart from them, only Alexandra knew existed. They named all the crags and headlands beaten by the waves in winter and split by the summer sun. They would arrange to meet there, by the Lion's Mane, the Butterfly's Table, or the Angry Horse. When they met, they would speak in gibberish, as if their language was entire, and burst out laughing at the ridiculous sounds spilling out of each other's mouths and the puzzled looks of whoever happened to be there with them, whether that was Alexandra, or Percy Howard or his brother Tom. There were always children to play with.

# CHAPTER

5

It was 1934. Christopher was fifteen. Rebecca was sitting at the kitchen table as he arrived home from school. It was not unusual to see her there. But this was different. She had a large bruise staining her left cheek, and she was crying. Christopher's father sat beside her at the kitchen table, his face taut with dismal anger. It was the same anger that Christopher himself felt when Rebecca's father beat her. He sat down beside her at the table. He wanted to be the one to comfort her. He felt a pang of jealousy that it had been his father she came to first and not him.

"Rebecca's been here for about half an hour," Christopher's father whispered in English. "We got her cleaned up, but she's still very upset. She hasn't said much."

"I can't take living there anymore," she said. "I'm leaving, I can't live there any longer."

"What are you talking about?" Christopher answered. "You can't leave. Where would you go?"

"I can't live there, not with him, not with them." Her head dropped down onto her arms where they lay folded on the table.

"Just slow down. What happened last night? What started all this?" Christopher's father said as he placed his hand on the spill of hair on top of her head.

"What did he do this time, Rebecca?" Christopher asked.

She lifted her head off her arms, her eyes reddened. She brushed the hair away from her face and sat up in the chair. "Can I have a glass of water?"

"Of course, get her a glass of water, Alex, please."

"Yes, Father," Alexandra answered. Rebecca took the glass of water in her hand and took a small sip.

"My father wants me to leave school. He wants me to get a job." She had both hands around the glass of water and raised it to her mouth again.

"What did your mother say?" Christopher asked.

"She agreed with him. She says we need the money."

"Perhaps if she got a job herself . . ." Christopher added.

"She hasn't worked since the textile factory closed down." Rebecca's voice lowered to a whisper. "She hardly leaves the house these days."

"Did she try to stop your father when he hit you?" Christopher asked.

"Yes, at first. But he tells her that it's the best thing for me."

"Does it hurt?" Alex asked.

"No, I hardly feel the bruises anymore."

There was silence for a few seconds. No one seemed to know what to say.

"Your hair looks pretty," Alex offered.

"My mother did it for me, like when I was a little girl, although she didn't do a good job at all. I had to redo it myself, after I heard her go into the bathroom and then the crash."

"What happened? Was she drunk again?"

Rebecca nodded. "I just wanted to run out of the house and come up here or anywhere else but there. I didn't want to do it, but I had to help her. She's my mother."

"Of course," Christopher's father said.

Christopher tried to remember his own mother. It was hard.

"Was she okay?"

"She's fine, just some cuts and bruises. I picked her up, cleaned her up, and put her to bed. My father arrived home later on. He blamed me for what had happened." She paused. Silence descended for a few seconds before she began again. "I had never seen him so angry. He picked up a poker from the fireplace and ran at me."

"What . . . what did he . . . ?"

"Let her speak, Christopher," his father said.

"He hit me on the arm and I fell onto the floor. He was standing over me about to hit me with the poker again, so I picked up a piece of coal and threw it at his head."

Christopher squeezed her hand. Alex was crying, the sound of her sobs clear over the absolute silence of the evening outside.

Rebecca seemed to ignore them. "He drew up the poker and said he was going to teach me a lesson I'd never forget, and then I saw my mother behind him, holding my father's shotgun. She said that if he touched me that it would be the last thing he would ever do."

"Did he back down then?" Christopher asked. Rebecca nodded slowly. She brought her hands up to her temples like blinkers on a horse.

Christopher's father let out a deep breath and stood up. Alexandra walked over to him and embraced him, pushing her head onto his shoulder as he held her.

"It's all right, Father," she said. "We'll look after her." His mouth moved, as if he wanted to say something in reply but no words came. He filled the glass with water and returned to the chair.

"I'm sorry, Rebecca, please continue," he said.

"That's the last time he'll ever hit me. I told him. I told him that I was leaving and that there was nothing he could do to stop me."

"You're really leaving?" he said, but Rebecca ignored him.

"I packed my things last night. I never even said goodbye, not even to my mother."

"Where did you stay?" Alex asked.

"I stayed with my friend Sarah Smart. She didn't tell her family I'd run away."

"I know the Smart family; they're good people," Christopher's father added.

"I went back to see my parents this morning. My father got angry and said that it was my fault that my mother had turned against him. He said that I had destroyed our family." Her last words were faint, as if she were far away, not sitting inches from them at the kitchen table.

"Where are you staying tonight?" Christopher asked.

"With my parents. My mother talked him into letting me come back."

They sat there for a while. Christopher felt the dread of a life without Rebecca creep through his entire body. How could she leave him? They were meant to be there for each other—always. He couldn't even look at her as they sat there. He was facing out toward the window. His breathing was stilted, his whole body rigid from the anger at her parents riddling him. Christopher's father didn't seem to know what to say. "I'm proud of you, Rebecca," he eventually whispered. He got up to walk away toward the countertop where the raw materials for that night's dinner lay untouched. He picked up the knife and pressed it down on top of the carrots, the blade hitting the wooden cutting board with a loud clack.

"Can I stay for dinner, Mr. Seeler?"

"Of course you can, Rebecca, of course you can." His words

were as dull as the dusk outside. "Christopher, why don't you take Rebecca and Alex down for a walk on the beach before dinner?"

They left him there, the cracking of the knife on the board ringing in their ears as they pushed open the front door and even as they stepped out into the front yard. Rebecca stopped talking as they left the house. The conversation slowed as the three children made their way past Rebecca's house on their way down to the beach. Christopher knew he shouldn't be walking past the front of their house with Rebecca. Somehow it didn't seem to matter anymore. None of them even commented that they were breaking their own cardinal rule as they shuffled past. They continued down toward the seafront, past the beach and along the coast, where they sat in a row, with Rebecca in the middle, overlooking the gray waves crashing against the rocks below.

He thought of what Rebecca had said about leaving, but never mentioned it out loud. He was too raw inside to speak of it yet. There was no telling quite what he might say. They spoke again about what had happened the night before, but no one had anything new to say. They'd been over it all before. They watched the waves roll back and forth, covering the rocks like a white tablecloth spreading out and then being drawn back again. They sat there in near silence for twenty minutes or maybe more, until the cold of the night air forced them back up to the house, where dinner was on the table. Rebecca took her usual place. Christopher's father let Rebecca stay much later than usual, well past ten o'clock.

He hugged her as she left. "Christopher will walk you home," he said. "Take good care of her, Christopher."

"Of course, Father," he said as they left.

The chill March air bit at his neck, and he flicked up the collar on his coat. The light had faded. All they could see was the outline of the house and the moon illuminating the sea beyond and a million shining stars above them. The light shone gray-white on

Rebecca's skin and sent shadows cascading from her cheekbones down along the bruise on her face. Her brown hair moved gently with the wind. "I don't ever want to go back there," she said, but still she walked on.

"I know. I . . . I wish there was something I could do. I wish I could get a job and take you away from here . . . and . . ."

"You've already done so much."

"Do you really think you'll leave?"

"I just have to get away. I can't stay here any longer."

"Where will you go?"

"I've been writing to my cousin, Mavis, in London. She said she'd take me in."

"Why didn't you tell me?"

"There are some things I can't tell anyone. Not even you."

His heart was beating so hard that he could almost feel it coming out through the skin on his chest. She didn't seem to notice. He reached his hand over to take hers but brought it back before he touched her. "So do you think you'll stay in London forever?"

"I don't know. Forever is a very long time. I have to look after myself," she said.

"I look after you, and so does my father. My sister looks after you. We all do." They were walking slowly, much more slowly than usual.

"I know you do, but you can't always be there. There were so many times when I needed you that you couldn't be there. I had to look after myself." She reached over and took his hand.

"I don't know what I would do without you. I just don't know what I would do if you left. I want to be there for you whenever you need me."

"You could come with me."

"My father would never allow that," he replied without thinking.

"Maybe when you're older, then."

The words swirled around within him. He thought of leaving with her, but those thoughts dissipated as soon as they came. "I don't want you to leave," he said as the lights of her house came into view.

She turned to him and took his other hand. She was facing him, just inches away. His eyes were used to the dark now and he could make out each curve and angle of her face and the outline of her long hair falling down over her shoulders. "I want to tell you . . ." She paused and looked at the ground, and he thought his heart would drop out. "I just want to thank you. You're my favorite boy, the best I could ever . . ." And he reached for her and felt his lips against hers and he felt their feather touch against his and it was awkward and perfect and he reached his hand up and put it behind her neck and gently held her head. She drew her head back with a smile. His body was electrified. He had no idea what to say. She shifted her feet and let go of his hand.

"I'd better get going inside."

"Okay."

"I'll talk to you in a few days. I need to wait until things settle down here."

"I'll leave a note for you under the rock on the beach."

"Okay. Good night, Christopher." She leaned forward to peck him on the lips again.

Five days later she was gone. Christopher left her a note and, when she didn't turn up, he knew that she had kept her word; her father would, indeed, never hit her again.

# CHAPTER

---

6

It was May 1937 when Uli came back, just in time for Christopher's nineteenth birthday. He still looked almost the same, with just a little more gray sprinkled through his hair. They sat out in the back garden in deck chairs, drinking cold beers as Alexandra prepared the dinner.

"It's been a while since you spoke German this much?" Uli asked.

"Not really. We try to speak it a little around the house. Father doesn't want us to forget where we're from."

"Nor should he."

"I can't believe it's been four years since you were here last," Christopher's father said. "It's been six years since I've been to Germany myself, not since Mother's funeral in '31. I had been meaning to go back, but who had the money then?"

"Times were hard everywhere. Germany was worse than most." There was a lull in the conversation for a few seconds before Uli began again. "And how about you, Christopher, how are you enjoying working for the old man? You like being an accountant? I hope he's not working you too hard."

"I thought it would be easy working for my father. I thought he'd let me go early every day, that I'd be rich, a gentleman of leisure."

"I do give you time off. It's called the weekend." Christopher's father laughed along with his brother.

"No, it's been great working for him. I'm learning a lot, and one day I'll open my own practice."

"You should come back to Germany, Christopher. There are plenty of opportunities there now."

"He is doing fine in Jersey."

"All I'm saying is that there are a lot of exciting opportunities for a young man like Christopher in Germany right now. . . ."

"We can talk about this another time," Stefan said.

"Okay, Brother, no need to get uptight. I see the old tree house is still there. Do you still want to live in it?" Uli said.

"I think this house has a little more room."

"Whatever happened to that sweet little girl? Rebecca? I know that she was in England for a while. Did she ever come back?"

"No, she never came back. We've not heard from her since," Christopher's father said.

"And she never wrote? You two were so close."

"No, she never wrote. She never gave us her address either."

"I'm sorry, Christopher. That must have been hard to lose your friend like that," Uli said. Christopher passed his beer bottle from one hand to the other before bringing it to his mouth.

"We got through it. He even has a new girlfriend now, don't you?"

"No, I don't," he said. "Every time I mention a girl, my father thinks she's my girlfriend."

"Don't worry about it. He still does the same thing with me, and I'm thirty-six years of age."

"Which reminds me, when are you getting married, Uli? What happened with that girl, Angela?" Christopher's father asked.

"She asked too many questions. Listen, Brother, I'll get married when you get married, okay?"

"I was married."

"Yes, but you've been a single man for almost thirteen years. What's your father's love life like? Ever find any strange women at breakfast?"

"He must sneak them out before Alex and I get out of bed."

Alexandra came out. She immediately made for Uli.

"Sunshine, you're getting too big to sit on my lap now. You're sixteen."

"I can still try," she said, and sat back on Uli's lap. Uli grunted and snorted, pretending that she was crushing him.

"All right, Alexandra, that's enough," her father said. "Sit down there, please." He pointed to the extra chair.

"We were just talking about your father's love life, or lack thereof. So what about you, Alex? Surely a beautiful young girl like you has hundreds of boys chasing after her?"

Christopher and his father both sat forward. "There's too many to choose from. I just can't make up my mind."

"I'll bet. You look just like your mother with those blond curls and pale blue eyes. Just don't end up with the kind of man that she did." Christopher's father pursed his lips slightly and scratched the back of his head, feigning annoyance.

"Is dinner ready yet?" he asked.

They went inside where the table was set. Alexandra brought the roast beef and potatoes and laid them out on the table. Christopher hadn't thought about Rebecca for a long time, but the mention of her name quieted him, and he remained silent through the dinner, watching the others speak. Uli was talking to Alexandra about her plans to go to university when his father interjected.

"Christopher, could you clear the table, please?" He took the plates, making sure to save the remaining food before placing the dishes in the sink. He stepped out into the garden and reached into his pocket for a pack of cigarettes and drew one out. "Are you smoking out there?" his father asked.

"Yes."

"Well, if you insist on indulging in that filthy habit, please go down to the end of the garden. At least that way we won't have to smell it."

Christopher trudged onto the grass without answering. The night was drawing in and the graying light was gritty and solid, as if he could feel it between his fingers. He walked to the tree house and reached up to touch it, to run his hand along the wooden surface. The paint he and Rebecca had applied to the inside of the tree house was flaking and cracked but still showed the garish red color she had insisted upon. He drew on the cigarette and watched the gray smoke billow up and merge into and become the night air. He wondered what she looked like now. He thought about their kiss, but then dismissed it. They were kids then. He wasn't a kid anymore.

"You know the government in Germany has proven the link between smoking and cancer? Herr Hitler himself has spoken out against the evils of smoking," Uli said from behind him.

"Is that right?" Christopher answered.

"Yes, the government has initiated a nationwide campaign to stop people from smoking. They say it causes heart disease and that it can stop women from becoming pregnant."

"Well, when I start trying to get pregnant, I'll quit."

Uli smiled and ran his hand along the window frame of the tree house. "This thing wasn't easy to build."

"I can remember seeing it for the first time. I can still remember getting the wet paint on my fingers and how hard it was to wait for it to dry. I was dying to get into it. It's not often I've felt like that since."

"I'm glad to hear that, but maybe you should get out a little more and not work so hard, eh?" They both laughed. Christopher threw down the cigarette and followed his uncle back up to the house.

The bottles of beer were piled up on the kitchen table, and Christopher's father opened the bottle of brandy he had been saving. It was the first time Christopher had ever seen his sister drink more than a couple of glasses, and the white wine she had been drinking had its inevitable effect on her. When she started asking her father when he was going to get married again and imploring him to get out there and meet someone, he stepped in.

"I appreciate your concern, but I think it's time you got off to bed now."

"Okay." She stood up. "Daddy, will you carry me, like you used to when I was a little girl?" she said with her arms outstretched.

"I think you're getting a little too big for that, and I'm a little old." He scratched his head. "I also think that the wine has gone to your head."

"Oh, come on, Dad, you can still do it. I know you can."

"You heard the girl, Stefan; carry her up the stairs," Uli said.

"Okay then, come on." He took her in his arms. Alex waved good night, then disappeared out through the door and up the stairs in her father's arms.

Five minutes later, Christopher's father arrived back in the kitchen, wiping a bead of imaginary sweat from his brow. "She asked me to read her a story after I put her to bed, but I had to draw the line somewhere." He sat back down and Uli began again.

"You have a fine life here. Yes, this is a very beautiful island, a very beautiful place. But you're always going to be the outsiders here, aren't you? You're always going to be the German family living on the English island," Uli said.

"This island is not a part of England."

"Come on, Stefan, you know what I mean."

"There were problems when we first arrived, but they're few and far between now," Christopher's father said, looking out into the black of the night outside. "It took me a while to persuade certain people that the war was over."

"I remember," Uli said, and picked up his glass of brandy. He swirled the brown liquid around in the glass for a few seconds before taking a sip. "Do you ever regret coming here?"

"No, not with what was going on in Germany when we came over here, and particularly with what has happened since."

"But Germany has changed now. It's a different place than it was when you left."

Christopher wondered if he should speak.

"Different how? Better or worse?" his father said.

"Oh, it's far, far better," Uli said. "Don't you read the newspapers?"

"Yes, I do, little brother. I read them every day."

"Then you must see what's happening in our country. These last few years since Hitler came to power have been the best in a long time."

"I see that Herr Hitler has banned all other political parties apart from his own Nazi Party."

"Yes, but what good did this democracy do us, Stefan? The years before Herr Hitler and the National Socialists came to power were the worst Germany has ever known. Utter chaos. You got out in time, but we weren't all so lucky. I am glad that you weren't there, my brother. I am glad that the children weren't there then, but it could be a wonderful place for them to grow up now."

"Jersey is a wonderful place for them to grow up."

"Yes, it was wonderful when they were children, but look at your son; he's not a boy anymore. This is an island, a tiny island.

It can't possibly offer them the kind of opportunity that Germany could."

"I would never stand in the way of what my children wanted to do. It would be their decision, not mine."

"All right then," Uli said, turning to Christopher. "What would you think of the idea of coming to Germany?"

"It's your life, Christopher. I can't tell you what to do. You're a man now."

Christopher could feel his eyes flitting around in his head like tadpoles in a glass. Both men were waiting for him to answer. It was hard to know what to say. Opportunity was a fine, exciting thing, but leaving Jersey? "I would certainly think that it would be a great experience. I mean, I love Jersey, but to live in Munich or Berlin? That would be incredible. Where would I work?"

"I'm sure I could get you a job in the bank. I've been there almost seven years myself," Uli said.

"Germany would be an amazing experience. I've never really thought about leaving Jersey before."

"You do know that other people, people like Rebecca Cassin, could never have those same opportunities in Germany?" his father said.

"What? What are you talking about?" Christopher said. Uli slugged back a massive gulp of beer. "She's not German."

"Think about it, Christopher. It's not because she's not German. It's because she's Jewish."

"I never knew," Uli said. "What difference would that make anyway? He hasn't seen or heard from her in years."

Christopher's father leaned toward his brother. "I do read the papers, Uli. I read them every day, and I know that Jews are being completely disenfranchised, completely removed from society. So that's the new Germany, Christopher, a land of opportunity for most." He turned to his son. "There is a new set of laws making it illegal for Jews to be German citizens or to marry non-Jews, or to own businesses or property. So make your choice, but make it wisely."

"I never knew Rebecca was Jewish. Not that it matters to *me*," Uli said.

"But in Germany it would matter to her, and it should to you too, Christopher."

"Maybe you should go to Germany. It's the only way you'll ever get Rebecca off your mind," Uli said, laughing.

Christopher wanted to argue that he was over Rebecca—that it was three years since she'd left—but they'd see through him like the beer in the glass in front of him. Unwanted images of Rebecca now flooded his mind.

"I haven't seen Rebecca for a long time," was the best he could muster in reply.

"But if you did want to be with her, you never could be, not in Germany anyway. Here in Jersey, we may not have all the opportunity of Germany, but we have some things."

"I don't agree with the Nazi policies about the Jews either," Uli said. "But what can I do? The government says that it was their fault that we lost the war, that they are enemies of Germany and are in league with the Bolsheviks."

"And what do you believe, Uli?"

"I believe that I remember Mrs. Rosenbaum who lived down the street from us and how she would smile at us and give us sweets when we were young. There is so much talk of the Jews these days. I had never really considered them before. I never knew it mattered to single them out."

Christopher's father stood up and poured himself another glass of beer before sitting back down. "I read what Hitler says about the Great War. The talk of these 'November Criminals' and the Zionist conspiracy, it makes me laugh, Uli, really it does. We stabbed ourselves in the back. There was no Jewish conspiracy. Some of the best men I fought with in that godforsaken mess were Jews, good Germans. Ernst Heppner, Hans Buchsbaum, Franz Bachner. They were all Jews, and friends of mine, all dead."

"The Nazis are not perfect, far from it, but things are so much better in Germany now. It's easy for you to sit here in Jersey and judge us in Germany. You weren't there when things went bad. You left."

"Yes, Uli, it is easy to be here, to sit in judgment of Germany and the Nazis, and that's why I won't go back and why I won't encourage Christopher or Alexandra to go back there, even if it is the country of their birth."

A silence settled across the room. Christopher wanted to say something to get the conversation moving but couldn't think. He lifted the glass to his mouth and took another mouthful of beer. His father breathed out heavily and looked at his watch. "I think it's time you went to bed, Christopher," he said. Christopher expected some reprieve but found none. It had been several years since he had been sent to bed, but as he looked at his father again, he understood, and got up from the table. Uli stood up and hugged him as if he were trying to crush him to death.

"Good night, you two," he said as he walked out. "Try not to kill each other." Both men smiled. Christopher said nothing. He turned and tramped into the hall and up the stairs, each step a minor triumph. His head felt like a thin raft, afloat on a boiling sea, and the top of the stairs brought a nausea that he had barely felt before. He fought past the bathroom door and sat down on the toilet seat, his trousers still up, his head in his hands. His eyes grew heavy and sleep overcame him.

When he came to, he looked at his watch. More than two hours had passed, and his legs were numb from sitting on the toilet. The image of Rebecca wandered somewhere into his vision. He turned on the cold-water faucet and splashed some water onto his face. The voices were still there, still downstairs in the kitchen, and he wanted to go back down. The towel was hard and cold and he used it quickly, finishing drying his hands in his armpits as he approached the door. He listened to the house, as he always did at this time of night. There was nothing other than the gentle flow of the wind outside and the muffled patter of voices through the floorboards. He would go down, if only to say good night, even though he had already done so.

Light filtered up the stairs and he followed it down, taking each step slowly. He heard them talking and sat down on the last step, not wanting to interrupt. He listened. The conversation had turned to their own mother, who had died six years before, their own father, who had died before Christopher was born, and Christopher's mother.

"All dead," Uli asserted. Christopher moved his head around the banister at the end of the stairwell. The door was open enough that he could see Uli sitting back on the chair facing his father, out of his view behind the wall. "I can't quite remember meeting Hannah for the first time; I was so young." He watched Uli wait for an answer that didn't come. "She was always so good to me, and even Father liked her, even Father." Uli's voice trailed off and he picked up the glass in front of him and took a gulp of the mahogany-brown liquid.

"She was the only thing I never had any doubt over. People say that I should move on. I don't see why."

Christopher's entire body was rigid.

"Perhaps it's time to let her go. It's been thirteen years now, Brother. You're not old. You've still got a life to live."

"Maybe, but maybe I just don't want to live it without her." Neither man spoke for thirty seconds, until his father began again. "Anyway, I've never met anyone who matched up to her. And bringing a woman back home to the children . . . They're not children anymore, I suppose, but I just couldn't do it. You know I met Hannah when I wasn't too much older than Christopher was when we moved here. Her grandfather was German. You knew that already, though."

"Yes, I did."

"You know I don't remember the first time I met her either. It was like she was always there, always with me, from even before I was born."

"I never had anyone like that. I never had what you had."

"You still can. It's all there for you."

"It's still there for you too."

"Christopher and Alexandra are more than enough for me. Christopher is . . ." Christopher moved to get a better view. "We're so alike," his father continued, "too much so sometimes. That's why I made the decision about Rebecca. When she left, I mean." Christopher froze.

"With the letters?"

His body went numb, as if he'd been tossed into the freezing winter sea.

"Yes. I knew that his feelings for her were blinding him. Sometimes I feel bad for her. She still doesn't know that he never saw the letters she wrote him. I glanced through a few of them myself, and I knew I had done the right thing. The things she said . . . It would have distracted him too much. He can be such a hotheaded boy. Who knows what he might have done?"

"I'm sure you did the right thing. I know it wasn't easy."

"Maybe I'll show them to him someday, when he's ready." Christopher's father stopped. His voice weakened. "I loved her as a daughter myself. There's nothing I want more than to see her back here one day, and if she was ready, with Christopher, sure."

"What if our father had done that to you? Barred you from seeing Hannah?"

"He never had reason to."

"What if he had?"

"I don't know, Uli, I really don't know. I think I would have found a way. I think . . ."

"Do you still send her money?"

"I can't. She moved, didn't leave a forwarding address. I lost touch. I must have written to her five times myself without reply, but she's gone. I wish I knew where. I feel bad for letting her go. I can't bear the thought of never seeing her again. She used to threaten to come back, but I knew she couldn't. If she could come back, I wouldn't need to keep her letters from him."

They were still talking in the kitchen, but Christopher couldn't hear them anymore, just the rushing of his own blood and the quickening pulse racing electric through his veins. He got up, stumbling up the stairs, and found his way to the top and into the bathroom. He crouched down into a ball, his arms wrapped around himself. He thought about Rebecca and the times when she needed him and he wasn't there. The times when she had reached out to him and he had not answered. Christopher heard a knock on the door.

"Christopher, are you in there?"

He waited for a few seconds, not knowing what to say, but then the surge came again. "Leave me alone."

"Christopher," his father said, his voice more faint and distant than before. "Are you all right in there?"

Christopher leaped to his feet and yanked the door open. His father was standing there at the door. He looked sick. "Where are the letters?" he shouted. His father jerked his head backward as Christopher thrust a finger in his face. "Where are Rebecca's letters?"

His father looked utterly shocked. He drew a breath and moved his lips but never made a sound.

"Where are the letters?" Christopher was square against his father now. He was taller than him. Not by much, but enough that he was looking down on him. Uli thundered up the stairs. "I asked you a question. Where are they? They're mine. . . ." He grabbed his father by the lapels.

"Don't you touch me," his father spat through gritted teeth. Christopher drew his hands away. The door opened and Alexandra was there, her eyes thin slits and her hair a mess.

"What's going on?" she asked.

"How could you do that?" Christopher roared. "How could you keep Rebecca's letters from me? She needed me, and I wasn't there for her. I said that I'd always be there for her. . . ."

"It wasn't an easy . . . I'm sorry. I thought you'd get over her and we could move on with our lives. I was going to give them to you when . . ."

"Where are the letters, Father? Where are my letters?"

"Just give me a chance to explain first. I had to try to do the best thing for both of you. You know I think of her as my own. I never wanted to lose her either."

"Where are the letters?"

"We've all had a bit too much to drink, and I think that it would be best if . . ."

"If you kept his letters, give them to him, Father," Alexandra said.

"Stefan, give him the letters," Uli said.

Christopher stood, his face a few inches from his father's. He had never stood this close to him before.

"Come with me," he said, and pushed past Uli on the stairs and down into his study. He walked into the study and stopped in front of the bookshelves above his desk. He reached up for a leather-bound box behind the picture of Christopher's mother. He opened a drawer, took out a key, and opened it. The letters were on top. "I had to open the letters to see if she was all right, and to get an address. I had to see . . ."

"Give me my letters, Father," Christopher said. The anger had given way to something far worse. He held out his hand and his father placed the pile, about five letters, into it.

"Go to bed, Christopher, it's time you . . ."

"No, Father, no. You don't get to tell me what to do anymore."

He left his father there alone in the study. He walked past Uli, still standing at the top of the stairs, and onward to his bedroom. He turned the light on and sat down on the bed, spreading the letters out on the quilt. He heard a knock on the door.

"Are you all right in there?" Alexandra said.

"Yes, I'm fine. I can't talk to you now, Alex. I'll speak to you tomorrow." He heard her mutter a faint good night, and then she was gone. He picked up the first letter. Rebecca had sent it almost three years before. He pulled out the piece of paper from the envelope and read the first few words, skimming through the lines, looking for anything important, almost too eager to finish and move on to the next to read the letter itself. Sentences stood out. She was working as a nanny for her cousin, Mavis. She was thinking of her parents more but had not contacted them. She was happy and said she might never return to Jersey, although she hoped she would. No address. The postmark on the outside said London.

He placed the letter down on the bed and opened the next one, written to arrive in time for Christmas 1934. He scanned through it and came to the address in the middle, somewhere in London he'd never heard of. She asked about Alexandra and his father. She said she missed them both, but especially him. He crumpled the delicate letter in his fist, the words that she had written to him. He took another look at the address before moving on to the next letter, dated February of 1935. Her first words were to ask why he had never written to her. She supposed that he was very busy, or that the letter might have been lost in the post. She wrote her address again in large letters decorated with colored pencils and lined with tiny blue flowers. She was doing well and enjoying her life in London. The letter was short. She asked that he write back again at the end and that he might even come to see her that summer.

He lay back on the bed, staring up at the ceiling and thinking of her as she wrote the letter. He ripped open the next envelope. This letter was only a few words.

*May 12, 1935*
Dear Christopher,
Please reply to this. I am worried. I can't come back to see you but wish that I could. Your father told me that you are trying to move on, but please just let me know that you are all right, that you don't hate me.

Love,
Rebecca

He came to the last letter, a full year and a half since the previous.

*November 13, 1936*
Dear Christopher,
This is not a letter I ever thought I would write, because before this, I could never imagine my life without you. I suppose I was naïve to think that you'd always be there for me, even when I left Jersey and even as I sit here, alone in this room in London. I knew that you would be angry that I left without saying goodbye and that it took me so long to write to you, but I never thought that you would be so angry that you would not reply to me, or never want to see me again. But I understand. Your father has explained everything to me. I know that I haven't been the easiest person to be around. I still remember

that first day we met, when you found me crying in the bushes, and I think that if you looked for me today, you would find me the same way, just in a different place. But I will be all right. You know me, I'm a survivor, and I am where I need to be at this time in my life. One day I will come back to Jersey, and we will see each other again.

I miss you. I always will.

Love,
Rebecca

The letter fell to the floor. He sat there for a few minutes before he finally got up. The night outside was black nothingness.

# CHAPTER

## 7

They arrived at Lehrter Stadtbahnhof, the main train station in Berlin, on a fine morning in April 1938, three days before the wedding that Christopher thought he'd never see. Uli had met a twenty-four-year-old teacher, Karolina. They had known each other for three months. Everyone was shocked except Christopher's father, who said that nothing his brother could do would surprise him anymore.

Seven years had passed since their grandmother's funeral. They had not been to Germany since. Christopher's father betrayed no emotion at the return to the city of his birth. "It feels like we're coming home, truly it does," Alexandra said as they stepped off the train.

"I love Berlin," Christopher's father answered with a tiny sigh. "But this isn't the Berlin that I knew." A horde of schoolchildren shifted past them across the platform, dressed in the light brown uniforms of the Hitler Youth. They stood and watched the children pass.

Alexandra shrugged. "It's no different than the scouts." Stefan didn't answer and picked up the bags. They followed beside him as he walked out to a tram, which arrived in a matter of seconds, and they pushed aboard to make for their hotel. The new German flag, the black swastika in the white circle on the red background, was everywhere. Twenty or more flickered in the wind outside the station in great thirty-foot swathes.

The tram was packed, and they stood with their bags at their feet, holding on to the straps draped down over the pole above. "This is so exciting," Alex said. Christopher studied the expressionless faces of the commuters. A young man leaned casually against the window, reading a newspaper. The drawing on the front of the newspaper was of an overdrawn, plainly Jewish man murdering a screaming child, and at the bottom of the page ran the headline, "The Jews Are Our Misfortune." Christopher stood in front of his sister, between her and the newspaper, as the tram continued.

Uli and Karolina were waiting in the lobby of the hotel when they arrived. Karolina hugged them each in turn. They had seen her only in faded black-and-white photographs, and always with Uli. She and Uli in a restaurant smiling, holding glasses of beer. She and Uli on the beach at Wannsee. She was a small woman, with long blond hair and bright blue eyes. She was young and pretty, only five years older than Christopher. Christopher's father looked like he could have been her father. Christopher hugged Uli, roughly bashing his shoulder with an open palm until his uncle let him go and stood back. Uli grasped Alexandra, lifting her into the air.

"It's wonderful to meet you all at last," Karolina said. "We have a packed afternoon of sightseeing ahead of us. No time to be tired, I'm afraid. So drop off your bags upstairs and get back down here. Is that all right, Stefan?"

"Of course it is, Karolina. We are all so eager to get to know you that we don't want to wait another minute."

They deposited their bags upstairs and within five minutes were all packed into Uli's car. Christopher's father sat up front with Uli. "I've never been to Jersey," Karolina said as the car started. "I would love to; it sounds wonderful, but this must all be quite different."

"Very different," Christopher answered.

"It's absolutely wonderful here," Alex said. "I never thought there would be anywhere like London, but this is even more fabulous."

Christopher wasn't listening to the conversation as they went. He could only stare out the window at the marvelous city he might have grown up in. He might have known the enormous avenues buzzing with cars, trams, and trains, instead of pondering them in amazement as a tourist. They parked the car and walked to the Stadtschloss, the royal palace.

"I'd say this compares pretty well with your Buckingham Palace," Uli joked. Alexandra was standing arms linked with Karolina.

"It's incredible," Christopher said.

They made their way to Unter den Linden and the Brandenburg Gate, where Uli took his turn as tour guide. "This is it, the column of victory," Uli said, gesturing to the huge structure and the chariot led by four horses on top of it. "This is the center of the Reich, the center of the new Germany." He took Karolina close to him. "This is the symbol of the new start for all of us." Karolina hugged him closer. "Look back down Unter den Linden. It stretches for as far as the eye can see."

The green trees, interspersed by the flags of the Nazi Party, stretched for miles.

"And look," Karolina said. "The changing of the guards; we're in luck." The gray-uniformed soldiers stepped in perfect time, their long rifles on their shoulders.

"I don't think I really want to see this," Christopher's father said.

"Okay, Stefan, it's getting toward dinnertime anyway. We have somewhere special to take you."

The evening was warm and clear, and they went to dinner in a café outdoors. Music from the live band floated around them as they ate. People got up to dance on the patio. Rebecca invaded his mind. They could never be together in this strange and wonderful place, warm and friendly to him, yet intensely hostile to who she was. *Not that we're together now, or ever will be.* He didn't know how to feel.

After dinner, Uli asked Alex to dance, and although she refused, he dragged her up with him. Karolina asked Christopher if he wouldn't mind if she danced with his father. "Of course not. It'll do the old man good." Christopher's father took her hand and led her out onto the patio. They danced as the lights flickered on, and the evening faded into night.

Uli's bachelor party was the night before the wedding. Alexandra stayed with Karolina's family as the others accompanied Uli and a horde of his friends into the Berlin night, for "one last night of debauchery," as Uli himself put it. Thirty-seven-year-old men, Uli's friends seemed to have more interest in talking about their children, or the wedding the next day, than the debauchery that he had in mind, at least at first.

Christopher was momentarily alone when Uli approached him.

"Having a good time with the old men?"

"Absolutely," Christopher answered. They clinked beer glasses. "He seems to be having a good time too." He gestured toward his father, sitting with two of Uli's friends in the corner.

"It's good to see him let off some steam." Uli leaned in close. "What happened in London? You never told me about that. You couldn't find her?"

"No. We went over a few weeks after I first wrote to her. Father had lost contact with her himself a few months before." Christopher turned around and placed his beer glass on the bar behind him. "She wasn't there. We went to the house. Her cousin, Mavis, had died suddenly six months before. Mavis's husband went back to Scotland without any kind of a forwarding address."

"What about Rebecca?"

"No sign. It was as if she never existed. No one even seemed to know her."

Christopher's father, unable to hear what they were saying, roared, laughing at something the man beside him said. "What about him?" Uli asked. "Are you two better now?"

"Now we are. It took some time. He admitted to me that he'd made a mistake, and that he shouldn't have kept the letters from me."

"And he tried to rectify it. It's not many men who'd do that."

"No, it's not. There's not many men like him."

"I think it's time to forget about Rebecca Cassin."

"Yes, I keep telling myself that."

Christopher found himself sitting at dinner between his father, who seemed genuinely determined to have a good time, and Uli's friend Werner, a lawyer, originally from Dresden.

"So what do you think of Berlin? It's quite a city, isn't it?" Werner's swastika badge signified his membership in the Party. Several of the men wore them.

"It's incredible," Christopher said. "I have never seen anywhere quite like it."

"It was so different, just a few short years ago. Before the National Socialists came to power, and while the Bolshevik threat was still lurking. It was a terrifying time. I'm glad you weren't here to see that. I can see why your father wanted you away from here."

"We've had a wonderful life in Jersey."

"I spoke to your father earlier—it does sound like the most beautiful place—but do you not find yourself intoxicated by the sheer surge of life in this city?"

"I'm feeling intoxicated by something."

"This is the most incredible time to be German. You should come back here and be a part of this revolution. The Party—we're trying to change the world, to work for a better future." He raised his glass of beer and took a deep swig. "Not everyone needs to join the Party. Your uncle says he never will, but he's as proud a German as you'll ever meet."

"I know."

Werner hardly seemed to hear him. "It's a revolution all right, a wonderful, bloodless revolution. Look at this city, everything's in order again, everything's clean, and the people are back at work. Finally it's okay to be proud to be German once more." Werner looked at him, most likely for a cue to continue. Christopher didn't feel like giving one to him. He wanted to ask why everyone couldn't be a part of this wonderful society, but he didn't.

"Why do you think he did it? What is so special about Karolina?"

Werner lifted the glass of beer to his lips. "I think time catches up with all of us sooner or later, Christopher. You're young now, but you'll understand one day. We all marry for different reasons: some for love, some for money or power, and some so they won't be forgotten or left behind." He offered a cigarette to Christopher before lighting one of his own. "But I've met Karolina several times now. She is a wonderful woman, and she'll make Uli very happy." Uli was downing the third of three straight shots of vodka.

"Why did you get married, Werner?"

"I think a little of each reason, my friend, a little of each."

# CHAPTER

8

Christopher awoke from a dreamless, dead sleep and immediately felt her beside him. It was the morning after his twentieth birthday. He was on his back, she on her side, facing away. He lifted up the sheet and saw the gentle curve of her back as she lay with her legs tucked up so far they were almost touching the elbows she held clenched together in front of her. Her gentle hair was carelessly spread over her shoulders, gold against the light brown of her skin. He had never realized quite how small she was, just how fragile. He went to reach his hand over to touch her hair but stopped himself. He drew his hand back and let it fall uselessly onto his belly. She kicked her legs slightly as she breathed out hard, almost as a snort, and then drew them back in. He was frozen, unable to leave as they were in his room in the apartment he shared with his friend Tom. He sat up in the bed, more as a reflex against the pain than anything else, and Sandrine stirred beside him. She turned over to face him and opened her eyes with a gentle grace he had never quite seen before.

"Good morning," she said.

"Good morning," he replied. He coughed and turned away. Several long seconds passed with neither of them speaking. He glanced back over his shoulder at Sandrine, who turned onto her back. He wished he could say something, or that she would. He got up out of the bed, naked, and pulled a towel over himself.

"How are you feeling today?" he managed.

"I feel fine, how are you?" Her voice was flat, almost emotionless. A steady drizzle was licking the windows, distorting the view outside. "Yeah, I feel fine." Christopher pulled on his underpants and, for some reason, picked up a comb. He put it back down immediately. There was a knock on the door. "Yes?" he said.

"You have a visitor. Your sister's here to see you," Tom said, and closed the door behind him.

"My sister, Alexandra, is here to . . ."

"I heard," Sandrine said. "I will leave if you just give me a moment to change."

"Let me go out and talk to her. I'll be back. I'm really sorry about this." She drew her knees up to her chest, the blanket up to her collarbone and draped down over her sides. He pulled on his trousers and sat back down. He reached out to her, to put his hand on her face. It felt good. Her skin was warm and smooth and she leaned into his palm. "Sandrine, I'm sorry. Perhaps last night was a mistake. I just don't know right now."

The knock on the door came again, louder this time. "She says it's important."

He drew his hand away and pointed toward the door. "Just let me see what this is about. I'll be back." He buttoned up his shirt and opened the door, just wide enough for him to slip through before closing it behind himself. Alexandra was sitting at the kitchen table with Tom, who looked nervous and immediately excused himself to his room as Christopher sat down.

"What is it? Is everything all right? You seem . . ."

"I need you to come with me right now," she replied. "Are you ready? I drove down to get you . . ."

"What's wrong? Is it Father?"

"He's fine. It's something else. I can't tell you now. I have to show you. Please, just get ready and come with me." He went back to his room. Sandrine was fully dressed and sitting on the bed.

"I have to go. I think there's something wrong."

"What is it?" Sandrine seemed genuinely concerned.

"I don't know. She wouldn't tell me, but I have to go right now." He pulled on the same socks he had worn the night before. "I'm sorry, but you'll have to see yourself out."

"I'm ready to leave. I'll walk out with you."

Christopher let his laces fall untied. "No, my sister is out there. There's something wrong. I don't want to upset her."

"Upset her? What are you talking about? Are you ashamed of me?"

He walked around to the bed where she was now standing and took hold of each of her elbows. "No, of course not, it's just that I don't want to complicate things. If there's something seriously wrong . . ." He took his hands off her. "Please, just let yourself out after we leave?"

"Maybe I should just climb out the window, shin down the drainpipe?"

"I don't have time for this," he said. She sat back down on the bed. He put one hand on the doorknob and turned around. "I'm sorry. I have to go now. Can we talk later?"

"Of course. You go. I hope everything is okay." She sounded distant, as if she were in the next room, talking through the wall.

"Okay. Goodbye." He left her there, alone on his bed.

He led Alexandra out the door and down the stairs to the street. She put her little umbrella up for the walk to the car.

"What is it, Alex? What's going on?"

"I don't know myself. Father told me to get you, that he had to tell us both together, and that it was very important. That's all I know, I swear." She pushed the keys into the ignition and the car rumbled to a start. "Christopher, who were you talking to? Was there someone in your room with you?"

"No, of course not. Come on, let's get home."

They didn't speak for the duration of the ride to the house. He thought about Sandrine, alone in his room, closing the door behind her as she let herself out to walk home.

The rain had slowed by the time Alex pulled into the drive. He waited for her at the front door before pushing it open and stepping into the silent house. She motioned for him to keep going toward the closed door to the kitchen at the end of the hall. Rebecca was sitting at the table. She was taller now, maybe about five foot seven and up to Christopher's shoulders. The picture of her he had harbored in his mind was nowhere near as beautiful as she actually was. She wore the full-length dress and hat of a lady, just like in the fashion magazines that Alexandra pored over.

"Surprise," she whispered. She kissed Christopher on the cheek and threw her arms over his shoulders and around his neck. There was a young man with her. He was blond, with a tanned face that looked somehow familiar. The young man was watching her as she pulled away. "Christopher, this is Jonathan. Jonathan, this is my oldest and dearest friend, Christopher Seeler."

Jonathan stood up. The handshake he proffered was firm, and he sat back down without saying a word.

"So?" Stefan said. "What do you think of your surprise?"

"It's amazing." *Who is this man?* he thought to himself. *What is he doing in my father's house?* "What are you doing here?"

"We got off the ferry last night." She was wearing makeup. He had never seen her wear makeup before. Her painted nails shone pink, and her hat lay on the kitchen table beside the chair she had been sitting in, beside the chair she had always sat in.

"It's such a pleasure to see you, and to meet you too, Jonathan," Christopher said, and stood back from her. "How long has it been?"

"Four years. We've a lot of catching up to do," she answered.

"Where have you been? We . . ."

"We happened to be in London," his father interrupted. "We tried to look you up, from the address you gave us in your letters. You weren't there. That was in June 1937, a year ago."

"You tried to look me up? I moved to Southampton in February 1937. Jonathan helped me to find a job and somewhere to live." Jonathan put his arm around her. "I can't believe we missed each other," she continued. "It would have been so wonderful to see you."

"Come on, Alex, let's leave these three to talk for a while," his father said.

"Well, I was hoping we could go for a walk," Rebecca said. "Down to the beach, the Lion's Mane or the Angry Horse?"

Jonathan was still sitting down. "Where are these places, Rebecca? I've not spent too much time in this part of the island before."

"You're from Saint Brelade?" Christopher asked, although he knew perfectly well where Jonathan Durrell, son of the former bailiff of the island of Jersey, was from. Everyone knew the Durrells' mansion.

"Yes, quite," he replied. "It was strange to have to go all the way to London to meet a girl from home, the girl that I'm to marry, but Rebecca captivated me from the first moment we met."

"It's not raining too badly. We're going to go out for a walk now," Christopher said. He felt ridiculous. It was ridiculous to feel like this, to feel the seething, serrated edge of jealousy that was slashing at him. It was hard to be here, and yet he had dreamed of seeing her all this time.

He led them out of the house and into the morning. It felt wrong to look at her. She was more beautiful than ever. They turned on the road down toward the sea, the road that led past her parents' house. Rebecca was in the middle as the three walked together. He had thought this would have been easier.

"I've missed you so much all these years I've been away," Rebecca began.

He could feel Sandrine against him and see Jonathan Durrell down on bended knee. "So you're getting married? That's wonderful."

"Yes, we've come back to get married. We'll live in the house to start, until my practice picks up, and then we'll find accommodation of our own," Jonathan answered.

"Congratulations," he managed. "I'm delighted for you both."

Rebecca's parents' house came into view. The front door had been freshly painted. "I'll leave you two to talk. I'm going to call back into the house." Jonathan shook Christopher's hand again and walked down the driveway.

Christopher had not been inside for more than ten years.

"He knows your parents?"

"They were over to visit twice in the last year."

"Things have changed. How are you getting on with them?"

"Better. It was easier not living there, not being privy to . . ." She took a breath to continue. "I'm glad I went to England. I had to do it. My cousin, Mavis, wouldn't see them when they came. She said that they were only interested in us because I had Jonathan as a suitor, and they were only there to see what they could gather up for themselves. But everything changed when she died and I moved to Southampton."

Christopher didn't answer. The wind was picking up and sweeping in across the channel. The smell was as familiar as any he knew. He wondered if it was still familiar to her. The wet sand of the beach was hard beneath their feet. "I missed you so much when you left."

"Why didn't you write to me? I never understood . . ."

"My father kept the letters from me. He hid them. I only found out about them by accident. I overheard him telling Uli about them one night."

"What?" She stopped walking. Her face tightened. "You never got my letters?"

"I only saw them for the first time last year. You'd moved out by that time."

"That does rather change . . . things." Her words were slow, coming almost as a whisper.

"When I found out that my father had kept your letters from me, I felt that I'd let you down, because I'd said I'd always be there for you no matter what."

"You were fifteen years old; you did so much. I never would have made it through without you." She took his hand. It felt wrong, but the pleasure of it was undeniable. Thoughts of Sandrine came to him, and the rational part of him tried to focus on her, not Rebecca. "I thought about you so much back then. I never forgot you. Jonathan had a lot to live up to. I never thought it would come to this, you and I here, back on this beach, and me living back with my parents."

"And you getting married to the son of the richest man on the island?"

"Yes. It seems like a dream sometimes. I feel like I'll wake up and we'll be back in the tree house with Alexandra."

"It's still there, hanging on for dear life. Uli did a good job. You know he's married now?" He longed for her to reach across to him, to take his face between her hands and kiss him. They talked for another ten minutes or so until Jonathan came to get her for their lunch engagement.

He stood there alone and watched them walk back toward the house. He stayed there on the beach, sitting alone, until a squall blew in off the sea, and the rain set in again.

# CHAPTER

---

9

He found the letter two days later, pushed under his door. Tom was bending to pick it up when Christopher stopped him. It was a single piece of paper folded. There was only one sentence written.

*Gunde de viznay bin Lion's Mane shces.*

It wasn't signed. It didn't need to be. Christopher held the letter tight. *She's getting married. What harm could come from meeting her?* Tom asked who the letter was from, rubbing nonexistent facial hair between three fingers.

"It's from Rebecca. She wants to meet."

"Be careful. She's engaged, and not to just anyone—to Jonathan-bloody-Durrell."

"I know what I'm doing," Christopher replied. He didn't mention the note to his father, though he would have liked to. He knew what his father would say, and he knew he would be right.

He arrived ten minutes early and she was already waiting for him. She wore a new dress that accentuated the curves of her body. Christopher raised his hands to his tie, pushing it upward as he approached. Her face enthralled him. Her eyes lured him in as a siren's call. She was sitting on a rock overlooking the Lion's Mane, a rocky outcrop about half a mile down the coast from her parents' house.

"Christopher, you look wonderful. I can't tell you how splendid it is to be back here with you."

"Why did we call this place the Lion's Mane anyway? It looks more like a bunch of black carrots cutting into the sea to me."

"I suppose the Lion's Mane was a better name. It flows off the tongue."

They were both facing out toward the endless fascination of the sea. It was hard to know what to say next. There was so much. "Tell me about your time in England. Where were you?"

"Mavis lived in Kensington. She married a barrister, and I lived with them and their baby son, Alfred. I worked as a nanny for my bed and board before I got a job of my own in one of the local restaurants. It was awful when she died. It was so sudden. I'm glad I didn't see it. Edward found her."

"What happened after the funeral?"

"I had met Jonathan several months before. We were courting by that time, although I wasn't ready for marriage yet." The words hacked at him like razor blades. He tried not to show it, and if she noticed, she didn't stop talking. "He arranged a job for me in the yacht club there, and found an apartment with some of the other girls who worked there. I lived there for more than a year, and now I'm back here, with you."

"What was it like when you left? You were just fifteen. You must have been terrified."

"I was, at first, but I think I could get used to about anything now. Mavis was so good to me. She was more of a parent to me than my mother and father ever were. I owed her so much."

"But you're back living with your parents now."

"Only until the wedding," she answered. "They're better now, most of the time anyway. My father dare not lay a hand on me. He knows how it would look in front of the Durrells, his new darlings. It sickens me how much my mother and father fawn over them, but they're my parents; I can't give up on them." She gazed out at the water extending out in front of them. The early June sun shone off the tops of the waves as they crested out like golden icing on some giant cake. "Their drinking is better now, although it seems hard to imagine it could've gotten any worse. I've really noticed the effect it's had on them. They look more like they should be my grandparents. They were so handsome once, at least from the old photographs I've seen."

He was sitting beside her on the rock, his hand only inches from hers. "It was such a shock when you left. I remember thinking that life just couldn't go on. It seems so ridiculous now, the things that children think?"

"No, of course not." They still hadn't touched each other. "No, Christopher, we were the center of each other's world. It's sweet when you think about it."

"But we were young then."

"Yes, of course, nothing ever stays the same."

"That's funny, I thought nothing ever changed. It doesn't seem like anything ever changes on this island."

"I came back, didn't I?"

"Yes, you did, and engaged to be married. Perhaps you are right after all." He felt good reiterating that she was engaged. Saying it out loud set a boundary for them both to be wary of, for them both to obey. "So how did you two meet? Where were you?"

"I told you I was working as a waitress in the yacht club. A friend introduced us when she heard he was from Jersey also. I can't say that I thought much of him at first." The feeling had gone from her voice, as if she were repeating a story she had practiced many times, and was now reciting to him. "But he wore me down, like every man does, I suppose. He found out where I lived and sent me flowers, and even befriended Edward, Mavis's husband, to get to know me better."

"What's he like? I hear his parents are very well thought of around the island. I've never met them myself, but my father has."

"He's not as outgoing as they are. He's shy, and can be rather serious, I suppose, but he was so good to me in England. I'm sure he'll make a wonderful husband."

"Congratulations."

"Thank you. What about you? You must have every single girl on the island chasing after you. You've grown up so handsome," she said. She put her hand on his shoulder, and just as quickly it was gone.

"Oh yes, every girl on the island. It's tough, you know, trying to keep them from waking my family at night. There's so many of them camped outside my house."

"No, seriously, I heard you were seeing that girl from the Red Lion, Sandrine? I've not met her, but I hear she's very pretty."

"'Seeing' is a strong word."

"You sound like Uli now. Is that what you're going to be, the eternal bachelor?"

"He's married now."

"You know what I mean. Don't dodge the question, Master Seeler."

"I feel like I'm being questioned by the police. Let's just say I'm still waiting for the right girl to come along. Sandrine is lovely, a really nice person, but . . . I don't think that she's the right one for me, not now anyway." The sun had disappeared and leaden clouds were extending over the land from the sea. He took a deep breath. *What do I have to lose?* "I suppose I thought you were the person . . . I know it sounds silly now that you've found the one that you truly want to be with."

"Oh Christopher, you're so sweet. Any girl would be so lucky to have you, truly they would. Perhaps things might have been different. . . ." He stood and she grabbed his wrist. "Sit down, please."

"So when is the big day?"

"There's no date set yet." Her voice came as a whisper this time, almost lost on the strengthening wind. "I'm not feeling sorry for you, there's no need for that. I loved you for so long, but I never thought I'd come back here. When you didn't reply to my letters . . . I tried to forget about you. I thought it best, especially for you. You didn't need me holding you back. Your father was right in what he did."

"You never held me back."

"I left, Christopher. I didn't want you to uproot yourself from your home and your family, for me. I wasn't ready for that. It was just a bad time."

"I understand." *There could never be a better reason to leave here.* "Things are better between my father and me now. It took some time."

"I'm glad." The rain began to spit down on them. It began first as a spattering that drove them to their feet, then as a deluge that soaked them through. Their clothes were stuck to them as they started back toward the houses. Rebecca took off her heels and went barefoot as she streaked ahead of him. She stopped outside her parents' house to wait for him. The rain was still pouring down, and Rebecca's hair was clamped tight to her scalp as she spoke, rivulets of water running down the smooth skin of her face. "Come on inside, my parents are not here. Trust me, they're out." She scampered down the driveway. He stood still. She pushed the front door open and disappeared inside.

She left the door open for him. He followed her. The lamp was on, casting a sparse light against the darkening evening outside. He had never seen anything quite so beautiful as she was. Without thinking, he reached for her and put his arms around her, hugging her tight to him. He felt her arms wrap around him. His hands were on the center of her back, and he could feel the wet ruffles of her dress between his fingers. The rain was beating down outside, but they were safe inside her parents' house. *Of all places to be safe inside.* It was thirty seconds before she drew her head back and they released their grip on each other. She mumbled the words. "We should get you dried off."

She led him through the hallway, seemingly freshly wallpapered, to the newly carpeted stairs. He stopped at the foot of the stairs. She waved a hand for him to follow. There was little light on the stairwell, only that of the dull hall lamp behind them. She was at the doorway to her room, her hand on the knob. He had never been in her bedroom before. She pushed open the door, and he saw the iron bed, still unmade from the night before, below the window and the old dresser with the mirror above it. They still hadn't spoken. She reached out to him, taking his hands in hers, holding them up so each could see them in front of their faces. He felt his breath quicken, could hear hers do the same. She held her arms in the air. "Can you help me?" she whispered, and he leaned back to undo the hooks on the back of her dress, unclasping each one in turn. She stood there wordlessly as he worked on the hooks and then the belt. He tried to pull the dress down, but she redirected him with a gentle, "not that way," and he pulled it up over her head. He pulled the slip up over her head the same way, and she lowered her arms and reached out to him, dressed now only in bra and underwear. She took his tie, roughly tore it off, and began to work on his shirt. Meticulously, she worked through each button and, once it was open, pulled it off him to reveal his bare chest. She took a towel from the chair behind her and rubbed his torso and arms, moving up to his hair. She was inches from him and handed the towel to him. He dried each arm first, before moving on to her hair and finally her breasts and flat belly.

He handed the towel back to her and she placed it over the chair behind her once more. They stood there for a few seconds. He wondered what to do next. She reached toward him and undid the belt around his waist, letting it fall to the floor with a clack. She helped him with his trousers and dropped them to his ankles. He lifted each foot in turn, and she picked the trousers up to throw them across the room. She removed his underpants and he was fully naked. She reached around her own back and undid the hooks on her bra. She pulled down her underwear and she was naked in front of him, her knees touching as she crossed her legs ever so slightly. He reached toward her, putting a hand on her shoulder, feeling her warmth. She put her hand on his, and he took a step into her and put his other hand around her waist. Then their lips were touching and he felt her tongue slipping into his mouth. Seconds slid into minutes, the only sound that of the rain outside and the sea below. They were still standing there by the bed when the sound of a car pulling into the driveway filled the air. He pulled away. "I thought you said they weren't coming back."

"I didn't think they were. You really need to leave, immediately. They can't catch you here." She was already pulling her underwear back on.

The noise was at the door now, and it opened. Two or more people walked though. "How am I going to get out? I can't exactly waltz downstairs and stroll past them." He had his trousers on now.

"Eh, the window, you can shin down the drainpipe." He walked to the window. It was less than twenty feet. There were voices downstairs now, both her parents and Jonathan. He was fully dressed within seconds. She was at the door, shouting that she would be down in a minute. He opened the window, stuck one leg out and then drew it back inside.

"What are you doing? You need to leave, please."

He strode across the room and kissed her again. "I had to say a proper goodbye."

He opened the window and let himself flop down into the sloshy wetness of the still unkempt back garden. She wasn't at the window. There was no wave goodbye. He cut through the bushes and ran back to his father's house through the driving rain.

# CHAPTER

## 10

He went through the motions of changing for bed. He climbed
under the covers and put out the lamp. But his mind was already
made up. He needed to see her. He bounced back out of the bed
and reached down for his clothes, folded neatly on the chair beside
his bed. He was dressed and ready to go within thirty seconds.
The light of the moon covered the apartment in a thin film of
luminescent white, just enough for him to find his way out and
he was gone.

He cycled past the lights of the town. The lamp on his bike
cast out a tunnel of white in front of him, illuminating the narrow
road and the bushes closing in around him. The warmth of summer hung thick in the night air.

He arrived at his father's house and climbed off the bicycle. The
handlebars were moist and clammy from where he had touched
them. He rested the bike against a bush and began walking down
toward Rebecca's parents' house. There was no light other than that
of the moon and stars.

Christopher stopped walking and took a pack of cigarettes out of his pocket. He placed one in his mouth. The box of matches in his hand was from the pub Sandrine worked in. He put them back into his pocket and threw the cigarette away. He understood the pressure Rebecca was under, but surely the best thing was to finally reject Jonathan Durrell and his proposal. His friends all knew what had happened. He reached around the back of his neck and took a piece of hair between his fingers and pulled. The pain jerked him back into the moment, standing there on that dark road. He walked on, and the house came into view over the black-green bushes that fenced the perimeter.

He ducked in through the hole in the hedge at the back of the house, ignoring the pricking of the twigs as they grazed his ears and the side of his neck. He crouched down in the overgrown grass at the back of the garden, surveying the scene, as he always did before he looked for suitable stones to throw up at Rebecca's window. There was a dull light on downstairs. That didn't mean anyone was awake. It was after midnight. She wasn't expecting him tonight, so he would need to find something big enough to wake her up, but only her, not her parents. He moved forward, feeling through the patches of grass and rough soil for stones. It took him a few seconds to find two or three good ones, and he threw the first up at her window in its solitary position on the second floor. His first throw was a good one and he crouched down again, waiting for her to appear. Thirty seconds passed. Usually she woke up with the first stone. He threw another, this time missing the window altogether. He cursed under his breath before throwing the third. This one hit with a loud clack and he bent down again, hoping that he hadn't cracked the glass. He waited, expecting an angry face to greet him. No answer came.

He dug his hands into the loose soil of the untidy garden. He got up to retreat through the bush back to his father's house. The back door of the house opened, about fifteen feet away. The twin barrels of a shotgun jutted out the door. Christopher ran toward the bush. The shotgun exploded, and he stopped cold, half expecting the slicing heat of shot fragments in his back.

"You there, stop now," Pierre Cassin said. "Turn around. That was a warning shot. The next one will be right at your head."

*Keep going. Don't stop.* Cassin was drunk, that much was clear from the slurred words that fell out of his mouth, and he only had one shot left. Christopher turned around with his hands raised. The light flooding out of the open door behind Pierre Cassin illuminated his face. *"L'Allemand."*

He stood there for a few seconds waiting for Cassin to speak. "I'm sorry that I was sneaking around in your back garden, Monsieur Cassin. I was only here to see Rebecca."

"Oh, I understand that," Cassin said, laughing. "It's heartening to know that love is still alive in the world, and creeping around my back garden of all places." Christopher didn't flinch, he hadn't moved, his hands still raised above his head, the wind licking at the top of his neck. "I suppose you're wondering what I'm going to do with you now? I should have you arrested for this."

"I'm so sorry, Monsieur Cassin. I won't do this again."

"You won't come to see my daughter again, just because I came out here and pointed a shotgun at you?"

He looked back at Cassin. His face was a dark hole illuminated only by the light curving around the sides. His hands seemed uncertain as they pointed the shotgun directly at Christopher's chest.

"Where is Rebecca? Is she here?" The wind blew hard against the house.

"No, she's not here. Come inside and I'll tell you where she is," he said, and gestured with the point of the shotgun to walk into the house. Christopher heard the crack of the door closing behind him. Cassin told him to keep walking, into the sitting room.

"I haven't seen you in this house for many years, but I'm sure you know it almost as well as I do," he said. He moved through into the sitting room, lit by a dim lamp in each corner. The room was covered in a flickering golden half-light, the corners dark. The once grand furniture seemed faded and worn, the walls were covered in Cassin's paintings of summer days and leaves blowing in the breeze. Christopher could make out only the dark shapes in the murky light. Cassin directed him to sit down on a chair by the fireplace. He sat down opposite him in a large armchair and picked up the whisky glass. His large shoulders slumped down as he sat, his tattered dressing gown draped across his shoulders like rags on a rotting scarecrow. Rebecca once spoke of how handsome her father had been as a young man and how her mother fell in love with him the first moment they met. That was hard to believe now. He was staring at Christopher across the firelight.

"Do you want a drink?" he said, holding up his glass.

"No, no thank you."

"Oh now, you don't say no when a man offers you a drink in his own house. Now, do you want a drink, young man?"

Christopher hesitated for a few seconds. "Yes, please."

"Good. I do so hate to drink alone." His French accent was still strong. He spoke as if he was just about to clear his throat, but never did. He reached over to the cabinet beside him and took out a whisky glass, filled it to the brim, and held it out.

"Thank you, Monsieur Cassin," he said, the brown liquid spilling over the edges. Cassin motioned for him to drink it and he held it to his lips, taking a sip.

"Is that the best you can do? Drink that back."

"Monsieur Cassin, this is a lot of . . ."

"I said drink it!"

Christopher looked across at him and the shotgun, cradled in his lap. He raised the glass to his lips and took the largest gulp he could manage, letting the whisky slide down his throat. It was vile, like drinking flaming gravel, but he didn't flinch.

"So let's talk about why you are here, despite the fact that you are not, well, how can I put this? You are not welcome?"

"I'm sorry, Monsieur Cassi—"

"You've said that, boy!" he shouted. "Don't you say that again! You're not sorry, no, you're not sorry. If it had been Rebecca who came out into the garden and not me, would you be sorry?"

"No."

"Well, then, don't give me that *sorry* line anymore. It's tiring. It demeans us both."

"I don't know what you want me to say." He held the glass up to his face and then brought it back down. Cassin narrowed his eyes into tiny slits and gestured for him to drink. He held the glass to his lips and sipped. "Okay, you're right. I'm not sorry."

"Now, that's the answer a man would give." Cassin's face was stiff, unyielding. He finished his glass before pouring himself another. "You like my daughter, then? Or is it love?" Cassin said. He lit a cigarette. The smoke hung thick and heavy in the air as Cassin leaned forward to speak again. "So, what do you know about love, boy? Tell me about love."

Christopher took another sip of the cheap whisky swirling around in the glass. "I don't pretend to be an expert," he said through his grimace.

"Let me tell you a little something about love," he spat. "It's pure lies, perpetrated by women to control the men of this world. I can see what you think you know, and it makes me laugh, boy. You love Rebecca and she loves you? You know where she is tonight? You know where?" Christopher shook his head. "She's at a reception in Lord Durrell's house. As you know, the young master Durrell has taken quite a liking to Rebecca." Christopher's heart dropped like a stone. "Now, what was that you were saying before, boy?"

Christopher stared down into the gray-black filth of the fireplace.

"She doesn't want you. You won't need to come creeping around my back garden anymore. Soon she'll be married into the richest family on the island."

"She doesn't love him. How can she?"

"There you go talking about that crap again. There's no love, boy, there's no love. There's only this," he said, pounding his chest. "And this," he held his glass aloft and took another sip. "There's no better reason to marry than money, no better reason, to look after your family, in their old age." His voice trailed off and he took a deep swig of the whisky in his glass.

"Are you going to let me go?"

"I haven't decided yet." He picked up the shotgun, cradled it across his lap. "Now, tell me, why do you think I don't let you see my daughter?"

"I don't know."

"Oh, come on now, are you going to make me ask every question twice? Are you man enough to answer a few questions or not? Now why do you think I don't let you see my daughter?"

"Because of my father, because you hate Germans."

"Good, good. That's a good start. There's also the fact that you're a filthy wretch scrounging around in my back garden like a little Nazi rat. Why would I let someone like you see my daughter? Why would I give her to you?"

"She's not yours to give."

Cassin laughed and drew on his cigarette. "What age are you, twenty? You are a naïve fool, aren't you? This love you speak of, I suppose Rebecca tells you that she loves you, that she wants only you?" The smile spread across his face once more. Christopher was about to speak, but Cassin began again. "Only today she was talking with her mother about how much she was looking forward to the wedding, and how much she wanted to take Jonathan Durrell as her husband."

The words hit Christopher like bullets. Cassin was lying. He had to be. Rising to the bait would only be letting him win. Yet the words lingered like scum floating on a pond. "What about you, Monsieur Cassin? You have it all worked out then, do you?"

"I know what exists and what doesn't." He drew on his cigarette again and leaned forward. "I left home when I was your age to go to Paris to pursue my art. I met Monsieur Monet and Monsieur Renoir, worked with them both. It was a wonderful time. A time . . . of discovery"—he held up his glass, staring into it as he spoke—"during which I discovered that I was never going to be good enough to be one of them. I had my talents, though. And my talent, boy? Women were my talent. Women were easy to me, and I soon realized that with my talents, it wouldn't matter that I wasn't good enough to be rich myself. There were so many ladies in Paris looking for a young artist to fulfill themselves with, and I gave them what they wanted. In return they gave me the freedom to pursue my art. I traveled all over Europe, from Paris to Rome to Vienna and Berlin. And there were always women, rich women."

Christopher looked up and around the room and wondered where all the money had gone. The lamp in the corner flickered, throwing shadows around Cassin's face. It was clear he was enjoying this. Christopher took another sip from the glass and stared back across at him.

"I was living with a woman in Paris, long before you were born, before the war. She was a wonderful woman. She was rich. My wife, Marjorie, Rebecca's mother, was her niece," Cassin sneered. "She was beautiful, but there was more. Marjorie was in line to inherit the family fortune. I began seeing her. Her aunt never knew, of course." Cassin took another sip and looked down at the floor between them. "That was a golden age, perhaps the best time of my life. But Marjorie moved back here to Jersey, to her family home."

He could hardly believe this man was Rebecca's father.

"She . . . she was gone, and I was left in Paris with her aunt. But then the war began, and I did my duty, served with honor in Flanders until I caught a bullet in the leg and went home. Let me tell you, many of my friends were not so lucky. Your father and his friends took care of a great . . . took care of many of them." Christopher stared back, unblinking. "And now that madman, Hitler . . . determined to destroy everything he touches. Is there no end with you people?" He almost spat the words out.

"I don't concern myself with politics."

"You think by living here you can change what you are? You are one of them. You really think I would give my daughter to you? A filthy Boche?"

"I was born German, but I live here. My mother was from Jersey. I have been living here since I was six years old."

"Oh, what difference does that make? You will always be one of them, you will never fit in here, and you know that." Cassin settled back in his chair, laid down his glass, and leveled the shotgun at Christopher. Christopher squirmed backward in his seat. "You know I could shoot you now, don't you, boy? I could shoot you and say that I caught you breaking into my house. No one would ever know."

"Please, Monsieur Cassin, I'm sorry . . ."

"I told you not to say that to me again!" Cassin roared. "I told you that already. Now, are you sorry?"

"What?"

"Are you sorry, you Nazi rat?"

"No, no, I'm not sorry."

"Okay, at least you admit that much. At least we're being honest with each other. Now get yourself together. See that piece of paper behind you on the dresser. Yes, see there, boy. Pick it up and the pen too. We're going to write a letter to Rebecca, telling her how you really feel. I think she deserves to know. Don't you?"

He reached back and took the pen and paper in his hand. The shotgun was still pointed directly at him. "Now . . ."

"Shut up. I'll do the talking from here. You write. You do know how to write, don't you? Yes, lean on that book. We don't want this to look . . . rushed." Cassin laid the shotgun back across his lap and picked up the whisky glass and began to dictate. "Dear Rebecca. Write it, boy, write!"

"Okay, okay."

"Dear Rebecca, I could not see you to tell you this face-to-face as I find myself overcome with guilt." Cassin's face was stern, unforgiving. "I have spent a lot of time of late contemplating our courtship. I am sorry to tell you that I can't see you anymore. I have found myself racked with guilt since sleeping with Sandrine." He looked up at Cassin, his mouth wide open. He stood up, forgetting where he was. Cassin smiled and gestured with the shotgun for him to sit down, and he let himself drop back down into the chair. "I take full responsibility for my actions and cannot blame them on my growing dependence on alcohol. I want you to be happy and now realize that I am not good enough a man to be with you, particularly bearing in mind the infection I have contracted since this occurrence." Christopher let the pen drop. Cassin raised the shotgun again. "You write the letter, or I call down to the police to tell them that I have just shot an intruder in my house. You choose, boy!" Christopher's muscles seized, and his whole body felt limp. Cassin began again. "I know that you have been contemplating the offer of marriage from Jonathan Durrell. This is some comfort to me that you have found a suitor who is worthy of you. I wish you all the best in your future with him. Yours, et cetera, et cetera. Don't try anything funny, boy. Sign it, and if I see anything strange about the letter, any kind of code . . ."

"There's no code, see for yourself, you twisted old bastard!"

"Pass it here." Cassin scanned through it. "Good, very good. This is going to be an unfortunate shock for Rebecca, but at least Jonathan will be there to comfort her. Along with her family, of course."

Christopher was drained, exhausted. He stood up. "I'm leaving now." He knew what he had to do. He wouldn't let Cassin win.

"Yes, get out," Cassin said. Christopher fumbled through the shadows and toward the front door, Cassin's words echoing and then fading as he walked out. "Stay away from my daughter. If I see you around her again, I'll kill you. You hear me? You hear me, boy?" Christopher closed the front door behind him, ran out into the garden, and bent over, sucking deep breaths into his lungs.

# CHAPTER

## 11

He stumbled back up the road, back toward the house, the wind churning around him and the sound of the waves crashing onto the beach ringing in his ears. His vision was dimming and the taste of whisky swirled around, mixing with the bile in the back of his throat. There was no light now. The moon and stars had left him. He led himself by memory up the road toward his father's house. He kicked something hard and crumpled onto the road. He pushed himself up and felt the dull pain in his knee. The pain in his left leg intensified as he tried to stand on it, and he hauled himself forward on his right, dragging the other leg behind him as he went. There was no stopping now. The house was ahead. He couldn't see it, but he knew it was there. The sound of the sea receded as he went, replaced by the sound of his own breathing and his pulse rushing electric through his veins. "I have to get to her," he said, perhaps out loud, perhaps in his head. The road leaned to the left and he followed it around, his eyes now adjusted to the black. The house was there. No lights on. He saw his bike, still resting against the bush where he had left it. It was no use to him now.

He reached up to his forehead, dripping with hot, salty sweat. The pain in his leg ran up through his entire torso, but he ignored it, or tried to ignore it, and dragged himself toward the front door of the house. The house was completely quiet except for the breath thundering through his lungs. He put both hands on the wall and edged along toward the kitchen. He was able to move more easily with the solid structure as support and was sure he wasn't making any noise as he moved. He sat down at the kitchen table, his pulse finally slowing. *I have to get to her, tonight. It has to be tonight. Now.*

The adrenaline was gone. The room was unstill, as if he were sitting on a rickety raft on some hot tumultuous sea. His left trouser leg was ripped, with dark bloodstains spreading out across the knee. He took a tablecloth, hanging over the back of his chair, and dabbed the cut through the tear in his trousers. The tablecloth fell onto the floor. He left it there. His knee was stinging, but it didn't appear to be broken. There was no sound from upstairs, and he continued along the wall and into the study. The car keys were on the desk. He placed them into his pocket. The house was absolutely noiseless as he struggled out the front door.

The Durrells' house in Saint Brelade was forty-five minutes in the car, during the daytime. He squinted at his watch. It was hard to tell in the darkness, but it seemed to be around one a.m., or maybe later. Rebecca and her mother were out very late, and the thought of waiting for them came to him. Where would he wait? He certainly wasn't going anywhere near that house again. The best thing was to drive down there. There must have been a party at the house. They would have made excuses for Cassin himself as he was liable to ruin an occasion like that. He turned the key in the ignition, the car coughing and spluttering to a start, and he looked up at the light going on in his father's room. The bedroom window opened.

"I have to borrow the car, Father. It's an emergency!" he shouted, and accelerated out of the driveway, not waiting for word of reply. The certainty of what he had done was with him as he drove away from the house. The certainty that what he was doing was the right thing propelled him on. Forgiveness from his father or whatever else would have to wait.

The lights on the car cast out thirty or maybe forty feet in front of him. The rearview mirror showed nothing but blackness extending behind. He thought about Cassin and the shotgun and the whisky. The headlights flashed onto a cow on the road for the brief second before he dragged the steering wheel to the side. The car swerved off into the dark, careering through a bush and into a ditch, and the steering wheel collided with his chest as the car flipped over and came to rest on its side. Thoughts flashed through his mind of Rebecca, her father, and the long drive left to Saint Brelade before he spiraled into darkness.

———

Alexandra was there with his father. She was crying. Christopher's father bent over farther, now coming into Christopher's view. Christopher could feel his left eye was closed. He couldn't open it, and then the pain came, trickling up his spine at first and then in great waves. He arched his back and saw the white sheet lift and fall with his chest. He felt his father take his hand, felt the warmth of his fingers. Christopher's words came as a splutter that rocked his head back and forth. His father quieted him, putting his hand on his forehead. He tried to sit up but fell back. His vision cleared as the pain increased, and he raised his fingers to feel his swollen eye.

"I'm sorry about the car, Father."

"No, no, I don't care about that. Don't worry about that."

"I had to do it. . . . I had to stop her." His vision dimmed once more, and the light magnified, blurring everything and everyone in the room. "It was her father, it was Monsieur Cassin, I had to . . ." The darkness descended upon him again.

He awoke to see his father and sister, both asleep in chairs on opposite sides of the room. His vision had cleared, and the pain was more regular now. He watched them sleeping for a while until he closed his eyes again.

Alexandra was there when he woke up. "Where is Father?" Christopher said. She touched her hand to his forehead.

"He had to leave. He'll be back soon. He was here with me all night. How are you feeling now?"

"I feel fine," he lied. His left arm and left leg were both in thick white casts and his head ached like nothing he'd ever felt.

"Is he angry about the car? What did he say?"

"He really doesn't care about that. We were just so worried. Why did you do it, Christopher? We have the clothes that they found you in. They stink of whisky."

"I . . . I had to do it. It wasn't something I had planned on doing." His pulse was speeding again as he spoke. "Who found me anyway?"

"Mr. Baines. You almost ran over one of his cows."

He was about to tell Alexandra to express to Mr. Baines how sorry he was when Rebecca walked in. She was alone, holding a bunch of flowers. "I suppose I should leave you two to talk," Alex said, and left.

Rebecca looked tired, her eyes swollen. She sat down next to the bed. He tried to sit up but couldn't.

"How are you feeling? I was so upset when I heard about what had happened."

"I'm feeling fine. The doctors say I'll be better soon. How are you?"

"I got the letter that you wrote. My father gave it to me." The evening sun was golden through the window, each speck of dust now a precious ingot. She was more beautiful than he could have imagined possible.

He tried to sit up again but felt a sharp dart of pain up his side, and he slid back down. "I didn't mean what I wrote in the letter . . . I . . ." She took his hand where it lay on the bed.

"Stop, Christopher," she whispered. "I know. I know who you are." She took his hand to her mouth, kissed it, and held it to her cheek. "Oh Christopher, how could you imagine that I would ever believe that? How could I believe what my father said? You've always been the best thing in my life. I always knew that; I just forgot for a while. You were always in my heart, from the first moment we ever met. I have loved you all my life. I was out that night at Jonathan's house telling him that the engagement had to end, that I didn't love him, and that I was going to be with you." Rebecca leaned up and kissed him. It hurt. Christopher didn't care. "It's always been you, Christopher. It always will be you."

# CHAPTER

---

## 12

Rebecca had nowhere else to go, or nowhere else she wanted to be. She moved into Christopher's apartment and was waiting for him when he'd recovered enough to join her there. She lived with him a week or two while he recovered. Once she had found a job, in a local hotel, she moved into an apartment down the road. It was close. She only slept there. They spent the rest of their time together.

By the summer of 1939, fear had begun to infest the island. That fear bred resentment. This was his home too. This was his island as much as it was theirs. Christopher, along with everyone else, was becoming more obsessed with the politics of the country of his birth. There was no escaping it. Even Uli admitted that the country might be headed toward war, after the rest of Czechoslovakia fell in March. He couldn't empathize with his uncle's excitement at reclaiming Germany's place among the nations of the world and making up for the crimes perpetrated against her at the end of the Great War. He could not be like him, could not share in the patriotic pride swelling in Germany at the rallies where Herr Hitler held the gigantic crowds in thrall and entranced them with his words. The Seelers were finding it harder to be German, to associate themselves with the book-burning hordes. There was no mistaking where they were from, though. Conversations about politics hushed when Christopher approached, as if his friends were unsure of his allegiances, even though they had known him all his life.

Uli knew what side he was on, even if Christopher didn't. Uli had rarely mentioned any measure of politics in his letters in the past, but as the year had worn on, it was a subject that was becoming more and more difficult to avoid. Uli truly seemed to believe that Hitler didn't want war and that he and his Nazis would stop once Germany had retaken the lands stolen from her after the Great War. Uli mentioned these truths, as he saw them, in passing, preferring to comment on Christopher's life and to recount stories of the domestic bliss that he and Karolina had launched themselves into. But Stefan saw things differently, and was becoming visibly upset by the situation in Germany. Christopher could feel the disapproving glances and hear the insidious whispers in the darkness of the movie theater as the encirclement and public humiliation of the Western powers by the Nazis played on the screen in front of them in the newsreels.

Only Tom, his old friend who still lived with him, would speak to him frankly. Tom was seeing Alexandra now. It had happened gradually at first, and then all of a sudden. They had all seen it coming, even Christopher himself. Tom joked about divided loyalties should he and Alexandra end up married. He looked at Christopher as he made the joke, as if trying to gauge his reaction. Christopher smiled back at him, putting his arm on his shoulder. No further words were exchanged on the topic. Two weeks later he proposed to Alexandra. They walked into the house on a Sunday evening in May to announce the news. Tom hugged Stefan, Christopher, and Rebecca in turn. Alex had never seemed happier. It was a wonderful time.

War was declared on a Sunday. They were in the pub. Tom and Alex were newly married, still reveling in the experience of their wedding the previous week. Alex broached the inevitable question of when Christopher and Rebecca were to be married just as the bar owner announced it. A hush came over the crowd for a few seconds. A few people cheered and shouted "God save the king" and "God save poor Poland." Christopher could only think of Uli in Berlin, and Karolina, pregnant with their first child. Tom tried to make a joke. Christopher barely heard him, and if Alexandra did, she didn't react.

"It will pass," Rebecca assured him. "It will all be over by Christmas."

He took another swig of beer. He knew most of the other patrons, at least in passing. They clinked their glasses together, toasting the king and wishing death to the Germans. There was loud cheering and then someone started singing "God Save the King." Most of the crowd joined in. Tom took Alexandra by the hand and stood up.

"Perhaps we should be leaving too," Rebecca said.

"No, I think I'll stay if that's all right." Rebecca kissed him, and the others said goodbye. He walked to the bar alone. He was standing beside Jacques La Marque and Sidney Morris, both men in their fifties, fishermen on the island.

"Some situation, eh?" Christopher began. Neither man replied. "Hitler just doesn't want to stop."

Sandrine pushed the beer toward him.

"It's on the house," she said. "I thought you could use it today."

"Thank you. I never congratulated you. When is the wedding?"

"Next year," she said, and walked away.

In the background, the sounds of "God Save the King" swelled and filled the room until all were singing it—except him. He thought of Uli in Berlin. Was he sitting there tight-lipped, as he was, as the crowd rejoiced and sang the national anthem? He doubted it somehow.

Jacques leaned forward. Both men had served in the Great War, and were now too old for this one.

"What's to happen now? It can't be like the last war."

"No, it can't be. It'll all be over quickly. Hitler will take Poland and be done with it. Britain and France are just too strong. The Nazis will know better."

Sidney took a long pull on his cigarette. "I certainly admire your sense of optimism."

Christopher lit a cigarette, staying silent, though he knew the words to the song. He stayed there for another hour before he went home to tell his father that they were at war.

---

The letter came six weeks later.

*October 12, 1939*
Stefan, Christopher, and Alexandra,
First of all congratulations to Alexandra on getting married! It seems like all the best people are getting married these days. What about you, Christopher? Isn't it time that you gave up your freedom forever and subjugated yourself to a woman? No, but seriously . . . Alex and Tom, we were so sorry that we weren't able to travel to Jersey for the wedding. It seems like these politicians have other things on their minds than my traveling for

your wedding. Thank you for the nice letter you sent me, Alexandra, and the photographs enclosed. It's amazing how your father could have produced a daughter quite so beautiful. Questions could be asked, but I don't suppose now is the time. I look forward to meeting Tom again as your husband, as opposed to Christopher's friend who used to scuttle around the house in those ill-fitting shorts that left little to the imagination. At least we know that your children will have fine legs when they do come.

On the subject of children, Karolina is doing very well; pregnancy seems to suit her. If it's a boy, we are playing with the idea of naming him Stefan, after Stefan Zweig of course, our favorite novelist. Karolina seems to want to come up with names for a girl, but really what's the point when I know I'm going to have a son? The question of what kind of a world my little son or daughter is to grow up in is an entirely different one, however. And this brings me on to the serious part of this letter. With all that's going on in the world at the moment, one has to decide what is worth fighting for, what is worth sacrificing for. I have been considering joining the army for some time now, just as you did, Stefan, when last our country called, back in 1914. I was too young then, but now I feel it's my turn. Once Germany has reclaimed the lands stolen from her after the last war, the German people will once more be safe from the threats of Bolshevism and our country will be able to take her place among the great nations of the world. The fact that conscription has been introduced for all able-bodied men up to the age of forty-one reinforced my decision. There is no escape from this. I am joining the Wehrmacht, and by the time you receive this letter, the process will be under way.

Try not to worry. I am sure this war will be over soon enough, and we will all be together again, in a better world for our children to grow up in.

Uli

"What do we do now, Father?" Alexandra asked.

"We do nothing. We stay here. We've nowhere to go, no place to be but here." He placed his hand on her head. "We haven't changed. Uli hasn't changed either. Christopher, you have Rebecca to think of now. The risk of the Nazis arriving here is too great. You need to leave." Christopher didn't reply, just stared down at his fingers and listened to the sound as he tapped them on the wooden table.

The line at the ticket booth for the ferry was out the door as Christopher arrived with Rebecca. He couldn't stand the thought of leaving. This in-between place was so perfect for him and his family, who were neither German nor English, neither one side nor the other in this new war. But Rebecca's touch as she held his hand reassured him. Staying here would be too dangerous. They had been standing in line for about ten minutes, deflecting questions from Mrs. Mesrine about their living arrangements, when Arthur Cooper, the ticket seller, got out of his booth. He walked down the line to them and motioned Christopher to come to him. Christopher knew him. Arthur was a decent sort but a bad drinker. Christopher felt the shock of nerves inside him as Arthur took him aside, away from anywhere their conversation might have been heard.

"I presume you're here to get off the island, to England?"

"Yes, of course," Christopher replied, trying to figure out what he was about to say. "Is there something the matter?" he asked as Arthur hesitated.

"Well, yes, there is. I'm sorry to tell you that since the war was declared, His Majesty's government has barred all German citizens from either entering or leaving the country or its protectorates." His mustache twitched above his mouth. "So I'm afraid I can't let you leave. Even if I did, they'd never let you into the country."

Christopher ran through what he could say or do, but there was nothing. "You're sure about this?"

"I've been dreading the day you or your family came in here. There's no one else this applies to on the whole island. I'm sorry."

"It's not your fault. There's really nothing to be done." Rebecca was still waiting in line. "We'd best be going, then. Thanks for taking me aside like this."

They were trapped. There was nowhere for them to go, nowhere for Christopher and his family to be except this in-between place. The war had seen to that, and, for the first time since he and Rebecca had come together, he felt as though he was losing control.

There was talk of war everywhere, and all over the island, young men up and left for the mainland to join up for their chance to have at the Hun. To those who remained on Jersey, the war seemed far away, like a storm out at sea that the fishermen would talk about while the sun still shone down on land.

The fear was everywhere. Everyone was scared—some hid it, but there was no getting past it. Two weeks later the German forces began their advance into Belgium, France, Luxembourg, and the Netherlands, which soon all capitulated. The British army was pushed back toward Dunkirk. The atmosphere on the island changed as rumor began to spread that the British forces stationed on Jersey were to be withdrawn. Christopher's father, who had been hoarding canned foods for several months, began to buy as much petrol as he could carry. Most people on the island had the same idea and it became harder to come by as the days went on. The local fishermen helped out with the massive evacuation of British troops to England from the beaches at Dunkirk. Tom began to talk about joining the army himself. His twin brother, Percy, had left several weeks before, along with Harry Locke, to enlist with thousands of others. The only thing that held him back was his wife and the thought of her not being able to flee to England like so many were now planning to do. Christopher waited, read and reread the last letter from Uli, looked at the picture of his newborn son, Stefan. Uli was in the advance, which seemed just days away from defeating France and perhaps pushing onward to the Channel Islands and England itself.

He worried about Rebecca more than himself. The reports filtering across from Europe about the Nazis' treatment of the Jews were too frightening even to imagine. The Jews in Europe were being stripped of their property, their homes, and even their citizenship. He remembered the headlines in the newspapers he had seen in Berlin in 1938. Now they were coming.

June came and Paris fell. Two weeks later, Winston Churchill, the new prime minister, announced that the Channel Islands were of no strategic importance and that the garrison stationed there was to be withdrawn to the mainland. They were to be declared an open town, and to be left for the Germans. But on the newsreel that night, there were no reports of such an occurrence. Christopher was driving home when he saw the green uniforms of the troops. They were being loaded into trucks. He asked the policeman directing traffic and was told that they were pulling out. There was no official announcement. The news was out. The roads were packed, and it took him more than an hour to make the ten-minute drive. There was panic everywhere. People were scuttling around like ants, carrying their possessions to God knows where. He went to the greengrocer and then the newsagent. Both were closed, their shelves already cleared.

He went to Rebecca. Since the time they had tried to leave, they had skirted around the conversation of what would happen if the Nazis were to invade Jersey. She, in particular, had become very good at avoiding the topic. They had never truly believed that it could happen, not until now.

"The troops are leaving."

"I heard," she replied. "We've been left to rot, to fend for ourselves."

"You know what needs to happen now. All the Jews on the island are leaving."

"My mother is leaving, although my father is being stubborn about it as always."

"I'm glad to hear she's done the sensible thing. As far as your father is concerned . . ."

"What about you?" Rebecca said. "I can't leave you."

"Never mind me. I'll be fine."

"No. I won't leave you. What have I got to go to in England?"

"What is this? Are you insane? The Nazis are coming. We've both seen the newsreels. We've both seen how they're disenfranchising the Jews in every country they set foot in."

"So I should disenfranchise myself? What about you? You haven't answered my question."

"You know I can't leave."

"That's why I won't leave. I won't leave you. Anyway, what makes England so safe? Who's to say that Germany won't be invading England next month or next week? Where do I flee to then? This is my home. Why should I leave?"

"You left before." Was he shouting now? It was hard to tell. He walked to the window in her apartment. There were people rushing back and forth on the streets below. Nothing like this had happened before.

"I was a child then. I'm telling you, Christopher, I'm not leaving. We're going to be together, nothing can change that."

"No, no way. I want to be with you, but not at that price, not at the price of your safety, your life." He took his arms away from her hips. "You're going to England and that's it. You're leaving before they arrive."

"Why should I give up everything I love, to run and hide?"

"Because they'll take everything you have. They'll take away your home, your citizenship."

"There's nothing for me there. If I leave, I'll lose everything. The only chance I have at any kind of a life is to stay here."

# CHAPTER

---

## 13

There were rumors everywhere. The British forces were coming back. The Germans were to bypass Jersey. The Germans were to invade and deport all the inhabitants to camps on the mainland and use the islands as a springboard to invade the south coast of England. People spoke of going, but few actually went. Rebecca still refused to discuss the possibility of her leaving. Christopher was in his father's house when she arrived.

"Rebecca, what are you doing here?"

"Oh, so you're talking to me now?" she countered. "You know I don't take orders from you or anyone else." He was wary of the argument that was about to occur. "I know you want the best for me, but who's to know what will happen? At least if I stay here, I'll be with you." Christopher's father got up to leave. "Please, Mr. Seeler, I'd really rather you stayed for this." He sat back in the chair.

"You're so pigheaded. You've got to realize the danger staying here puts you in," Christopher said.

"I have to agree, Rebecca. Staying here is insane. I know you want to be with Christopher, but there will be a time for that, after the war is over."

"When the British win?" Rebecca was exasperated. "How are they going to do that? They were routed at Dunkirk. The French were beaten in weeks." She sat down beside them at the kitchen table. "They'll probably be in England in a month. If Christopher could come with me, I would go, of course I would try. What's the point of a few more weeks of freedom without him?"

Christopher put his head in his hands. "Don't you see you have to try?" he said, his words muffled by his palms. "Who knows what they'll do if you stay here? We've been through this before!"

"We can't force you to do anything." Christopher's father's voice was level and sober. "But if you do stay, you will be putting yourself in an unreasonable amount of danger. We will do our best to protect you, but the Nazis' hatred of the Jews is like nothing I've ever known. They blame the Jews for everything. We may not be able to protect you from them."

"Rebecca, you get on that boat, and you leave this island. I told you what those newspapers I saw in Germany said. What can I do to convince you?"

"Stop fighting me on this. I'm not leaving the island without you," she said, and left.

The German bombers came on Friday afternoon, June 28, 1940. Dozens of people waiting on the harbor to be evacuated were killed. Christopher knew some of them: Mrs. Shearer and her son, Norman, just fifteen years old; John Barrow, who had served in the Great War; and old Tom Frost, from Saint Savior. The next day, the main British fleet arrived to take away the remaining evacuees.

Christopher had not seen Rebecca since they'd fought in his father's house the day before. The morning of the evacuation, he had been to her apartment, anticipating another fight, but had not found her. Two suitcases lay in the middle of the floor, fully packed, ready to go. The feeling of hollow satisfaction he felt at seeing those suitcases was unlike anything he'd felt before. Bitter relief swept through him.

The ships were waiting in and outside the harbor, strewn across the water like leaves on a pond, waiting for the swelling crowds on shore. There were thousands of people, whole families lined up along the stone jetties, waiting for their turn to squeeze onto the tiny rowboats that would take them out to the larger ships moored farther out. Some people weren't leaving. Defiance spread through the crowd. Children who were forcibly pushed onto the boats were jumping back into the water, swimming back to parents who tried to feign anger as they toweled them dry in the summer sun.

The Jews were leaving. Christopher's father embraced his friend Albert Gold when he left with his family. They all left: the Fogels, the Levis, the Kleins. Mrs. Cassin arrived alone. She struggled with her suitcase as she made her way to join the line of people waiting for the boats. A young man went to her and helped her along. She got into the boat and sat down without saying a word to anyone. She never looked back.

Christopher waited there for several hours. Thousands had left the island. Many thousands more had decided to stay. Still there was no sign of Rebecca. The crowds on the harbor diminished as the day went on. He and his father stood, waiting. Most were too wary of the German bombers coming back to risk seeing their neighbors evacuated to the mainland. Tom's family arrived, his parents and little sisters. Christopher and his father said their goodbyes, not lingering too long as Alexandra and Tom were there. Tom stood stoically by, holding his mother's hand as she cried. He took her in his arms and then each of his sisters. His father shook his hand and they left. He was alone, his entire family gone. Alexandra was all he had left.

Rebecca never came. She was there at the apartment after the final ships had left. He pushed open the door, and she was sitting on the couch, pretending to read. Her suitcases were still on the rug in front of her, untouched from when he had seen them that morning. He didn't speak, just shut the door behind him. The couch creaked as he sat down next to her, and he put his arms around her, bringing her head close into his chest. "You really are quite mad," he whispered.

"I love you," she replied in a whisper, and they sat there for several minutes, not talking.

The next day, the Germans came with two divisions of men, and the five-year occupation of Jersey began.

# CHAPTER

## 14

Rebecca clutched Christopher's hand as they stood watching the columns of troops march past. The swell of people, three deep on both sides of the street, made no sound. The only noise was that of the marching songs.

"What are they singing? What do the words mean?" Rebecca asked.

"They're singing, 'On, On to Battle,'" he answered.

"People are staring at us."

"Don't be ridiculous."

"Surely these people have more to worry about than the fact that you happen to be German," she said. They stayed another five minutes until, their curiosity satisfied, they left.

Two weeks later a car pulled up outside Christopher's father's house. "Rebecca, go upstairs and close the bedroom door behind you. Don't come back down until they've left," Christopher's father said.

"Perhaps we picked the wrong day to visit," she said as she walked out.

A German soldier held the door of the car for the officer, who looked up and down the road before making his way toward the house. He knocked on the door and stood back. Christopher stood up, but Stefan put his hand on his shoulder and walked toward the front door. They were speaking German. The officer asked if he could come in. Christopher's father led the officer into the kitchen and asked him to sit down at the table. The officer was sat upright in the chair, hat on the table in front of him.

"Christopher, this is Captain Voss, he asked to see both of us."

Captain Voss stood up and smiled. "So good to meet you," Voss said, proffering his hand. Christopher shook it, his eyes drawn to the iron cross on the gray uniform.

"Christopher, make the tea, please. You'll have some, Captain Voss?"

"Yes, of course."

"So, Captain Voss, to what do we owe this pleasure?" Christopher's father said.

"Straight to the point, eh?" Voss laughed. "Well, as you know, we intend the occupation of Jersey to be an example for all the rest of the countries now under the control of the Reich." There was a silence, as if Voss expected them to reply but neither did. "We wish to have a good working relationship with the people of Jersey, and hence have left your local government, or the States, as you call them, in place. My Kommandant, Doctor von Stein, has asked for the cooperation of the people of Jersey and we expect it to be forthcoming. We know that life will be different under the guardianship of the Führer, and that war always brings hard times."

Christopher brought the tea over, set it in front of the two men. Voss took a few seconds to pour cups for the other two men before his own.

"That's all very well, Captain Voss, but what does this have to do with us?"

Christopher was thinking about Uli, how he had sat in that same seat so many times and how now he was wearing that same uniform. Two weeks ago the Seelers were the only Germans on the island, but now there were thousands, almost one for every three islanders. This was the first time he had spoken to one of them.

"We were looking through records of the people on the island and were very pleased to see that there was at least one German family living here. Doctor von Stein sees this as a way of introducing ourselves to the local people."

"What would we be required to do?" Christopher's father asked.

"Nothing more than to act as a go-between and to facilitate the smooth running of everyone's affairs on the island."

"Captain Voss, I'm sure that you'll understand that we've been living here for many years now. We've integrated with our neighbors and made many friends." Christopher's father picked up the cup of tea.

"What are you getting at here?"

"We may need to refuse this duty." Christopher's father placed his teacup back onto the saucer. He hadn't drunk any.

"Why on earth would you refuse? This is an opportunity to help out your neighbors as well as the Fatherland. This is a unique chance. And, of course, helping Doctor von Stein in his duties will bring certain rewards."

"Do we have a choice?" Christopher asked.

"I understand you've been here most of your life and this must make this even harder for you. I also understand your uncle, Uli Seeler, is serving with the Third Panzer Division in France." He held the cup of tea in front of him, and took a sip. "Your uncle certainly has no doubts where his loyalties lie. You yourself would make a fine addition to the Wehrmacht. Perhaps you might like to speak to someone about serving your country as your uncle does."

"Where do we go from here?" Christopher's father asked.

"Report to this address," he said, drawing a small piece of paper from his pocket. "You will be expected to be there at eight a.m. tomorrow morning. You may ask for me." He stood up and put his hat back on. "I expect you will be more accommodating as time progresses. I'm sure you'll see that we mean the best for the population of the island. Oh, and you may drive down tomorrow morning." He strode out of the kitchen and toward the door. Christopher came to the door as Rebecca came down the stairs, staying out of sight. He had the piece of paper in his hand and waited until the car had left before reading it. The address was the Durrells' mansion in Saint Brelade.

The next morning, Christopher and his father arrived at the gates of the mansion at about ten minutes to eight. The sentries shouldered their rifles as they approached the car window. Christopher's father explained their business there and the guard waved for the gates to be opened. It was the first time they had been in the car for almost two weeks. A few days after they had arrived, the Germans had barred all civilian use of cars and tractors, and suddenly bikes were very valuable items. The mansion, the former home of the Durrell family, was now the official residence of Dr. Gottfried von Stein, the Kommandant of the German occupying forces on Jersey.

Christopher's father pulled the car to halt. "Remember, this is not the place for rebellious words; keep them in your heart." The sentry led them inside. There was no sign of Lord or Lady Durrell, just German soldiers strolling around the beautiful gardens. The sentry led them inside the foyer and told them to wait. They stood on the polished marble floor, looking at the paintings of Lord Durrell's ancestors and the portrait of Hitler, newly installed beside them. Captain Voss came down the stairs to greet them. "Hello, gentlemen, so glad you've decided to join with us." He led them into a small office upstairs and sat them down. He regretted that

Dr. von Stein had not the time to see them and that he would keep it short. Their job would be to translate the ordinances passed down from the German occupiers to the States, the ruling political council on the island. They would be required to translate these ordinances, not to explain them. For their work, they would be well paid and would receive the privilege of the use of one car for their family. The whole meeting took less than five minutes. Captain Voss told them that they would start work the next day in an office building in town.

Christopher and his father began their new enforced role. There were no other fluent German speakers living on the island, with the exception of Alexandra, and both were happy to keep her as far away from the Germans as possible. News of their new appointment soon got out. They were in the pub one evening after work when Dewey Leonard, a local fisherman, now unemployed, like hundreds of others due to the German ban on all fishing boats leaving harbor, approached them at the bar. He was drunk, blind drunk. "Traitors," he hissed, "profiting from the invasion of the island. You've been waiting for them to come for a long time now, haven't you?"

Christopher went to step forward, but his father put an arm across him. "I can assure you we're not happy either. The sooner they leave and we can return life to normal the better." No one else spoke up. Dewey walked away, cursing under his breath. Two days later they found the tires on their car slashed outside the office. Christopher confronted Dewey, sober this time, on the street a few days later, but he swore he was on the other side of the island visiting his mother that day. They never reported the incident.

The Durrells were still living in their house. They were now sharing it with the Kommandant and his staff. Everywhere on the tiny island was suddenly very crowded.

# CHAPTER

---

## 15

The ordinance about the Jews came in October 1940. All Jews on the island were to register at the Chief Aliens Office in Saint Helier. Christopher read down through the document, his pulse quickening with every line. Jews were defined as any person that belonged at any time to the Jewish religion, or who had more than two Jewish grandparents. People on the island who had never considered themselves Jews would be included. Realizing what was coming, he felt his hands turn to blocks of ice. Until then Christopher and his father had been taking stock of every chicken, cow, hen, and pig on the island and what each farmer was growing, translating letters to and from the people for the Kommandant and, of course, translating whatever decree Dr. von Stein happened to want to pass down that day. There had never been anything about the Jews. Somehow Christopher had convinced himself, and Rebecca too, that the Nazis would treat the Jews on Jersey differently. Christopher's father walked over to him and picked up the sheet of paper, written in German and signed by Dr. von Stein at the bottom. He handed the sheet back.

"One thing's for sure," he said. "Rebecca is not registering."

The door opened behind them. Lance Corporal Steiner came into the office the Nazis had provided them in Saint Helier. Steiner was from Frankfurt, a young, handsome man, only a little older than Christopher. He was perpetually cheerful, and that day was no different.

"How are we this morning, gentlemen?"

"Do you know anything about the order for the Jews to be registered?" Christopher asked.

"What need have you to worry about that? It's just a part of the process of cleansing the population."

"What do you suppose will happen to the Jews on the island?" Christopher asked.

"Who knows? But for the time being, it's important that we know who they are, so that we can watch them." He put down some papers he had been carrying. "It's so good to have some fellow Germans here; it makes our job so much easier. The British are a most civilized nation of people, not like the Slavs. I was in Poland, you know, when the invasion took place. Those people . . . those people are very different. They barely have running water. And the Jews there, they're as close to beasts as I've ever seen, more like vermin. The British are very different, however. It seems a shame we have to fight them. I'm sure one day we'll all be on the same side. Don't worry about the Jews, Christopher. They certainly don't worry for you. They're the cause of all this war anyway." He reached into his pocket for a cigarette and put it in his mouth. "Are you feeling all right, Christopher?"

"He's not been well all day," his father said. "Is it all right if he goes home? He only lives a few streets away."

"Of course, it seems like you're almost finished for the day anyway."

Christopher didn't wait for any further permission and nodded as he picked up his belongings. He waited until he was out of sight of the office building and ran around the corner.

Rebecca was reading when Christopher burst in. The radio was off. It was rarely on in those days: the prescribed radio stations spewing Nazi propaganda were of little interest to either of them. Some people on the island dared to listen to the BBC still, even though being caught would mean a night in jail.

"You're out of work," she said. "Did the Nazis let you out early? What is it? Attila the Hun's birthday?"

"The Jews on the island have been ordered to register. There was an ordinance passed down today. I translated it myself."

"Where do I have to go? When?"

"By the twenty-fourth. Next Thursday. They set up some office downtown, but don't worry. You're not registering. That's not going to happen."

"I'm not ashamed of who I am."

"I know, Rebecca." Christopher took her face in his two hands. "They have this . . . idea, this perverted notion that Jews are vermin, rats or the like."

"What about my father? He's registered as a Jew; he's on the voting lists. He'll have to register for sure."

"I don't know about your father. I can't do anything for him."

"Oh no." He took her in his arms and she buried her head in his shoulder. "I have to see him. I have to tell him."

*Why? He would never do that for you. He's probably drunk, cradling that shotgun. He deserves to die alone.* Christopher hadn't been back to the house since the night Cassin forced him to write the letter. He and Rebecca had discussed that night many times and, although she fully believed him, she couldn't hate her father for it.

She hadn't been to see him in the few months since the Nazis had arrived. She said she thought of him often, alone in that house in Saint Martin, surrounded by the short-lived gains of her courtship with Jonathan—his retirement plan gone awry.

"I know we don't owe him anything. But I have to tell him. He's still my father."

"Okay. Let's go and see your father, together, today."

They set off on their bikes, out toward Saint Martin. The roads were full of German soldiers, hundreds of them, scuttling around on motorbikes and in trucks, their weapons slung over their shoulders. Once Rebecca was identified as a Jew, there would be nothing he could do, but how would the Nazis know? There were no synagogues on the island. She could pretend to be someone else, could take someone else's identity, maybe even Sandrine Mallard, gone to England with her new fiancé. Well, maybe not Sandrine, but there were many others. *There are ways around this, no need to panic,* he told himself as they rode past another truck of German soldiers. Cows had wandered out onto the road ahead, and the soldiers had jumped out. Christopher stepped off the bike and walked ahead, weaving through the soldiers littering the road. Rebecca walked through the soldiers with her head high.

It was five o'clock when they arrived at the house. A gray curtain of clouds drew in over the coast from the sea. They dropped the bikes in the driveway beside the brand-new car that never left the driveway, a gift from Jonathan Durrell to his mother-in-law-to-be that never was. Rebecca knocked on the door. Gentle music wafted through. She knocked again. They waited for another thirty seconds, neither of them speaking, until the door finally opened.

"Hello," Rebecca said. "Can we come in?"

"So it's true, then. You stayed, with him? There are twenty thousand Germans on the island now. You have plenty to choose from."

"Can we come in, Father?"

"If you must."

The hallway was clean, and the mirror above the side table was brand-new, the remnants of the price tag still clinging to the corner of the frame. Rebecca led them into the living room. Christopher felt like he was returning to the scene of a crime. There were a couple of whisky glasses strewn around the tables, and the ashes from last night's fire were still in the fireplace, but, apart from that, the room was well kept and clean. Rebecca took a seat, the armchair beside the fire where Cassin had made Christopher sit. Her father was in the armchair opposite, and Christopher sat on the couch facing the fireplace itself.

"I'm glad to see that you're keeping the place in good order," Rebecca began.

"It's been easier since your mother left."

"We're not here for a social call," she continued.

"Oh no? Say what you have to say and leave me alone. I've no wish to see you again, not after the way you betrayed your own family. The sight of you disgusts me."

"I really don't care what you think of me, because I know you've never cared for anyone your whole life, not me, not Mother, not even yourself. I'm just here today to tell you that the Germans are going to order that all Jews on the island are to register."

"Is that it?"

"Come on, Rebecca, let's go."

"What do you mean 'is that it'? The Germans want all the Jews on the island to register. Don't you care?"

Cassin's eyes fell down to the floor. He didn't speak. He just reached into the cabinet beside him and took out a crystal decanter. He took off the top and poured himself a drink.

"I really think it's time we left," Christopher repeated.

Rebecca got up, as if in slow motion. Her eyes never left her father, yet he only glanced toward her. Christopher took her by the hand. Just as they were walking out, they heard his voice.

"Rebecca . . ." he said. "I . . ." He raised the glass to his mouth. Christopher took her hand to leave.

A few weeks later, Christopher read through the names of the people registered as Jews on the island of Jersey. There were several he had never known as Jews and who had been known to regularly attend the local Anglican church. At the top of the list, he saw the name of Pierre Cassin and the note below that his family had been evacuated to England before the invasion.

# CHAPTER

16

The ordinances coming down from Dr. von Stein became more and more draconian. Curfews came earlier, and more freedoms were curtailed. Hitler had seemingly become obsessed with the defense of the Channel Islands. Massive building works began in 1941. The Todt workers, slave laborers from the continent, built gun emplacements, anti-tank walls on the beaches, and hundreds of bunkers and batteries that jutted gray out of the green hills overlooking the coast all around the island. The conditions the slave workers lived under belied the apparent good intentions of the countless Nazi officers who Christopher and his father saw in their office.

The Todt workers, named after the founder of the forced labor organization, Fritz Todt, came in February of 1941. The first batch, forty or so of them, represented the closest thing Christopher had ever seen to the horrors of hell in front of his eyes. The workers had no proper shoes, and their ragged clothes betrayed their bony, starving bodies, swelling joints, and sagging white skin. They coughed and wheezed as if trying to clutch on to the very air around them. Rebecca held out a piece of bread to a worker shuffling past, a young man, probably no more than eighteen years old. She had just managed to slip the tiny morsel into his hand when the guards saw them. The nearest German soldier ran toward them and struck the young worker in the head with the butt of his rifle just as he stuffed the bread into his mouth. His body crumpled to the ground like an empty sack flopping onto the pavement. Rebecca screamed, and the guard forced her back with the flat side of his rifle. Christopher tried to grab at it but felt himself held back by another soldier behind him. The guards shoved them both backward, away from the road. The other workers picked up the young boy and carried him somehow. They hardly looked as if they could carry themselves. The workers shuffled on. All that remained was a pool of blood on the pavement, which washed away moments later with the coming of the rain.

Many times after that, they stood outside his apartment, watching for the chance to give the Todt workers whatever food they could spare. Sometimes they were able to, but all too often the guards forced them back, and the workers marched on defeated.

---

It was a hot rainy night in July when Christopher arrived home with a letter his father had given him. He felt his tattered, dirty clothes sticking to the sweat on his skin. Soap was rare, and new clothes were a memory by that time. Rebecca was sitting by the window. He went to her, putting his hand through her hair and onto her neck. "I can't take this anymore," she said.

"You can't take what?"

"This isolation, this stunted life." The rain outside was pelting the window. "I have ambitions. I want to get married, to you."

"This isn't the time for wedding talk. What would we make the cake out of, sand?"

"I know. I know that can't happen until the Nazis leave. I just never thought they'd be here even this long."

"Rebecca, you need to be patient. Once the war ends . . ."

"I'll be able to leave the house again? I'm going insane in here."

"You know we have to be careful. If the Nazis catch you with no ID papers . . . We've been through this a million times."

"I know, I'll have to register as a Jew, but what are they going to do to me then?"

"You really want to take that chance? You've seen the way the Nazis treat the Todt workers. Do you want to end up like one of them, a walking skeleton, a slave?"

"My life seems to have stopped since the Nazis arrived."

"Is your life so terrible?"

"No, I didn't mean that. I'm happier now with you than I've ever been. It's just that you're the only good thing in my life. I want to go to university; I want to have a job and a life and children. I want to have children with you and be your wife." She led him to the couch, where she sat on his lap.

"We can have all those things. You can have your education one day. I want children too, but this is no time to bring a child into the world, not here, not now."

"What's going to happen if I register? Nothing has happened to the other Jews so far. They're all getting on with their lives. They can leave their apartments . . ."

"It's not a good idea, Rebecca. If we can just wait . . ."

"For what exactly? Whether or not I register is my decision, not yours. I'm not ashamed of my heritage. Anything's got to be better than scuttling from my apartment to yours. I don't even have a job anymore. All I do is hide." *Perhaps she is right.* "At least I'll be able to have some kind of normal life if I do register."

The letter from Uli weighed heavily in his pocket. It was probably the first letter that any islander had received since the enforced blockade of the island had begun, since the Nazis had arrived.

"What's the matter?"

"Nothing is the matter. I got a letter from Uli, smuggled through on one of the transports by one of the German soldiers."

"Being German does have its benefits here after all. What does it say?"

He reached into his pocket and handed the envelope to her. She held it in her hand for a second before opening it. She smiled as she read the first line.

*June 27, 1941*

Stefan, Christopher, Alexandra, Tom, and Rebecca (I hope),

I trust everyone is well. If the people on the chain of getting this letter to you are as good as their word, this should reach you by the time I get to Russia. We received the orders last week and we are to ship out tomorrow. The other officers are talking about this being the final push to win the war, and that this could be all over by Christmas. The Russians are a disorganized rabble, and should be easily defeated by the combined forces of the Reich, or so everyone says. In my mind I can't help thinking of another overconfident general called Napoleon and what happened to him on his excursion into Russia, but we will see.

I miss home more than I ever thought possible. I long to see Karolina and hold Stefan. I think about them all the time, and sometimes find myself staring at the photos she sends me for hours at a time. Stefan is running around now supposedly and even has a few words.

Karolina tells me that he knows who I am by my photographs and can point at them and say "Papa." That is enough to make my heart melt and to forget there is anything else in this whole world.

I can't say I enjoyed my time in France. I suppose it's difficult for the people here to see that we're here to prevent bloodshed and loss of life, not to cause it, but I don't think they'll ever understand. Maybe if we do win this war, which everyone says we will, they will appreciate us some day, and we can all live in peace alongside one another. I just don't know. I'm just a soldier, although now I'm a major myself. They must be running out of people if they're promoting me. But I'll just do what I always do, keep my head down and run when the bullets start flying. Please try not to worry about me.

I hope you are all well and I hope that Tom hasn't joined the British army! No, but seriously there are some words of warning I have to impart. From the last of Christopher's letters that I received before Jersey was taken, it seemed that Rebecca wanted to stay, to be with him. And while that filled me with joy, I must warn of the laws that the Reich has regarding Jews. Just be careful, Rebecca, if you read this. If anything happens, I will use as much influence as I can with the friends I have in the SS, some quite high up, but there is only so much I can accomplish. Keep your head down and this will all blow over eventually.

I will try and write again soon, but I don't know how good the postal service in Russia is going to be.

Love to all,
Uli

She let the letter drop into her lap. The thirty seconds before she spoke drew out excruciatingly. "I can't believe Uli is fighting for the Nazis. I can't believe he's one of them. He was such a kind person."

"He still is."

# CHAPTER

---

17

Christopher met Dr. Wilhelm Casper, the new Kommandant of the German garrison on Jersey on July 19, 1942. Christopher was working in the office in Saint Helier on a day like any other. They had not heard from Uli in the year since he had been posted to Russia. They only knew he was still alive through reports from the clerks working in Dr. Casper's office. Uli was still listed as active and serving on the Eastern Front. They were the only people on the island who had received any news of the outside world since the occupation had begun. Rebecca was still hiding in the apartment and had barely left in months. She was still as optimistic as he imagined anyone in her situation could have been. As he held her at night, he noticed the bones jutting out, tightening against her skin. They had both lost weight. Everyone had, even the German soldiers themselves.

Steiner walked into the office, leaving the door ajar behind him. He went directly to Christopher's desk, where he was poring over the ordinances of the day.

"What's going on?"

"Doctor Casper wants to see you, immediately."

"What is this about?" Christopher's father said. The flecks of gray were clearly visible in his hair now, his thin face weathered like the rocks on the shore. "I'm sure that any query Doctor Casper has can be ironed out with me. I see him several times a month, albeit briefly . . ."

"The orders were quite clear. He wants to see the boy." Christopher was all of six months younger than Steiner.

Christopher stood up. "I'll be back in a few minutes. I'm sure this is nothing more than a trifling matter," he said in English, a language Steiner didn't speak. "Isn't that right, Steiner?" he said, switching back to German.

"What, what are you talking about?" Steiner said.

Steiner led him out the door. He had never been summoned to see the Kommandant before. His father had, but not like this.

Steiner held the car door open for him. The journey out to Saint Brelade, to the Durrells' mansion, was about fifteen minutes. The only other cars on the road were German troop transports. Steiner sat beside him for the duration of the trip, but neither man spoke. The fifteen minutes seemed to last years, and Christopher was sweating heavily as the car finally arrived at the gates of the mansion where the Durrells still lived, although in a tiny corner and cordoned off from the rest of the house. He hadn't seen them since the day of the evacuation, over two years before. Few people had. The gates opened and the car moved slowly up the driveway, coming to a halt just outside the main entrance to the house. Steiner got out. Christopher opened the door himself, stepping out onto the gravel in the summer sun before Steiner could move around the car in time. His feet crunched on the gravel as Steiner led him into the house and upstairs. Steiner told him to sit down outside the Kommandant's office, which had once been one of seven guest bedrooms in the house. He sat down on the soft red velvet couch and waited. His shirt was sticking to his back. He imagined Rebecca at home, the guards coming for her. He imagined her in this house, where she could have lived. The door opened.

Dr. Casper stood at the door and extended a hand to Christopher. He was a stout, almost portly man with a round face and thinning hair sprinkled across the top of his rounded head. Christopher felt the strength in his wrist as he shook his hand.

"Herr Seeler, good to meet you. Come through into my office," he said in English.

Christopher took a seat in an antique wooden chair facing the large desk. Hitler's portrait watched over the wood-paneled room.

"We really appreciate the work you and your father do for us here on the island. It is most important that the people know that we are not here to enslave them or anything of that nature. It is most fortunate that we have pillars of the community such as your father and yourself working with us."

"Thank you."

"My predecessor, Doctor von Stein, set up an efficient system here on the island and, despite some difficulties, I think we are achieving our goal as a model of German occupation. There are always problems, however. You are aware of the laws in the German Reich concerning the Jewish population, are you not?"

Christopher's blood froze. "Yes, Herr Kommandant."

"Please understand that this is not my decision; this has been passed down by my superiors all the way from the Führer himself. You understand that, don't you?"

"Yes, of course." The muscles in his neck felt like steel rods.

"There has been much pressure on me from above to register and control all the Jews on the island. Not just some of them, you see, but all. You understand, don't you?" Christopher's legs were shaking, and he could see the fabric on his trousers waving like a flag in the breeze. "It's very important that we have the full cooperation of everyone on the island on this matter, particularly such close colleagues as the likes of yourself and your father, don't you agree?"

"Of course, Herr Ca— I mean Doctor Casper."

"Let's not stand on the ceremony of titles here, Christopher. I want you to think of the German occupying forces here as friends, after all, are we not all German?" *She's alone in the apartment. I'm stuck here.* "Anyway, it's been brought to my attention that there are several Jews on the island that have not registered with the pertinent office. It is of utmost importance that these Jews be registered with the proper authority. I'm sure you understand this as much as the States, your local government, does, and it was with this in mind that they gave their cooperation to us in this matter. It didn't surprise me that little protest was raised. They realize what an important job this is." Casper got up and walked over to the window. He gazed outside for a few seconds before turning back to Christopher. "Is there anything you want to tell me? I understand mistakes can be made, but for you and your father to retain your jobs and the privileges that go along with them, I do expect a certain amount of loyalty." Casper sat down at his desk again. Christopher hadn't moved. "I won't ask you again. Have you anything to say to me?"

"No, I don't, Doctor Casper."

"You disappoint me, Christopher, really you do. I trusted you with great responsibility, and you betrayed that trust. Rebecca Cassin registered with the local authorities as a Jew this morning. I'm told you know her, intimately. I deliberately called you in here before she would have had a chance to tell you herself." Casper clasped his hands in front of him on the desk. "They have a way about them, don't they, the Jews? They have a way of looking into you, almost seeing your soul, what your weaknesses are. I don't blame you, Christopher. I feel sorry for you. You really should be treated by a doctor for the sickness she has inflicted upon you. By registering, she has done you a service, just as I am going to do by not telling my superiors about this. There will be no record of this unfortunate incident to hold you back in your future serving the Reich."

"What are you going to do with Rebecca?"

"What are we going to do with Rebecca Cassin? Nothing. We're just going to see to it that she's registered and then, of course, she will be subsequently bound by the rules concerning all Jews on the island."

"What about resettlement? Are you going to take her away . . . ?" Every guard was down now.

"Enough questions, Herr Seeler. Unfortunately I have had to relieve not just you of your position with us, but your father also. It is regrettable, but necessary." Casper stopped and the door opened. "That will be all, Herr Seeler."

Casper had him removed. The guard walked him down to the car, where Steiner was waiting to drive him back into town.

# CHAPTER

## 18

The last six months they had together were a strange mix of joy and fear, trepidation and contentment. They rarely spoke about their present; the scarcity of food, the deportations, and Rebecca's complete lack of freedom. She had moved in with him. It was safe to do so now. There were no glares of disapproval from the neighbors for those who never went out. By that time, the registered Jews on the island were allowed out for only one hour a day, between the hours of three and four in the afternoon. She had been caught out after curfew before and spent the night in jail. It was the last time she did it. Christopher never mentioned the fact that she'd registered herself. At the time it had seemed the right thing to do, and he saw no sense in dredging up the mistakes of the past. Instead, they spent their days dreaming of a shining future. He stayed with her most of the day, as there was little work available. Christopher's father would often stay with them, and Alexandra and Tom also. The walls of the apartment and the island itself seemed to close in further and further, the vise tightening on them from all sides.

The deportations began in September of 1942. A number of Jews were taken, as well as hundreds of non-Jersey-born citizens. There seemed no reason why Rebecca was not chosen to leave. As nonnatives of the island, the Seelers were also eligible. They were passed over for deportation, perhaps as some remnant of the protection they had once enjoyed, but perhaps not. The Nazis seemed to have little logic in their decision making.

The letter arrived on January 12, 1943, typed in brief, formal language and signed at the bottom by Dr. Wilhelm Casper. Rebecca had been selected for deportation to Germany. The boat was scheduled to leave on February 13. She was told to gather one bag of belongings and to be at the Savoy Cinema at two p.m. on that day. That was all. Christopher tried to go to Dr. Casper, but he refused to see him or his father. Captain Voss feigned sympathy but promised nothing. There was nothing he could do, he explained. There was no court of appeal. The decision was already made and had come down from the Führer himself, and who could question the Führer himself?

It was easy to fake it, to pretend that the day would never arrive, to live in denial, and that is what they tried to do, at first. As the day drew closer, her demeanor changed. They went through the plans about escaping; trying to get to France or England. It was impossible. They tried to think of somewhere she could hide for the duration of the war. How long would that be? Months? Years? There was nowhere, and with little enough food to keep themselves alive, no one was willing to hide her. The acceptance of what was to happen gradually came over them, and the mourning began. They didn't know what was to happen to her. There were rumors everywhere of concentration camps and slave labor. They saw film of the camps in the local cinema and saw well-fed, happy-looking Jews bounding around, busy with outdoor activities and healthy pursuits. Rebecca was filled with brief hope, but even in his wildest dreams, Christopher couldn't believe it to be true.

She cried for days, only happy when he was holding her. On the third day she stopped. It was as if she emerged from a fever with a new clarity. She began taking risks, for as she rightly pointed out, what had they to lose? They began leaving the apartment together and went to visit Tom and Alexandra, Christopher's father, and their other friends still left on the island. There were so many good-byes. Those still brave enough to listen to the BBC had heard of the Allied victories in Stalingrad and El Alamein and assured her that the war would be over before long. She and all the other deportees would be back soon. There was nothing else to say.

Christopher awoke early on the morning of Friday, February 12, 1943. She was already awake, sitting by the window, watching the orange glow of the sunrise as it came up over the sea and flooded the streets below them. She tiptoed back to him across the cold floor, barely covered by the thin carpet, and put her arms around him. He felt her kiss him. He couldn't respond and, as he looked into her eyes, the pain inside grew, and he heard himself whimpering. She held him against her for a minute or more before pushing his head back. She took his face between her two hands, drying his tears with her thumbs.

"Oh, be quiet now. Don't cry. We'll be together again when all this is over, and then nothing will ever come between us again."

"This is all my fault. If it wasn't for me, you would have left and you would have been safe in England."

"Christopher, you are the best thing in my life, the only thing I've ever had that was truly worth living for. There is no life for me without you. Don't you see? This isn't the end for us." She leaned down to kiss him, and they made love, under the covers, safe against the cold of the morning all around them in the room.

They lay there in silence for a few minutes afterward, holding each other, her thin, frail body against his.

"I want to go out," she said, jutting her head upward. "I want to go out walking along the cliffs. I want to see the island and the sea. What are the Germans going to do to me if they catch us? Deport me?"

Half an hour later they were on the street, she on the crossbar of his bike as they cycled past columns of German soldiers and out of the town into the countryside toward Christopher's father's house in Saint Martin. It was cold, and he felt the scythe of wind cut through him. They arrived at Christopher's father's house. He was there, and took Rebecca into his arms, holding her under his chin, kissing her on the top of the head. He looked every one of his forty-eight years.

There was no small talk. Stefan prepared the tea in silence. It was watery and weak, the tea leaves almost completely drained of flavor.

"I'm here to say goodbye. It's tomorrow that I leave and . . ."

"I know that, Rebecca, I know why you're here. I'm just so sorry we couldn't do anything to prevent this."

"It's my fault," Christopher said. "If I had told Casper that Rebecca was a Jew, if I had told him . . ."

"If you had betrayed her, you mean?" his father replied. "This is no one's fault but the Nazis themselves. Rebecca, you have to be brave. You were always such a brave girl. The strongest person I ever knew."

She reached for Christopher's father and hugged him. He was silently crying.

They stayed for lunch, a thin turnip soup that Christopher's father had managed to concoct. They talked about the future and how the Seelers themselves were likely to be deported to Germany at any time. They talked about the possibility, or the seeming impossibility of escape or finding places to hide on the tiny island,

and food to sustain them while they hid there. The conversation fell silent until she began to smile again.

"I see the old tree house is still hanging on," she said. The wooden structure, built over a morning by Uli almost twenty years before, was clinging to the tree he had nailed it to. It was completely weather-beaten, the original paint all but faded to the wooden gray underneath. They talked about the golden sun of their youth for an hour or more and then left to walk the beach together. Christopher's father stayed in the house.

Their clothes were faded and old, hardly able to keep the cold out, and they huddled together as they walked down to the beach. They were passing Rebecca's father's house. "Wait here," she said. "I'll only be a few minutes," she said, and slipped out of his grasp.

He walked down to the end of the road to where barbed wire writhed around fence posts hammered into the ground. It had been a while since they had been here, more than a year, not since the barbed wire was put in place and the mines laid down along the beach. Somehow Christopher found it hard to imagine a full-blown amphibian invasion of Jersey on the beach by his father's house in Saint Martin, but the Germans had. He waited ten minutes for her.

"What happened?" Christopher asked.

"He's on the same ship as I am tomorrow. We're being deported together."

They walked along the line of barbed wire as it snaked along the coastline. They followed it for several miles, just walking. It was enough just being there and together. They made their way back as the evening drew in and the gray of the clouds turned black over the sea. The rain came down, swept in on the cold wind. They shivered together as they tramped back up the road toward Christopher's father's house.

Tom and Alexandra were there when they arrived. They embraced Rebecca with tears in their eyes. They couldn't find the joy they had all shared for so long. Tom would soon be the only one of them left on the island. Somehow Christopher felt worse for him to be left behind.

They made their way back into town before curfew, set at eight p.m. They passed by some troops on the way back. Christopher made sure to look as casual as he could as he passed, and not hurl the hatred at them that was burning a hole inside of him.

They arrived back at the apartment and locked up the bike outside. They made their way upstairs and tried to act as normal as they could. She prepared dinner of some carrots, a potato, and some thin soup cooked in seawater for extra flavor. The salt had long since run out. He held her as she cooked, his face buried in the back of her neck. They ate the meal together under a blanket on the couch.

He fell asleep at around four. The heavy yoke of tiredness overcame him, robbing him of his final hours with her and the final sunrise they could have had together. They woke up at around noon. She packed her bag. He couldn't watch. It was too much. He walked her down to the Savoy, where her father and the other Jews were waiting, herded together by enough German troops to guard hundreds. The soldiers stood back wordlessly, glaring at the Jews as they arrived. There were thirteen altogether. Rebecca was the thirteenth. Christopher motioned to her father. Cassin edged his way out to him. He looked like a very old man. He was drunk.

"Look after Rebecca. She is still your daughter. This is your chance to make up for the past." Cassin shook his hand. Christopher turned to Rebecca, the same frightened girl he had found by the beach almost twenty years before. He took her in his arms. The German officer came over. It was Voss. He glanced at Christopher, didn't acknowledge him.

"All right," Voss said. "We need to get moving now." He pulled her away from him. She motioned for him to come back. He leaned in to her.

"Next time I see you, we're getting married. The next time . . ." A German soldier cut her off, forcing her onward. She said it again. "You hear me, Christopher? The next time we meet."

The thirteen were marched down to the harbor. He walked alongside them. He wanted to be strong for her, but it was more than he could bear. They marched straight out and onto the ship. She turned to him standing alone on the jetty. She was on the gangplank and shouted something back to him. It was lost in the wind. He saw her red face, saw her tears one last time through his own before she disappeared inside. He stood up to watch the ship as it left. There was no one else there. He stood on the jetty completely alone, watching the ship as it moved away until it disappeared into the gray of the horizon.

# CHAPTER

---

## 19

*Auschwitz-Birkenau 1943*

The screams from the crematorium faded into silence. Christopher was pacing back and forth in some kind of attempt to control the shaking infesting his body. The yard was empty now. He steeled himself, trying to block out the horror of what he had just witnessed. There had been no way of knowing that this was what went on here, or that this is what he would find. He heard Müller's voice directing the Sonderkommandos and saw him looking over. He breathed deeply in through his nose, trying to slow down his heart, blackened and damaged by what he had just seen. He felt a hand on his shoulder. "It takes a bit of getting used to, Herr Seeler," Friedrich said. "These ways are so much more humane than they used to be."

"More humane for the prisoners?"

"What are you talking about? No, no, that is an irrelevance. More humane for the SS men tasked with this important duty. There were too many affected in the early days, before we streamlined the process. You will get used to this, Herr Seeler. There is strength in you that I can see, that all who meet you can sense. Use it, and you will be doing the Reich a great service here."

"Yes, Herr Rapportführer."

"Excellent, now get to work. You are needed inside the changing room. Make sure all valuables collected are put into the appropriate boxes and piles, and, above all, make sure that they all find their way back to the Reich, and not into the filthy hands of the prisoners themselves."

He saluted, and found the strength to walk back into the crematorium, following the path that the people had taken just minutes before. Müller and Breitner were already inside, directing the Sonderkommandos as they sorted through the piles of clothing. Flick arrived with several prisoners, each carrying a separate box. Breitner did the talking, reminding the Sonderkommandos to go through all pockets, to check the lining in each coat, to turn out every suitcase, and to place the currency in one box, gold and jewelry in another, watches into another. Christopher walked among them, watching each as he went by, trying to look officious and fearsome. Coats were taken down off the hooks where their former owners had left them, and neatly folded clothes were flung into piles. He picked up a child's doll, ragged and worn with one eye missing, its blond hair streaked with dirt, and placed it back down on the clothes of the little girl who had left it. The SS men walked up and down, shouting at the prisoners sorting through the goods, urging them to go faster, faster. It was all done with speed and efficiency. Boxes of shoes, coats, underwear, wallets, eyeglasses, gold and jewelry, bottles, medicines, food, and, of course, cash, were placed on trolleys, ready for transportation back to the warehouses that he was to oversee. The SS officers were pleased at what had obviously been a good morning's work. Christopher made his way past the guards and prisoners and through the now-cleaned-out dressing room, and saw the box full of dolls by the door, collected and sorted along with everything else, waiting to be "redistributed back to the Reich." Nothing was not worth stealing.

He walked out into the yard as more SS men moved in. The Sonderkommandos made their way into the gas chambers to transport the bodies, the "stiffs," as the guards referred to them, upstairs to be burned. Christopher thought of the thousand or so corpses, freshly murdered, and had no intention of waiting around to see what happened next. He hurried each of the prisoners along as they jogged toward the warehouses, the carts packed with the boxes they had sorted themselves. He watched them as they pushed the carts, perhaps twenty of them, toward the warehouses. A voice came from behind him. "You know what they call the section where we sort through the goods? The section you're now in charge of?" Breitner said.

"No, I don't."

"They call it Canada, the land of untold riches," Breitner sneered, revealing brown, chipped teeth.

"Thank you, Herr Breitner," Christopher replied, and began to walk back toward Canada, following the last cart as it departed from the crematorium.

There were no markings on the warehouses. There was no sign above the door for the warehouse that held the shoes or the glasses of the recently murdered, yet the Sonderkommandos seemed to know almost instinctively what warehouse to bring each pile of stolen goods to. They never made a mistake. He thought about Rebecca as he walked up and down the lines of warehouses. Every so often he would stop and look inside, gesture to the SS guards on duty or frown at the prisoners working inside. There was no way they could have killed her as soon as she arrived at the camp, was there? He shook these images from his mind, forcing himself back into the moment. *She is alive*, he told himself. *I will find her.* He would not allow her to share the same fate as those people. The more he thought about her, the more the panic set in, so he tried to wipe his mind clean of her. There was nothing he could do, not yet, not until he gained the confidence of the administration here.

He turned and walked back down the line of warehouses and walked inside one, where prisoners were sorting through spectacles, bottles, and what seemed to be medicines. The guard on duty saluted him. Piles of tiny brown-and-white bottles were littered across the wooden tables. None of the twenty or so women working in the warehouse looked up at him. He walked over, fighting the urge to introduce himself to the prisoner working at the table. Most of the prisoners in Canada seemed to be women, better fed than the others he had seen in the main camp, and, no doubt, content to have avoided more arduous and dangerous work. He picked up one of the bottles. The writing on the white label was in Czech. He found another, written in German, "Take once daily, for rheumatoid arthritis." He put the bottle back down with a shaking hand. It fell onto its side and rolled off the table, hitting the concrete floor with a crack as it smashed. The guard in the corner whirled around and started to shout something. Christopher held his hand in the air. "Take no notice; that was my fault." The woman at the table stared up at him, her brown eyes swimming with fear. She had thick, brown curly hair, and her weathered face could have been beautiful in another time or another place. "What is your name?" he asked.

The woman seemed surprised to be asked such a question. "Katerina Lehotska," she answered in a thick Czech accent.

"Work hard and stay safe, Katerina. I am the new Obersturmführer of this section. You can tell the other workers that things are going to change around here." He immediately regretted what he said and felt an icicle of fear sliding down his spine. Katerina looked puzzled and brought her eyes back down to the broken bottle on the floor. He resisted the urge to pick it up himself and walked back toward the door. A gunshot cut through the air, and he hurried toward the sound of it. Breitner was standing outside smoking a cigarette. "What was that?" Breitner shrugged. Christopher ran past him and into the warehouse where the shot had come from. The dead body of a woman in her thirties was strewn on the concrete floor, her head pumping out ugly black-crimson blood. "What happened here?" An SS man stepped forward as he placed his pistol back into its holster.

"I saw her place a ring into her pocket, Herr Obersturmführer," the soldier said with the air of a man boasting to his boss about a job well done.

Christopher gritted his teeth as he looked down at the corpse. None of the other workers looked up, all still sorting the jewelry on the tables in front of them. There was nothing he could do. The frustration burned within him. "Get this body out of here!" he shouted. "Let this be a lesson to you all, there will be no stealing." He stormed back out, but there was nowhere to go, nowhere to escape to. There were only the wires and the warehouses, the crematoria and the shadows of the prison hospital. He stood back as several Sonderkommandos jogged inside and emerged carrying the corpse of the middle-aged woman. Once outside, they threw it onto the cart with the nonchalance of the fishermen that he had watched in Jersey as a child, slinging their nets that were writhing and wriggling with gray-scaled fish onto carts to be brought to market. The woman's body was taken away. The guard stood back at his post as if nothing had occurred. Christopher walked back inside the warehouse, making sure to step over the pool of blood coagulating on the warehouse floor. The soldier who killed her was standing back against the wall. He saluted as Christopher approached him. "Now hear this," Christopher explained. "These prisoners here are skilled workers." The soldier looked completely perplexed. "There should be no summary executions here. If there is a problem, if someone has stolen, you will come to me. I don't want the guards taking the rules of the camp into their own hands. Only anarchy will follow that way. It is of vital importance that we maintain discipline at all times. Do you understand me?"

"Yes, Herr Obersturmführer." The soldier saluted again, seemingly convinced.

The Sonderkommandos were already cleaning up the pool of blood. The other workers, eight of them, all women, remained working. One of the women's heads was bobbing back and forth, only slightly, like a cork on the end of a fishing rod. She was crying. He had the urge to go to her, to tell her that he was Obersturmführer in charge of these warehouses now and that they would all be safe. No one could give that assertion, not here. The smell of blood, of death, was thick in the air. It followed him outside as he walked down toward the crematorium. Breitner was standing outside the last warehouse, carrying a small box full of what seemed like tiny gold nuggets.

"Herr Obersturmführer," Breitner called out. "You should probably take these. The last Obersturmführer here insisted on handling all the gold and jewelry himself."

Christopher took the box from Breitner. It was full of gold teeth. "Thank you, Herr Breitner. I'm sure in a few days' time I'll be up to speed with all the processes."

"There is someone else you will need to meet, Herr Obersturmführer." A particularly healthy-looking prisoner in a black uniform was standing behind Breitner. "This is Ralf Frankl, chief Kapo of the Economic District." Frankl was a stout, strong-looking man with pockmarks on a brutal face.

"It is a pleasure to make your acquaintance, sir," Frankl said with a heavy Bavarian accent. "I am here to help you maintain discipline at all times."

"How do you explain what just happened in warehouse six?" Christopher asked.

"These Jewish dogs have to be kept in line, Herr Obersturmführer. Force is the only thing they understand."

"What were you sent here for, Frankl?"

"Double murder, Herr Obersturmführer," Frankl replied, looking surprised at the question.

"You'll fit in well, then," Christopher muttered under his breath in English. The two men were perplexed. "Well, Frankl, I am in charge here now, and there will be no summary executions, no executions without my say-so, is that understood?"

Frankl's eyes opened wide. "But, Herr Obersturmführer . . ."

"Don't make me repeat myself, Frankl," he said, and walked away, leaving the two men to argue among themselves.

Christopher went to his office at the end of the line of warehouses, there for the express purpose of counting the booty looted from the murdered. A box of gold teeth, three boxes of cash, three boxes of watches, necklaces, earrings, and other assorted pieces of jewelry seemed a paltry return for the murder of over a thousand people. He wondered how much the Sonderkommandos, prisoners, guards, and his own subordinates had skimmed off the top for themselves. He sat there for the rest of the afternoon counting the reichsmarks, dollars, pounds, and other monies of the people from the train that morning. He divided it into neat bundles, wrapped in elastic bands, and placed them into a suitcase. The code for the safe was written down in one of the drawers. He memorized the code before ripping up the piece of paper it was written on. He placed the suitcase full of cash along with the suitcases full of jewelry into the large safe, which was about three feet wide and as tall as he was. He locked the door behind him and returned to his desk. *Who's going to help me? I can't do this alone.*

# CHAPTER

## 20

Christopher arrived back at his room after eight o'clock. Today had been a very normal day according to Flick. Just average. Many days were much busier. The murder of a thousand people was normal. The hatred for the Nazis burned through him, but he controlled it, smothering the flames as they ignited. *Control is the key.* Lahm was out. He was thankful for that as he took off his jacket. There was a letter on the bed. He picked it up, almost able to smile as he tore at the envelope. He drew out the letter and laid it flat on the bed as he sat down. It was from his father.

*September 22, 1943*
Christopher,
We have missed you while you were in training. We are settling in better now; although Alexandra still misses Tom, she understands that it is not forever. We are doing as well as can possibly be expected. Berlin is different from the city that I grew up in, but we are gradually

finding our way, and I am sure I will have regular work soon. Alexandra is now working in a local factory. Cousin Harald has been very good to us since we were released from the hospitality of the Reich. It is wonderful to finally get to know Karolina, and little Stefan is a joy. I hope that your new posting is what you wanted and expected it to be. I'm sure if you remain calm and focused you will achieve your goals, and the Reich will be much the better for your efforts. We are well. Do not worry about us. I received a letter from your uncle yesterday. He is safe and well and fighting bravely on the Eastern Front. He is due back on January 28th for three days of leave. You are in our thoughts always.

Your father,
Stefan Seeler

He read it and reread it. The censors were everywhere. He almost laughed at how his father had referred to the internment camp they had been kept in, and then released from after only a few days. The foreign-born, non-German citizens deported from Jersey with them had not been treated nearly as leniently. They would likely be there for the rest of the war. There could be little truth either in the offhand way in which he had referred to Alexandra's feelings about Tom. It had been difficult to see her in the pain that the separation from him had caused her.

The door opened. He resisted the instinct to hide the letter. It was Lahm.

"How was your first day in the camp? What are you doing again?"

"I'm in the Economic District."

"So, you're the man to know. What's it like?"

"What's what like?"

"Canada, the land of untold wealth, we've all heard the rumors."

"It's just a lot of warehouses. I'm just trying to do my job like everyone else."

"Oh, right. I understand if you can't talk about it. Have you had dinner yet?"

"Yes, I ate earlier."

"Would you like to come for a few drinks tonight? There are a few of the boys getting together later. There's a movie on too, or a showing of some play, I'm not sure what's on."

"Okay."

"Great, we're playing cards later on too. It'll do you good to wind down; sometimes the work here can get pretty stressful."

Christopher folded up the letter and placed it on the top shelf of his locker and followed Lahm out of their room. Lahm was smaller than he, blond, and about twenty-two years of age.

"What do you do here, Lahm?"

"I work in the main camp, here in Auschwitz. My duties vary from day to day, but I mainly work in Blocks 10 and 11. It's not an easy job, but I find it satisfying, you know, to be doing something so important for the Reich."

"What goes on in Blocks 10 and 11?"

"They're the punishment blocks."

Christopher walked beside him out into the yard outside their block. The lights of the camp cast down harsh beams of white, and Christopher raised a hand above his eyes. Auschwitz was silent, the thirty thousand or so prisoners, only a few hundred yards away, making little sound. He wondered about the conversation he'd had with Breitner and the Kapo, Frankl. Was it too soon to stand out? He remembered the words of Friedrich and knew that by showing any kind of sympathy to the prisoners, he was risking his own life, and more importantly, the chance to save Rebecca's. But it was impossible to do nothing. How could he do nothing and still be himself, still be human? There had to be some way of affecting this. He was only one man, but he had some power, and there would be money. He thought of the masses of currency he had seen just that day. There would always be money.

Lahm led him across the yard. There were SS men passing them on all sides, milling back and forth. Most were slovenly dressed, their collars open and shirts untucked, some seemed drunk, meandering from side to side. Lahm greeted several of them and introduced Christopher to one as they reached their destination. Christopher tried to be as cordial as he could as he shook the man's hand. He walked behind them as they chatted. They led him to an open room at the end of the hallway where seven or eight SS men sat around a wooden table. There was money in the center, and each man held cards in front of his face. A thick haze of cigarette smoke filled the air. Beer glasses and bottles of vodka were strewn all over the table. All the men greeted Lahm as he walked in. "Everybody, this is the new man over in the Economic District, Christopher Seeler. Where are you from again, Seeler?"

"Berlin originally, but I grew up in Jersey."

"Jersey, isn't that in Britain?" a soldier asked from across the table.

"Not anymore!" the man beside him shouted.

Lahm sat down, Christopher beside him. "Do you play cards, Seeler?"

"Not well."

"Perfect, and working in the Economic District too, you'll fit in very well here," the same SS man who had made the comment about Jersey said. "Deal that man in." The comedian's name was Ganz. Two hours later and having said almost nothing, Christopher had almost doubled his original stake in the game. The other SS men were not as friendly as they had been when he sat down.

Ganz dealt the cards again. There were seven of them at the table, all drunk, all smoking. Christopher felt his eyelids get heavy, and the cards were blurry in front of him.

"Hey, new guy, you gonna give us back our money?" Sturmer, one of the guards, said. He was a thin, blond-haired man, about Christopher's age.

"Can't accept the way the cards fall?" Lahm slurred.

Christopher looked at his hand, and took a drink from the glass of vodka in front of him on the table. It slid down his throat and began its assault on his stomach lining. He looked around the table. His father had taught him this game. It wasn't about cards, but people. If they could see through him at the card table, why couldn't they see through him during the day, in the camp? He pushed another pile of chips out into the middle, raising the ante. The cards in his hand were nothing, but that didn't matter, it wasn't about them. He studied the faces through the smoke. There had been little talking during the hands for the last hour or so, just drinking. He watched as the faces around the table dropped. Each man folded. It was just him and Lahm. Lahm went to put down his cards and smiled, picking them back up.

"I think that you're a fake. I can see through you," he said, and Christopher felt the chill run through his entire body. "Let's see what you have." Lahm laid down his cards, three kings and a pair of sixes. He reached out and gathered the money in, sweeping it back toward himself with outstretched hands. "In fact, don't even bother showing me your cards. I know you don't have anything."

# CHAPTER

---

## 21

He dreamed about her on the beach in Jersey, the wind sweeping through her hair, and he could see her, but only as a dark outline in the gray sky. As he ran toward her, she turned to him and smiled. The blue of her eyes shone through the dark and outward, bright until he could see nothing else. Her face was in front of him, soft and smooth and beautiful, and she was laughing as she skipped toward the Butterfly's Table as a child. He followed her down to the sea, boiling and booming, throwing white water high in the air. When he arrived, she was gone.

Lahm was still asleep as Christopher awoke. The bare floorboards were cold as he stood up, and he quickly pulled on a fresh pair of socks and the gray trousers of his SS uniform. They slid on easily, now more comfortable than they had been the previous week or even the previous day. He approached the mirror in the corner of the room above the simple sink covered in Lahm's shaving materials and soap. He ran a gentle finger along the length of a bloodshot vein in his eye, poking through scarlet in the pool of gray white.

There was a great pressure in his chest, a weight inside him. He sat down to pull his boots on. He stood back up and made the effort to shave before buttoning up his shirt and pulling on his jacket. He shut the door behind him and made his way down the hallway to the latrine. There were two other SS men in the bathroom. One greeted him as he brushed past. The other man ignored Christopher and continued washing his hands, scrubbing them harder and harder under the hot water.

The cold of the October morning bit at his exposed skin. Winter was coming. The smell of it was heavy in the air. He tried to imagine how it would be for the prisoners when the snows came. He had stolen brief glimpses inside their living quarters. He had seen them huddled together, four prisoners in a cot made for one, their emaciated bodies huddled together to try to stave off the cold. *Focus on Rebecca.* Auschwitz, with its massive prisoner population and its centralized administrative unit, seemed like the best place to begin the search. Perhaps she was in the camp; perhaps he could see her, but then what? He walked around, past the Blockführer's office to the front gate. He flashed his papers to the SS guard on duty, who yawned as he bade him walk through. It was almost eight o'clock. The first shipment was due in less than an hour. He cursed himself for oversleeping; once the train arrived, there would be no time for anything other than theft and murder.

The block housing prisoners' records and the lists of those murdered as enemies of the Reich was just inside the main gate. He had no real reason to be there. SS men were not encouraged to wander around the camp. His role as Obersturmführer in the Economic District gave him some leeway, but not to be nosing around in the camp's records for a Jewish prisoner. There was another guard at the door, and Christopher presented him his papers.

"You're a long way from Birkenau, Herr Obersturmführer. What are you doing down here?"

"Listen, I've got plenty of better things to be doing, but my Rapportführer over in the Economic District wants me to speak to . . . a Karl Liebermann, whoever that is."

"The head of prisoner records?" the guard sneered. "Herr Liebermann is a busy man."

"And so am I."

The guard shook his head and stood aside to let him pass. Liebermann was sitting at his desk and looked up as though he had just been caught doing something he shouldn't have been. Christopher took the chair in front of Liebermann's immaculately clean desk before he could even say anything.

"Who are you, and why are you in my office?" Liebermann said. He was in his late forties and had a healthy double chin and rounded glasses falling onto the tip of a straight nose.

"My name is Obersturmführer Seeler, and I need your help. I heard you were a man with power in the camp, power that could help solve a little problem that has come up for me." Christopher paused, waiting for Liebermann to speak. He didn't. "I am looking for a particular prisoner, and I don't know if she is in this camp or . . ."

"She? Obersturmführer Seeler, why are you looking for this prisoner?"

Christopher took out a packet of cigarettes. "Do you mind if I smoke?"

"Yes."

He placed the cigarettes back in his pocket. "I suppose I can wait."

"If we could get back to the business at hand, Herr Seeler . . ."

"Okay, we're all busy. I understand. You could say that I have a vested interest in this prisoner. Her family contacted me, made me an offer for information."

"This is highly irregular. These people are enemies of the state. You know that, Obersturmführer Seeler."

"I understand my role and your role in this camp. Understand this, Herr Liebermann: This Jew is rich, very rich. The idea that I have any attachment to this . . . person is laughable."

"Sifting through prisoner records would take time."

Christopher felt the bulge of cash in his pocket from the wages he had just received. He took his hand out, left the notes on the table. Liebermann's eyes moved to the money. Christopher felt the sweat pooling in his palms.

"I don't accept bribes, Herr Seeler."

"I don't offer bribes, Herr Liebermann."

Liebermann took a piece of paper and placed it down on the desk on top of the wad of bills. "I'll see if I can find this person in our camp. Have you a name for this mysterious lady?"

"All the details are here." He pushed a piece of paper across. "There is no time to waste. The family will not pay much for news of a dead daughter."

"Come back tomorrow morning, and I'll see if we have some news for you."

"Excellent. I'm sure you are busy, and I need to get to my own duties." Christopher got out of the chair.

"Herr Obersturmführer, I'm sure I don't need to mention the sensitive nature of this matter," Liebermann said as Christopher reached the door.

"Of course not." He walked out.

The next shipment came less than an hour later and the gruesome spectacle played out in much the same way as before. There were more for the gas chambers later that day and more for the women of Canada to sort through. Christopher had not the strength to leave his office the rest of that day. He was disgusted at himself for feeling a sense of hope in a place where none could exist. His quest seemed so tiny, so utterly inconsequential in the face of all of this death, like chipping away at the edge of a glacier with an ice pick. He was determined, more determined than ever, to rescue her, but it didn't seem like a satisfactory end, even if he could somehow smuggle her out of the camp to escape. He had no idea how he would do that, even if he did find her. *One thing at a time.* He would find her first, and then worry about what the next step was to be. He was trapped here himself, trapped in this SS uniform, masquerading as one of them. He tried to remember the words his father had left him with: to always remain true to who he was, to not let the perverted ideals of the SS invade his being and corrupt his soul. That was already proving impossible. He was already changed. What good was it to find her but lose himself?

The rest of the day drew out slowly and painfully, like pulling an arrow out of an open wound. He ceded power to Breitner and remained in his office, counting and recounting the pile of currency that found its way to his desk. They brought the wooden crates of gold and jewels in, and, after a while, he didn't even acknowledge them. There were lockets with pictures of dead loved ones, beloved of people who would never see them or anyone again. All dead.

He didn't join Lahm and the other SS men later on for what seemed to be their nightly drinking session, instead claiming a stomachache. He lay in bed, not able to sleep at the thought that Rebecca might be in the camp herself, clinging on to life. Each day of life in the camp was likely to be a prisoner's last. He had already waited as long as he dared. There was no time to waste.

---

The next morning came. He returned to Block 24 in Auschwitz. The guard seemed to be expecting him this time and waved him through. Christopher's nerves were on fire as he walked down the corridor to Liebermann's office. He wiped the sweat from the palms of his hands before he knocked on the door. He pushed on it, not waiting for permission to enter, and Liebermann was as he had left him the previous day, sitting behind his desk, papers neatly stacked on each side.

"Is there any news?"

"You seem very eager."

"If you knew the sums of money being spoken about, you would be too."

"Well, I did have occasion to search for your acquaintance yesterday. There is no record of anyone named Rebecca Cassin, from Saint Martin, Jersey, ever being admitted to this camp or the camps adjunct to it."

"So what does that mean?"

"I should have thought that much was obvious, Herr Obersturmführer. Rebecca Cassin, is not, nor ever was, here."

"What about the other camps?"

"I have no idea," Liebermann said. He drew a piece of paper from a pile beside him and began to scribble on it. Christopher didn't move. "I have no idea where your friend is, Herr Seeler."

"She is not my friend, Herr Liebermann. Is there a way we can check the other camps?"

"Good day, Herr Obersturmführer."

"Answer the question."

"That would be a massive undertaking, a waste of my time. Now please get out of my office before I have you reported." There was nothing more to say. Christopher left without another word.

# CHAPTER

---

## 22

The intense hatred for everything around him began to infest him like a swarm of locusts. Every breath burned in his lungs, and the urge to rip off the uniform was almost impossible to resist. He slammed the door behind him as he walked into the office, where Breitner, Müller, and Flick were attending to their paperwork. He was immediately aware that he was under the spotlight once more. He was the new Obersturmführer in Canada, only in place a few weeks. If he didn't produce results, he would be replaced, and likely shipped off to the Eastern Front. He looked at the ledgers on his desk and the figures from the previous day's shipments. There were another two due that day, from Czechoslovakia. He thought of the people, huddled together on the cattle trucks, their throats raw from thirst, clinging to the children who would soon be dead. He stood up.

"Get in here, all three of you." They stood to attention in front of his desk. Christopher remained seated. "What is this I read? We had seven executions in the last week?" He looked at the three men, who seemed puzzled. "We killed more than one percent of our workers in the last week?" He stood up. "How can we possibly operate efficiently if we keep killing off our experienced workers?" The three men remained silent. "Why did this happen? Müller, perhaps you can explain."

"The executions are carried out by the guards, Herr Obersturm-führer, we have very little to do with that. . . ."

"Don't give me that. We oversee the operations in the Economic District." He had to stop himself from calling it Canada. "We make the rules there. What were the prisoners executed for?"

"Some for stealing jewelry, some for stealing food." Müller was calm as he spoke. Breitner was playing with his pen, looking down at it as Christopher spoke.

"There will be no more executions without my say-so."

"You've already made that clear, Herr Obersturmführer," Müller replied.

"Yet I see that there was another execution yesterday. Have the guards been informed?"

"Perhaps you should address them yourself," Breitner said.

An hour later, the seven most senior guards in Canada stood in Christopher's office. They didn't react as he spoke to them. They did not question the orders they were given, merely saluting after he had finished speaking. Christopher made his way down to the railway station. Less than a hundred were spared. They were to be worked to death. For the rest, death would come that day. Christopher walked through the changing rooms, overseeing the Sonderkommandos as they pawed through the clothes left behind by the soon to be murdered, who were at that stage packed into the gas chamber. He left the changing room as the gas was poured into the adjacent gas chamber, the sounds of screaming more than he could bear. He walked back to the warehouses and watched as the mountain of clothes arrived. He watched the women, their heads bowed as they worked. He could only imagine the yoke of the prospect of instant death that they worked under on a daily basis. And these were the lucky ones.

He walked over to a table where several women sat, sorting through undergarments. One picked out a diamond necklace, sewn into the hem of an old pair of trousers. She held it up before walking back to a table behind her where she dropped it into a wooden box. She sat back down. He walked over to her. Her long black hair was tied back. It was unusual to see prisoners anywhere in the main camp with long hair, but for some reason it was allowed in Canada. There seemed no logic to it, or to any of this. She did not look up as he stood next to her.

"Well spotted," he said. "That seemed well hidden." He bent down. "What is your name?"

She looked up at him, drawing her eyes away from his as soon as they met. "Helena Barova, Herr Obersturmführer."

"Have you heard about me, Helena?" He was sure that none of the guards could hear him. "Have you heard that things are going to change here?"

"I just do my work here, Herr Obersturmführer," Helena whispered.

"Tell the others; tell the other women, there will be no more summary executions without my express say-so." Helena looked back at him as if he were insane. "There are new rules here. Tell the others." He walked out of the warehouse.

He kept his head down as he walked past the prisoners milling around, carrying suitcases or pushing carts overloaded with clothes. Their defeated eyes were all fixed on the ground as he walked past them. He opened the door to the Economic District office. Müller was sitting at the desk, going through some ledgers. Christopher walked past him and into his own office, shutting the door behind him, but then turned around. He pushed the door back open and approached Müller at the desk.

"We haven't really had the chance to speak yet."

"No, Herr Obersturmführer, not yet."

"I think in order for us to maintain the most beneficial system to the Reich, we need to understand one another."

"Of course."

"Where is my predecessor? What happened to him?"

"Obersturmführer Groening? He was transferred to the front. He applied for the transfer himself. He said that the nature of this work wasn't to his liking."

"What about you, Müller, is it to your liking?"

"Yes, I'd say that it was. I was a bookkeeper before the war. This is the work I know and the best way for me to serve the Führer." Christopher picked up a paper clip from the desk and pressed it into his hand. The view through the window was only of the side of the warehouse next door, where the ladies of Canada worked.

"Is this your family, Müller?" Christopher picked a framed photograph up off Müller's desk of a woman in her late thirties, sitting in her Sunday dress, with two blonde girls standing on either side of her.

"Yes, my wife and two daughters in Hildesheim. Have you been there, Herr Obersturmführer?"

"No, no, I can't say that I have. I hear it's a very beautiful place."

"It is. I look forward to the day this war ends and I can return there."

"Thank you, Müller. Now let's get back to work. Heaven knows we have enough to do." Müller picked up the ledger once more and began poring over the lists of murdered.

Christopher went back to his office. He closed the door behind him. The safe, full of money and jewelry, was the first thing he saw.

He sat down at his desk, directly in front of it, but could still feel it behind him. He ran his hands through the papers on his desk in some futile attempt to distract himself. Rebecca came to him once more. What was the point of coming here and not doing everything he possibly could to find her? How would they both escape? He didn't know how many camps existed, or even where they were, just that this camp was now the biggest.

He looked around at the safe and the ledger he had written, which no one else had checked. He looked at the figures he had written. There were thousands of American dollars, reichsmarks, and francs. Every currency he had ever heard of. It was all sitting in that safe. A tiny fraction would be enough. Friedrich had warned him about corruption, but what punishment could they give him worse than what he had already seen? What was worse than the corruption of his soul? It wasn't stealing if he didn't use it for himself. There was no other way. He turned around to the safe. He reached across to touch it. There was a knock on the door behind him. He whirled around in his chair and set himself just in time to see Rapportführer Friedrich open the door. Christopher stood up to salute. Friedrich saluted back with a more casual wave of his arm and took his seat in front of Christopher's desk.

"It's been quite the baptism of fire for you these past few weeks, Seeler. The organization of the Economic District has improved, even in the short time since you've arrived. I hear you've instituted new rules for the guards there and established your authority over your sphere of operations." Christopher was trying not to squirm. "I understand that you've banned on-the-spot executions. What's the reason for this, Herr Obersturmführer? Are we to let the prisoners do as they please? There is a huge importance in making sure the prisoners know that stealing will not be tolerated."

"The workers are aware of the penalties for stealing, Herr Rapportführer. The guards were executing some of my best, most productive prisoners, oftentimes with little cause. I thought it better to impose a system whereby I would arbitrate the situations that present themselves. That way we can . . ."

"And how many executions have there been since you instituted this new system?"

"Well, none, Herr Rapportführer. There has not been the need for any executions."

"I understand that you want to assert your authority over the section, but it is I, as head of the Economic District, who should be making these decisions."

"Of course, Herr Rapportführer, but you are so busy. You have much more important duties to perform than the minor matters of executions and the like. I also am on the ground. Canada, as the guards refer to my section, is where I spend most of my time. I am in a better position, literally, to make those on-the-spot decisions."

Friedrich sat back in his chair. He looked tired. "Perhaps. I have an enormous job here, massive responsibilities."

"Everyone is aware of the enormity of your role in the camp's administration, Herr Rapportführer, and many of us are modeling ourselves on your example." There was silence for a few seconds. "Was there another reason that you came to see me, Herr Rapportführer?"

"Yes, there was, Herr Obersturmführer. You have the reclaimed currencies stored in the safe behind you?"

"Yes, there are suitcases full of dollars, pounds, reichsmarks, and several other currencies."

"All sorted, accounted for, and ready for their return to the Reich?"

"Of course, Herr Rapportführer."

"Good, good, because I have another job for you. The monies will need to be transported to Berlin. This is to be done with minimum fuss and with utmost secrecy. Your predecessor was trusted with this task, and so far you've proved yourself to be an exemplary SS officer." Christopher felt disgusted with himself for being described as such, but didn't show it. "I want you to transport that money to Berlin. You will drive, alone, once every second week, to transport the suitcases to SS headquarters in Berlin, where you will meet a contact who will relieve you of the suitcases and apportion it toward the war effort."

"Yes, Herr Rapportführer." The thoughts and possibilities of being out of the camp for one day every two weeks flooded through him, the possibilities of seeing his family and Uli's son, perhaps even Uli himself. Leave was still months away. The drive to Berlin was almost six hours; he might even be able to stay overnight.

"You are not to tell anyone about these trips. If anyone does inquire as to the purpose of these journeys, you will tell them that you are reporting to SS headquarters about the progress of the Economic District here in Birkenau. Is that understood?"

"It is, and thank you, Herr Rapportführer." Christopher stood up behind his desk and clicked his heels together as he saluted.

"No need for that. You will make the journey tomorrow and then every other Thursday. You will leave at six a.m. and make your way to official SS headquarters in Berlin where you will ask for Standartenführer Kohl, who will relieve you of the suitcases. Is that understood?"

"Yes, Herr Rapportführer."

"That will be all, Herr Seeler." Friedrich stood to salute. There was a picture of Hitler on the wall. Christopher made sure Friedrich noticed him saluting toward the Führer himself. Friedrich closed the door behind him. Christopher remained in the same position, his arm outstretched, staring at the door long after Friedrich had left. His breath quickened as he thought of the safe behind him, and he glared at the photograph of Hitler, watching him. But he was the only one. There were no other checks in place. There was no way for him to be caught, was there?

His hands were shaking as he turned the dial on the safe. The acids in his stomach seemed to be eating him from the inside. He stood up. The sound of the camp orchestra playing Wagner drifted around him. He knelt back down in front of the safe and thought of Rebecca. He drew down the window blind. The safe opened easily. There were several suitcases piled high, one on top of another. He picked off the top suitcase, the one full of US dollars. He had filled it himself. He had filled them all. He placed the suitcase on the table and drew his hands apart to open it. It had not seemed like money before, not money that he could spend. It had never seemed like actual currency to him, just units to be counted and accounted for, but these hundreds of crinkled used bills held together with rubber bands were different. Somehow they were different.

He reached into the case and drew out a wad of bills and held it in his hand for a few seconds, and then placed it onto the table. The bills came off easily, several hundred dollars. The sweat on his palms was running onto his fingers. He tried to count the notes, pressing them down under his thumb, but every noise from outside drew his eyes to the window adjacent to his desk. The sharp noise of metal grinding against metal snapped him back into the moment. A prisoner, one of the Sonderkommandos, shifted past, pushing a cart piled high with pots and pans. Christopher pushed the bills into his pocket and replaced the wad in the suitcase. He put it back into the safe and pushed the door shut again.

He could not remember having stolen before, not even as a child. The money felt heavy in his pocket, his feet like concrete as he stood up. The pistol on his hip smacked against the table, making a loud noise. Müller, Flick, and Breitner were all there as he walked out.

"Is there something wrong, Herr Obersturmführer?" Flick asked.

"No, why should there be?"

"No reason, you just look a little . . . unwell," he said.

Christopher raised his wrist to a clammy forehead. "It must have been something I ate—that fish for lunch." Christopher walked past them out the door. Evening was setting in, the air growing cold as the sun died. He climbed onto the bicycle outside his office and made his way along the warehouses of Canada and past the prison hospital, the gypsy camp, and the men's camp. He cycled on the other side of the road as he approached the women's camp. He passed the hordes of emaciated, wretched figures barely identifiable as women, returning from their day's services to the Reich. The family camp, where the propaganda films he had been shown had been filmed, and where certain prisoners received privileged treatment, passed on his left. The quarantine camp, where new female prisoners were kept before they joined the main population, was the last camp he passed before he reached the main gate. The land outside the gate was barren, stark against the gray sky above. There was not a tree or a bush to be seen, just marsh and meadowland stretching out on either side.

It was a further five minutes to Auschwitz. Just inside the main gate stood the administration building. It was the same guard outside the door. The guard looked at him as if he'd never seen him before. It was the third time that Christopher had presented his papers on the way here. The guard waved him past. The door to Liebermann's office was closed. He didn't wait for an answer after knocking, just pushed the door open.

"What are you doing here, Obersturmführer?" Liebermann's rounded cheeks turned a crimson hue. "We've already been through this. . . ."

"Well there have been fresh developments with my search," Christopher interrupted as he sat down at the desk. "I need you to find this woman. And I need it done soon."

"Have you any idea how busy I am here and how much time that would take?" Christopher threw the wad of banknotes down on the table.

"No, I don't. How much time would it take?"

"That's hard to say, to search the whole camp system . . . and there are new camps coming up all the time. It would be a difficult task."

"I have faith in you, Herr Liebermann." Christopher stood up and took a piece of paper out of his pocket. "Here are the details you'll need, and I'll call in to you when I can. I have to go to Berlin tomorrow, but I expect some kind of news on Friday when I get back."

"I'll see what I can do."

Christopher got up to leave, a hope renewed inside him. He turned around to thank Liebermann. The money was already gone.

# CHAPTER

## 23

Christopher was fresh as the alarm rang. He had resisted Lahm's protestations the night before and gone to bed early. Lahm was asleep in his uniform above the covers. One of his boots was by the door and the other still on his foot. His belt and baton were on the table. Christopher picked up the belt to place it on the chair. There were teeth marks on the baton. The belt slipped out of his hand back onto the small wooden table. Lahm stirred at the noise, but quickly fell back asleep. It was still dark outside, the shine of the searchlights illuminating the cold air. There was little activity other than the lights and the shadows of sentries patrolling the wire. The convertible two-seat car was parked outside, waiting for him. He would have no support, no armed guard. No others were to know where he was going or why. No preparations were to be made. It was a few minutes up to the office in Birkenau, and once there, he filled the trunk of the car with four suitcases full of money. He signed them out and marked off the ledgers, even though there was no one else there to check. It was all down to him and his word. His word as an SS man was to be enough, or was it?

He pulled the top down, the chill of the morning air biting at his exposed cheeks. He started the car and left. He presented his papers at the front gate and showed his orders. They didn't search the car, just waved him through. He drove clear of the gates onto the long empty road stretching beyond. It was strange that a world still existed outside. The camp seemed to envelop everything in his mind, whereby it was the entire world. He had only been there a few weeks, but it seemed hard to remember a time before the selections, the gassings, and the executions. The memories of his old life, his life before robbery and death had become his daily currencies, were dissipating like ripples expanding on water, fading into nothing. The prospect of six hours alone with his own thoughts as he drove scared him. The pressure within his chest was building again, and he drove for a few minutes until he thought it safe enough to pull over. He stopped the engine and silence fell upon him. The only sound was that of his breath, ragged and torn. Everything was gray: the sky, the land, the bare trees, and the uniform on his back. He sat back on the seat, gasping for air, trying to swat away the memories as they came to him, trying to keep the image of Rebecca in his mind, desperately trying to believe that she could still be alive. He thought of his father and sister. He started the car again.

The streets of Berlin were busy, clean, and ordered. There were no starving skeletons pushing carts piled with stolen booty. There were no crematoria. No smoke billowing thick into the air. The camp seemed a hundred worlds away. It seemed real. This seemed like a façade. He pulled up outside the headquarters of the SS and Gestapo. He asked for Standartenführer Kohl at reception. The pretty blonde receptionist asked him to take a seat while she called him. Kohl took less than a minute to arrive. He was a tall wiry man with gray hair extending into a greased widow's peak. He shook Christopher's hand with an overly firm grip. "So, you're the new man in Auschwitz? How much have you got this time?"

"Well, we have so many different currencies. . . ."

"No, no, let us worry about that, how many suitcases?"

"Oh, four suitcases this week."

"Times are good in Auschwitz, then?" They walked out to the car together, Kohl making small talk about Christopher's trip as they went. They unloaded the cases as if they were taking them out after a vacation and brought them inside to Kohl's office. They set them down on the floor by Kohl's desk, and Christopher stood there, waiting for something else to happen. "Thank you, Obersturmführer Seeler."

"Can you sign for them so that I've something to show my superior?"

"Of course, show me the ledger." He signed with a slapdash scrawl and handed it back. "We'll see you again in two weeks. And keep up the good work."

He felt like he'd just been mugged. Reichsführer Heinrich Himmler's office was on the same floor. Christopher nodded to the secretary as he walked past, noting to himself to speak to him next time he was here. It was just after one o'clock as Christopher walked out onto Stresemannstrasse. He had not been given an exact time to be back. He had not been given instructions about his return at all. There was no one he had to call or check in with. It was he alone. Harald's house was less than half an hour away and on the way back to the camp. He hadn't expected this level of autonomy. There should have been someone there with him, watching him, making sure he didn't abscond with the money, but there wasn't. There was no one to stop him seeing his family either.

He felt ashamed of his uniform and pulled up the top on the car, even though it was a fine day. Harald lived in a large five-bedroom house with his wife, his children having grown up and left years before. Christopher hadn't seen Alex or his father in almost three months. He should have been happier. Harald's wife, Steffi, answered the door. "Isn't this a wonderful surprise. What are you doing here? Your father will be so happy, come in, come in, Christopher, look at you in your uniform. Don't you look handsome?" She threw her arms around him. He stepped inside the house where he had stayed himself for his first few weeks back in Germany. That felt like a lifetime ago. "Stefan, Stefan, you'll never believe who's here." His father appeared. Christopher's father took him in his arms. "I'll leave you two to talk," Steffi said as she edged away.

He stood there with his arms around his father for a minute, or maybe more. His father's hair was almost completely gray now, his blue eyes shining through against the lines on his face. "Is Alex here? How is she?"

"No, she's at work. She's doing as well as can be expected. What on earth are you doing here? Is everything all right?"

"Yes, I'm fine. I was sent up to Berlin on . . . on an errand."

"What kind of an errand?"

"I'll explain everything. Is there somewhere we can go?"

They walked into the dining room where they sat down at the table. There was a color to the house he hadn't seen since he had joined the SS, bright flowers captured in paintings and orange curtains over the windows.

"Christopher, are you all right? You seem . . ."

"The camp where I work is called Auschwitz-Birkenau, or Auschwitz II." It suddenly felt cold. He lowered his voice to a whisper. "Is it safe?" Christopher said as he looked out toward the kitchen where Steffi was.

"As safe as anywhere, I suppose. You look ill, Christopher. Have you eaten?"

"I've no time for that, I shouldn't even be here."

"Is there news of Rebecca?"

"No, no news. Well, I do know that she was never in Auschwitz. I just have to find out where she is now." It was hard to talk, the words sticking in his throat as his voice became thicker. "Father, what do you think has become of our house in Jersey? Do you think that the house is still in one piece, waiting for us?"

"I do, Christopher." The pause lay heavy in the air. "The house will be there after all of this ends."

"It doesn't seem possible. It doesn't seem possible that places like Jersey exist anymore."

"They do, Son."

"I just can't believe they do anymore."

"How is your new posting? Is it where you need to be? Are you able to help with the resettlement of the Jews, at least?"

"There's no resettlement," he said, concentrating on each word, fully aware of his oath of silence to the SS. "There's only murder. Auschwitz-Birkenau is a death camp. It only exists for the purpose of murder and theft. And I'm in charge of the theft, the robber-in-chief. That's what I was doing in Berlin this morning, depositing the funds of the murdered with the Reich."

"What? Is it a punishment camp? Are the inmates being executed criminals?"

"Their only crime is that they're Jews or political prisoners or gypsies or Soviets. It's murder. I've been there less than a month, and I've seen almost forty thousand die, herded in on trains and gassed by the hundreds." Christopher took a pack of cigarettes out of his pocket and placed them on the table. "Women, children, the elderly, they're the first to go. Those fit enough to work are kept until they're executed on a whim or starved to death. And I'm one of them. I walk amongst the butchers and the murderers there. I eat my meals with them, drink with them at night." He lit the cigarette.

"How can this be?" he whispered. "You're not one of them, Christopher. Listen to me. You're not one of them. You're there for a reason."

"I don't know if she's still alive. I don't know if I can do this. I never thought the camp would be like this. No one else questions it. They're all completely convinced that what they're doing is right. I have no one to confide in."

"You have me and the rest of your family. How many prisoners do you oversee?"

"About six hundred, almost all women."

"Are you able to look after them at least?"

"To some extent. I've banned summary executions, and my commanding officer seems okay with that; he only seems to care about keeping the money flowing."

"Well, then, you've got to use that power, whatever power you have to make things better, even in some tiny way. And to find Rebecca."

"How can I? What can I do? One person? There are thousands of SS there, with the whole country behind them. There's nothing I can do. I can only hope to find Rebecca, and even then I've no idea how I'm going to get her out of that hell. That's what it's like—hell. No worse place on the earth."

"You have to be strong, for the ladies you oversee, for Rebecca, for yourself. There are always ways to influence things. You're in charge of the money? Money is influence."

It was after two o'clock. "I have to go. I have to go back there. Is there any news from Uli?"

"No, but no news is good news."

"Tell Alex I said hello. I'll be coming to Berlin on this day, every two weeks. I'll come back, at the same time."

His father hugged him. "I'll be here waiting for you. Don't forget who you are."

# CHAPTER

———

## 24

The days wore on with no news of Rebecca. She was always with him, hovering in his mind like a mist. He saw her face in every woman in Canada. He tried to stay among the women in Canada, to leave the selections to Breitner, who was always eager to be seen at the train station. Breitner was thirty-one, six years older than Christopher, and had been a member of the SS for three years. It must have galled him that a younger man, raised outside the Reich, took the position he saw rightfully as his. There was a reason. Breitner's work was sloppy, the accounts and ledgers rushed and often incomplete. He had had problems with alcohol in the past. He seemed sober now. He never engaged in the drinking sessions that the rest of Christopher's colleagues seemed to have almost every night. Christopher never saw him after work, never knew what he did. He was a hard man to know.

About eight hundred Slovak Jews were in the changing room of Crematorium III, sufficiently calm after the lies of the SS men. It was good for Christopher to be seen close to the action. He walked along the benches in the changing room, about two hundred feet long, watching the people undress, trying desperately not to make eye contact with them. An SS man named Northen, a guard from Hamburg, walked with him. Christopher tried to walk ahead of Northen, but every time he did, the SS guard would catch up. He was telling Christopher about his dog. He wished he would shut up. A middle-aged man with a graying mustache, dressed in a white shirt with a thick brown tie, stood up and took Christopher by the arm. He was much smaller than Christopher, only up to his shoulder.

"Excuse me, sir, but we're not meant to be here."

Christopher pulled his arm away. "I'm sure you're where you're meant to be." He thought to say the standard line about the hot bowl of soup and a life of labor on behalf of the Reich, but he couldn't do it. In just a few minutes he would suffer a horrific, agonizing death. Christopher had seen the piles of bodies by the doors of the gas chambers, all having tried desperately to force their way out into the air, to force themselves back into life. "Calm down, sir, everything is in order."

The man grabbed his arm again. "No, you are an officer. I must speak with you. I'm very concerned about what's going on here. We were meant to be on a train to Switzerland, we were to be released there. We have all paid for this right. We have all paid a lot of money for this and were promised safe passage to Switzerland."

"This is only a stop on the way to your final destination," Northen interjected. "You're here to shower and be fed. The Swiss government has spoken to our administrators at length about this. We have to make sure there are no lice or infectious diseases on any of the passengers before they are transported." Northen looked at Christopher, a twinkle of mirth in his eye. Christopher had not been outside in the yard when they were brought in, had not heard the latest round of lies.

"We are from Czechoslovakia. Why were we brought northeast? Why were we brought away from the logical route through to Switzerland? It doesn't make any sense."

Northen shifted his holster to the front to show an air of menace, but the man snatched for the gun and a shot rang out. The bullet burrowed into Northen's chest. Christopher dived to the ground as the man trained the gun on him. He felt the bullet graze his arm and braced himself for the pain. Panic spread through the changing room, filling the enclosed space with terrifying screams. Half-naked bodies moved and merged together and clothes flew through the air. Christopher was on the ground, a slight burning sensation in his arm. The man disappeared. There was another shot. The front door of the changing room slammed shut. The other SS men had fled. He was alone. He drew his pistol. There was a Sonderkommando about ten feet away, also lying on the ground. To his right, Northen lay gurgling his last few breaths. The screaming was subsiding now and the crowd of people that he had expected to attack him hadn't come. The man was nowhere to be seen. The lights went out and the screaming began again. It was absolutely dark. There was the sound of another gunshot. The floor was cold against his cheek. Several seconds passed before he heard the voice next to him. The Sonderkommando had crawled over to him.

"Where is he?" the Sonderkommando said.

"I don't know. I don't think there's any SS left inside. Northen is finished." He couldn't see the Sonderkommando's face in the dark, but he doubted that he was upset about Northen. "Let's try and make for the door." The two men stood up and felt their way along the wall toward the door, but it was over a hundred feet away, and there were eight hundred people in the changing room with them. Christopher barely breathed. The Sonderkommando was whispering prayers. The doors flew open and the harsh glare of searchlights penetrated the black.

"All remaining SS guards and Sonderkommandos are to exit the changing room immediately!" The voice was Kommandoführer Kuntz, the head of the detail that worked in Crematorium III. Christopher dashed past the huddling masses of people and through the door. The Sonderkommando and several of his colleagues were right behind. Ranks of SS men were milling about outside, fully armed. It was night. Lahm was at the front, his rifle pressed against his chest. Several heavy machine guns were moved down toward the door. Christopher put his hands on his thighs, bent over, trying to catch his breath. Lagerkommandant Höss, the head of the entire camp, was standing in front of him. Höss nodded toward him. Christopher pressed the pistol back into his holster and saluted. The clump of a grenade going off in the changing rooms preceded the pounding of machine guns, which were almost loud enough to obscure the screams of the people caught in the bloodbath. The lines of SS men moved past him to join in the massacre. He felt the hole the bullet had ripped in his uniform. More gunshots went off, and still the armed SS poured down the steps into the changing room. Lagerkommandant Höss stepped back toward him.

"You were inside there, Rapportführer?"

"Yes, Herr Lagerkommandant." Christopher's heart rate was slowing, his breathing almost normal as he spoke.

"What happened?"

"One of the prisoners snatched Sturmmann Northen's pistol and opened fire. I'm pretty sure Northen is dead, Herr Lagerkommandant."

"And how close were you, Rapportführer?"

"I was directly beside Northen, Herr Lagerkommandant."

"I see you had a close shave yourself." He gestured to the rip in his sleeve.

"You could call it that, Lagerkommandant."

"Rapportführer, I need to attend to this, but I want to speak to the officers in the yard afterward. Stay close by, I want you to stand with me as I speak to them."

Christopher milled around the yard, listening to the sounds of massacre for the next few minutes. It was all over quickly. It was just a matter of killing them all. The SS men began to come out of the changing room, the smoke billowing around them as they emerged. Some were covered in blood. It took several minutes for all the troops to come out of the changing room. Once they did, the Sonderkommandos went back down to herd the few remaining prisoners, those who had managed to hide behind pillars to avoid the carnage, into the gas chamber, for there was no escape for anyone once they entered the changing rooms. Christopher walked toward the entrance to the changing rooms in Crematorium III. Kommandoführer Kuntz was standing at the top of the steps looking down.

"This is some mess," Christopher said. "We'll be up all night cleaning this up." It took him a few seconds to realize what he was saying and a few more for the deep sense of shame to come over him.

Kuntz looked around at him. "You're the new man in Canada? You were right there when it happened?" He gestured down toward the changing room. "You're lucky to be alive. Maybe not lucky, maybe you were good."

Fifteen minutes later Christopher stood beside Lagerkommandant Höss as he addressed the crowd of officers in front of him. Friedrich was there at the front, along with Kommandoführer Kuntz of Crematorium III, Kommandoführer Strunz of Crematorium IV, and Kommandoführer Roehrig of number five. There was a crowd of about twenty, with Breitner, Flick, and Müller skulking at the back. All twenty stood in rapt attention as Höss spoke.

"Tonight is an example of what can happen when we let our guard down," he began. "The Jew is always looking for any chance to save itself, to inflict damage on us. Let this be a lesson to one and all that a lack of vigilance will end in tragic consequences. The death of a young SS man tonight should be a lesson to all. His lack of alertness to the dangers the Jew presents was his undoing, but conversely, Obersturmführer Seeler's quick thinking and alertness in the face of great danger is an example to us all." Christopher felt Höss's hand on his shoulder and the shame of the warm feeling it gave him. "Without Obersturmführer Seeler's quick reactions, this could have turned into a wider tragedy. His instincts as an SS man were solid and served him when he needed them most, these same instincts that every SS man in this camp should possess."

When Höss left, the Sonderkommandos marched back inside to clean up the mess of what remained of hundreds of people who paid for and were promised safe passage to Switzerland. Their blood-soaked, shredded clothes were piled on carts to be transported across to Canada, though Christopher doubted they would find much that hadn't been destroyed by grenades and gunfire. The bullet-ridden body of the man who had killed Northen was found and dragged outside. Christopher wondered if it was a better or worse fate than the gas chamber. His body was hung up in the men's camp in Birkenau, a few hundred yards away, with a sign around his neck that read, "Look at me! See what happens to those who try to escape, and now the other 800 on my transport are dead too!"

# CHAPTER

## 25

The next day he was walking through the warehouses in Canada, on the endless rounds he made, watching the prisoners, watching the guards. There were twenty or thirty women in the room, sorting through an enormous pile of clothes in the corner. He felt a tug on his arm. She was probably twenty, but it was hard to tell. Her face was creamy white skin leading up to high cheekbones and piercing green eyes. Her brown hair came down in a curl at the front beneath her headscarf. He had not seen beauty like hers in a long time. Not in this place. The guard in the corner began to shout something before Christopher held up his hand. He reached down and brushed her hand off the sleeve of his jacket. "Herr Obersturmführer, can I speak to you?" Her voice came as a whisper only he could have heard. The guard was now looking out through the open doorway at the rain driving onto the ground outside. Christopher walked on. "Herr Obersturmführer, please." He walked back toward her. The guard was still looking away.

"What is it? You've no reason to be speaking to me. Get on with your work."

"Please, Herr Obersturmführer, if I could just speak to you for a few seconds."

"What is it?"

"My name is Martina Culikova, please to tell you that my sister is arriving on the train this afternoon. She has her two children with her. Please, Herr Seeler, they say you are a good man."

"Who says this?" he snarled. He thought to strike her across the face, as much from the real anger inside him as from the act of being ruthless and cruel.

"It's just that she would make a wonderful worker. She was a seamstress back in Malinovo. She arrives this afternoon." Martina grabbed Christopher's arm once more, pressing her face into the sleeve of his SS jacket. Her tears left tiny marks on the gray. "Her name is Petra Kocianova, she arrives this afternoon."

"How dare you?" Christopher roared. "How dare you assume such things?" He felt the red hue in his face rise, and suddenly he was very hot. One word from him and the guard would kill her instantly. Just as easily he could kill her himself, just draw his pistol and fire. There would be no judgment passed, just one more body to dispose of. Martina was shaking, her whole body in convulsions as the waves of tears jarred her. The guard was walking across, his pistol in hand. Christopher held up his hand and the guard stopped. There were two other guards and perhaps twenty-five other prisoners, and all had seen and heard what happened. "Come with me!" Christopher shouted, and took her by the arm. The lady next to Martina whimpered and grasped for another overcoat, running her fingers through the lining faster than Christopher had thought possible. The guards reholstered their pistols. Martina Culikova had stopped crying, as if resigned to her fate.

She fell down. He didn't stop. She got back to her feet to save herself being dragged along the rough concrete floor. She was so light, like dragging a child.

They stepped out into the driving rain. He had no idea what to do next. He knew what he would have been expected to do by both the prisoners and the guards. Where had the prisoners gotten the idea that he was a good man? That was tantamount to a death sentence here. There was no room for good here, no place for pity or remorse. Rain ran down his face, mixing with his tears. He could not bear to look back at her. He just kept walking. She tried to speak, but he couldn't make out the words. They went past several warehouses. There was no one around, just some prisoners scuttling about, pushing carts overloaded with clothes, suitcases, porcelain vases, ragged human remains. Satisfied, he dragged her around the side of the second-to-last warehouse. She immediately fell to her knees and closed her eyes. She raised her hands and took off the headscarf. Her brown, straggly hair came free.

"Who told you that I was a good man? I am an SS officer."

Rain ran down the smooth skin of her face. "They say you are different," she whispered.

"Who says this?"

"The ladies in Canada.

"They say since you arrived, the executions have stopped. They say that you are the one who handcuffed that monster, Frankl." He drew his pistol, his hand shaking so much the gun almost slipped out. *If the other guards see that I spared her . . . I'll never find Rebecca. This has to happen.* She shut her eyes again. The pain in him was building again. It was almost unbearable.

"Why did you approach me like that, in front of the other prisoners, the guards?" The pistol felt like a thousand tons in his hand.

"I had to do something to save my sister and her children. I would rather die here than not try." Her eyes were closed, head down, her hands behind her back, ready for what they both knew was about to happen.

"What is her name?" He replaced the pistol back in his holster. She opened her eyes. "Petra Kocianova, she's from Malinovo, she's coming with her two sons, Patrik and Karel. If you could . . ."

"On your feet." He was almost a foot taller than her. "Never approach me again like that in front of the other prisoners. Go into the warehouse next door, where they are sorting the eyeglasses." He gestured toward her striped uniform. "Rip the edges of your clothes. Sit down in the mud before you go in." She scratched her face, leaving a long red line across the white of her cheek. "Come on." He undid his belt and dragged her back around and into the warehouse. Ganz, the card player, was on duty. Christopher threw her down on the floor in front of him.

"What's this?" Ganz asked.

"She thinks she can grab my uniform in front of the others, thinks she can ask me for favors. I drew my own favors from her. Put her back to work." Ganz grabbed her by the scruff of her neck and dragged her toward one of the sorting tables. The other ladies didn't look up from their work as he threw her to the floor. She raised herself to her feet and limped to the table. Christopher walked back out into the pouring rain.

It was still raining when the shipment came in. He had seen no one, done nothing since he'd seen Martina that morning. The damp of his hat was cold against his skin as he put it on. He slipped his arms into his coat. Breitner was preparing to go down to the train station with Flick when Christopher emerged from his office.

"I'm going to go down for the selection this afternoon. Breitner, you stay here and go over yesterday's ledgers. And Breitner, no need to look so surprised." Breitner slipped off his coat and murmured something about being glad he wasn't going out into the rain. Flick followed Christopher outside.

"Is there something wrong, Herr Seeler?" Flick said on the short drive down to the train station.

"No, I'm fine. It's just the pressure of the job. There's always something to worry about." He wanted to go on, to actually talk to this man, but he stopped himself.

They arrived at the train station a few minutes late. The selections had already taken place. If he were to do it, it would have to be now. She would be in the women with children line. That line meant death. He dispatched Flick toward the suitcases the Sonderkommandos were hauling off the train. The rain had thickened, and the smell of damp was everywhere. The line of healthy adults selected for labor was moving off toward the main camp in Auschwitz. The other line waited. The camp doctors were hurrying back toward Auschwitz, their selections made, their jobs done. He stopped one, a tall, fit-looking middle-aged man. "I'm looking for a prisoner," he shouted, his voice almost lost in the pounding of the rain. The doctor gestured toward the Rapportführer on duty, a huge man with a black baton in his hand. *This isn't what I came here for. This isn't smart.*

"Herr Rapportführer, I am Obersturmführer Seeler, from Birkenau. I work in Canada."

"Ah, the new Dollar King?" The Rapportführer let the baton fall by his side. Several seconds passed. "What is it?"

"You have one of my prisoners."

"What? Who?"

"Her name is Petra Kocianova. She is one of my ladies in Canada."

"What's she doing mixed up with this lot?" The rain was flowing down the angle of his cheek.

"She was transferred out and then came back with her children. She's one of mine, though. I would really appreciate if you did this for me. I wouldn't forget it."

"This is most irregular."

"I would be very grateful if you did this for me, very grateful."

"Herr Obersturmführer . . ."

"Very grateful."

"All right then, my name is Heinrich Schwarz. I expect something in return for this."

"Of course."

Schwarz caught the sleeve of Christopher's coat as he went to walk away. "And, Herr Obersturmführer, the children, they stay with me."

Christopher tried to think of something, some way around this. A thousand thoughts flashed through his mind. There was nothing he could do. He walked on. He called out to the line of people moving toward the crematoria, called out her name. She was about his age, with long brown hair and stained white porcelain skin. Her two children huddled close to her, one holding each leg. "Petra Kocianova? Come with me." She moved to come with him, the children clinging to her. "No, sorry, just you."

Her two boys were both under the age of six. "What about my children? I won't leave them."

"You can see them later. You can see them after their shower and disinfection. They are going to be taken to our kindergarten, just behind your own living quarters. You'll be able to visit them every day." The lies tore him inside. The line was moving off. The officer in charge was staring at him. There were only seconds left to do this. "We need to get you away from here." The two boys were crying now, clamping their arms around her thighs. He gestured toward an elderly woman. "Will you take care of the boys, Mother?" The old woman went to take the two boys, but they moved around their mother's legs to get away from her. The line had moved on. Rapportführer Schwarz was walking toward them, shaking his head. "Please, you need to come with me, right now." His voice was shaking.

"I won't leave my boys."

"Come with me, right now!" He grabbed at her arm. The old woman managed to grab a hold of the younger boy, who looked about three years old. Petra knelt down and hugged her sons. She whispered something to them as she gripped them tight to her.

He took her up to Canada as the workday was ending. Martina Culikova began crying as she saw her. He wondered when she would tell her that she would never see her children again, that today had been the last day of their short lives.

# CHAPTER

## 26

The children stayed with him. The act of saving Petra Kocianova seemed futile. He saw her in the warehouse over the following days, her face lifeless and ashen. There seemed little point to any of it. All of this would end someday. When that day came, who would ever believe what he was here to do? All the murderers would be making their contrition. One more from him would not be noticed. He was guilty, by association or otherwise, and that guilt was starting to erode him inside. There had to be more he could do. There had to be more than just preventing the casual murder of his workers. There was no way he could stop the beatings. They still continued on a daily basis. The ladies in Canada regularly limped into work with gaudy purple bruises covering their faces.

He had been counting the hours until his next trip to Berlin, but when the day arrived, he greeted it with little relief. Nothing was enough now. His mouth was dry when he awoke, the taste of whisky still on his breath. Drinking with Lahm and his friends seemed the only way to sleep now. It was easier to go along with them, easier just to drink than to resist the constant goading. Lahm was asleep as Obersturmführer Seeler pulled on his uniform. The jackboots slid on easily. They fitted him like a second skin and made little noise as he walked on the floorboards. He lifted the lapels of his SS coat to ward off the freezing winter cold. Prisoners were marching to work, the SS soldiers and Kapos snarling at them as they went. The distinctive crack of a rifle sliced through the air. He felt the pain rising in his chest. There was a starling on the hood of the car. Its brown plumage almost shone in the dull early morning light. It had a sprig of green in its mouth that twitched and shook as it moved. After a few seconds it took off and disappeared into the sea of gray sky above.

He thought of the children all the way to Berlin, the way they had clung to Petra's legs, longing for the protection that she could no longer provide. He tried to assure himself that he had done a good thing, that he had saved a life, that it was better that she survived, but it was no good. He cried for them as he drove. He thought of the boy shot in the face at selection and the man that had killed Northen. He thought of Rebecca, trying to push aside all else. He tried to remember the times before all of this, when the sun cast long beams through the kitchen of his father's house, illuminating her hair as spun gold.

They were expecting him at the house this time. Alexandra ran to him and swallowed him in an embrace. Karolina stepped out of the house, holding little Stefan's hand. Alexandra kissed him. His father wrapped still-strong arms around him. He broke free and picked up his cousin, embracing Karolina once Stefan was in his arms. The pain inside subsided, washed away. Alexandra came up from behind him to take his hand and led him inside. Harald and Steffi were there, standing just inside the door.

"Welcome to the returning hero." Harald smiled.

"I'm so happy to see you all. I just wish I could stay longer. I have to get back to the camp."

"Come on, you can join us for a cup of coffee at least," his father said. Alexandra pushed him into the living room. She sat down beside him with his father on the other side. Karolina smiled and hugged him before claiming she had to take Stefan out for a walk. Harald and Steffi made their way into the kitchen. Christopher's father closed the door. Alexandra's face changed.

"Oh my God, Christopher. Are you all right?"

"Of course I am. What are you talking about?"

"It's your skin; you look ill." She raised a hand to touch his cheek. "You look cold and gray."

"Thanks. I'm fine. It's a long journey here. How are you? How is your job? You must be missing Tom terribly."

"This life we're leading now is worse than I ever could have imagined."

"These certainly are hard times," their father said.

"Father told me about the camp."

"Were you planning to keep it from her?"

"No . . . I don't know. What good is it that she knows?"

"It can't be real. A camp set up to murder people?" Alex said. She looked thin. The lines on her face were far more pronounced than they should have been for a twenty-three-year-old. Her eyes had dulled, and her hair was lifeless and limp.

"It's very real."

Christopher picked up the empty cup in front of him and held it up, regarding the intricate patterns on the china. They were still silent when Steffi came in with the pot of coffee. She set it down on the table and backed out slowly without saying a word. Their father picked up the coffeepot and poured for each of them. "Are you safe there?"

"Yes, quite safe. I am getting quite adept at hiding my true self. As long as I keep the money flowing, I will be safe."

"Is there news of Rebecca?" Alex asked.

"No, not yet, my contacts are still looking."

"I'm sure she's out there," his father said.

"I hope so. What of Uli?"

"Nothing, no letters, no word from the Wehrmacht. He's still on the Eastern Front."

"How many people are dying in the camp?" Alexandra asked. "I just can't believe it. I cannot believe that they could do this. It's monstrous. I knew the Jews were gone, but nobody ever talks about them. It's as if they just disappeared into nothing."

"I've seen close to sixty thousand die, maybe more. That's in the eight weeks I've been there. It's like no circle of hell I ever could have imagined. Somehow finding Rebecca doesn't seem enough anymore." It felt good to talk about it, like pouring water over the massive fire inside. "I've tried to help the ladies that work for me. There are six hundred of them. I'm trying to keep them alive."

"But now you want to do more," their father asserted.

"Yes. I have to."

"What if the SS find out that you're helping the prisoners?" Alexandra asked.

"I'll be executed." Alex instantly began crying. "But I think that I'd choose that over doing nothing. I couldn't live the rest of my life knowing that I did nothing."

"Is there anyone in there you can talk to? Any confidant? What do the other SS think of what goes on there?"

"There's no one. The other SS think they're doing a job for the Reich, for the world. They're deluded enough, poisoned enough, to believe what they're doing is justified." He took a sip of coffee. It was too hot and it burned his lip. "What happened to these people, the other SS men, I mean, that they can do the things they do? You wouldn't believe the things I've seen. Women and children slaughtered . . . How can they do it? That question is burning a hole in my mind. I know these people. I eat with them. I play cards with them and drink with them. At night they seem normal, like regular guys, people you might enjoy drinking with if you didn't know who they really were."

"It's amazing what years of conditioning and propaganda can achieve," his father answered. "No one is born with that brutality in them."

"I often wonder if I'd be the same as them if I'd been subjected to the same."

"You could never be like them," his father said.

"I don't know. If I do nothing, I'm no different than they are. Carrying out orders, that's all the other SS men are doing there. There are plenty of killers, people who love what they do there, but most of the SS are passive. They're just doing a job."

"A job where they brutalize and murder innocent people?" Alex asked.

"Yes."

"No one speaks out?"

"No one. If anyone did they'd be shipped off to the Eastern Front, hauling bodies. There's no one else. I'm completely alone."

"You have us."

"I can't tell you how good it feels to talk to someone. I feel like I'm drowning in there."

"So, what are you going to do?" his father asked. "You're right; you do have to do something."

"I really don't know what I can do. I do have the money, and there are no checks. There's no one after me to check the money. There's a river, a monsoon, of money flowing through the camp."

"Use it," his father said.

"I think we should slow down here. He could be executed," Alexandra asserted. "I just think he needs to be careful."

"I've already banned any summary executions in my section of the camp. There have been no workers shot in my warehouses for a month."

"That's good. Is there anything else?" his father asked.

"There has to be something I can do for them."

"You're right, Christopher. There has to be."

# CHAPTER

## 27

Christopher sat perfectly upright, absolutely still. It had been surprisingly easy to get the appointment to see Lagerkommandant Höss. It seemed the Lagerkommandant was eager to meet up with him once more. Christopher coughed and smoothed out his collar, although he knew it was absolutely pristine from the time he had spent pressing and re-pressing it. He ran his hands over the smooth skin of his face and smiled across at Höss's secretary. She smiled back. Höss's office was just outside the fence of Auschwitz I, right beside the administration building where the Economic District's official, but rarely used, offices sat. Höss opened the door.

There was nothing extraordinary about this man, the Kommandant of all of this. He was of medium height, smaller than Christopher. He had a full head of brown hair. There was nothing striking or outstanding about his face, no scars or war wounds. He was a completely average man in his early forties. He was the type of man one would walk by on the street without passing a glance at or paying any attention to, yet he was the master of all this horror and death. Christopher felt physically ill just looking at him. Höss gave a lazy salute back to the young Obersturmführer. Christopher entered the room as Höss directed him and took a seat in a plush red leather chair, one of three facing Höss's massive leather-topped desk. The portrait of Hitler was looking down on them as Höss began.

"I was in Berlin last week," he said, lighting up a cigarette. He offered Christopher one from a sterling silver cigarette case. The initials engraved on the inside of the box were not Höss's. "I met with Standartenführer Kohl, of the SS headquarters. I believe he is your contact?"

"Yes, yes, he is. I've met him twice now." *How much is Kohl skimming off for himself? How much is Höss?* "I've not had the chance to meet him properly yet. . . ."

"Yes, he's a charming fellow. I've known him quite a while now. Are you a member of the Party yourself, Seeler?"

"No, I'm not."

Höss picked a file off the desk in front of him. "Yes, I remember seeing that in your file. You're from . . ."

"Jersey, Herr Lagerkommandant." He thought of the dead, the festering bodies awaiting cremation.

"Yes, of course. You were liberated in 1940. No divided loyalties, I hope?"

"None whatsoever, Herr Lagerkommandant."

"Of course not," Höss said, throwing down the file. "There's no room for that here, where the most important work in the entire Reich is taking place. Standartenführer Kohl tells me that production is up, significantly up, since you began here. Berlin is happy, and that makes me happy."

"I'm glad, Herr Lagerkommandant."

"Yes, I joined the Party in 1922 myself." He was looking past Christopher now, as if peering back to those halcyon days.

"I read about your record in the last war, how you were one of the youngest noncommissioned officers in the German army. I know you started off as a concentration camp guard yourself in '34." Höss didn't answer. "My own father served in the war also. I'm grateful now for my opportunity to serve the Fatherland."

There was a tumbler of whisky on the desk. "I'm glad to see such dedication. I have been most impressed by the work you've done in the Economic District so far. But, as you know, I am a busy man. What is it that you've come to see me about today?"

"There's been something troubling me ever since I arrived in the camp."

"And what might that be, Obersturmführer Seeler?"

"Corruption, Herr Lagerkommandant." Höss took a sip from the tumbler on his desk. "I have no idea what went on in my department before my arrival, and I certainly don't want to pass judgment on my fellow SS soldiers who operate in the Economic District, but I have heard some things. I have seen some things also."

"It's a sickness," Höss said. "I have little doubt that it's a disease spread by the Jew himself, the sickness of greed. It's true that some of the men have succumbed to it. It's up to men like you, dedicated SS officers, to provide the example these men need."

"That's what I'm here to speak to you about."

"Go on."

"There has to be a tighter system of checks and balances put in place. Too much wealth is being lost before it has the chance to make it back to the Reich, to where it can do the most good." Höss poured Christopher a tumbler of whisky and without asking him, pushed it across the desk. "There needs to be someone on the ground with access to the ledgers, to the monies, to the warehouses, and who can watch over the prisoners, and yes, the guards themselves, to make sure that any improprieties are stubbed out as soon as they occur." Christopher took a sip of whisky from the glass. "I have been watching the entire Economic District, every minute of every day since my arrival, and I think that the results have been evident. But it's still not enough. I estimate that ten percent, or more, of all the wealth to be apportioned to the Reich never arrives. I have worked out that for every two thousand prisoners that pass through the crematoria on a daily basis, we only collect about forty thousand reichsmarks, not including the gold and jewels the prisoners are carrying. Logic dictates that the prisoners are carrying more than this. They have to be. I want to make it my job, my responsibility, to make sure that none of this wealth is lost."

"Is this not already your job, your responsibility?"

"It's one of the many roles that I undertake, but I want to be custodian of the ledgers, to check and recheck the staff, the guards, and the prisoners themselves. I need a mandate to search any guard or any locker, any truck, and under any bed of anyone I suspect of stealing and hoarding wealth meant for the Reich."

"You want to take personal responsibility for all of the issues with corruption in the Economic District?"

"Nothing would make me happier, Herr Lagerkommandant."

"Corruption has been a problem in the camp for too long now. I was speaking about it only last month with Herr Himmler himself."

"I would like to make weekly reports about it, to you only. There should be no one else involved. It's too important an issue."

"An interesting idea, Herr Obersturmführer." Höss stubbed out his cigarette. "It's certainly something I would like to think about. A young committed officer like you could do much to stem the insidious hand of corruption." Höss stood up and held out his hand. "Well done, Herr Obersturmführer. Give me some time and I will get back to you."

"There is something else, Herr Lagerkommandant."

"You have my attention, Herr Obersturmführer. You have had my attention since that night you showed your bravery in Crematorium III."

"Well, what I wanted to ask about was . . . the children passing through the camp."

"What about them?"

"I was considering that we might be able to repatriate some of them, the babies perhaps, the ones that have not been poisoned by the Jewish ideologies and lies yet. We would be able to impose some of our Aryan ways upon them, to purify them as it were. A mission of mercy."

"I understand what you're saying, and I've had that thought myself before, but the sad fact of it is that they are just as much enemies of the Reich as their parents. It's in their blood. They have no choice. A Jew will always be so, nothing more, nothing less. They must be eradicated."

"I understand that, but how about the young children, the three-, four-, and five-year-olds? They could be put to work in the factories, cleaning out pipes, getting into machinery; their fingers can reach places adult hands cannot. I mean, what chance do we adults have?" He smiled. "It's just economic sense. The one thing that I cannot stand is waste."

"A compelling argument indeed, Herr Obersturmführer, but unfortunately Jewish blood is Jewish blood."

"We keep hundreds of able-bodied Jews every week to work for the Reich. I just don't see the sense in there being an age limit, that's all. I think in black-and-white, economic terms. It's my father's fault; he is a very logical man." He felt ashamed for mentioning his father in this place.

"I have very much enjoyed meeting you today, Seeler. You are an exemplary young officer, with many good ideas. The idea of making the children work? Well, again, it's something we could give thought to. But now I must bid you goodbye."

He shook the Lagerkommandant's hand and clicked his heels together to give the Nazi salute. Höss did think about it for three days. Christopher was to head up a task force to investigate corruption in the camp and to have recommendations in place for a new system to prevent monies being siphoned off at source within two weeks. There was no mention of the children and his idea to make them work, not yet. Christopher looked out as the sun was setting over the horizon. He thought of Rebecca, the children that he couldn't save, and the thousands of faceless murdered that he had seen pass through this place. For the first time in a long time, he felt hope.

# CHAPTER

---

## 28

The guards greeted Christopher as he walked into the dull, smoky room. They were all there: Lahm, Ganz, Meyer, Schlegel, Dreier, Bruns, Mohr, and Grüne, as well as two other SS that Christopher hadn't met before. They had kept him a place. The table was littered with the usual mix of cigarettes and all kinds of booze pilfered from the stores. Grüne pushed a glass of whisky across to Christopher.

"I trust we are all well tonight, gentlemen," Christopher began. He was greeted by a series of grunts from around the massive table. "And I hope you're all ready for me to take your cash." There was a large pile of money in the middle of the table, mainly reichsmarks, but also British pounds, US dollars, and Polish zlotys. Christopher sipped a glass of whisky, waiting for the next hand. "I don't think I can stay too late tonight. I have to be up early tomorrow morning for a meeting with some of the top brass. I'm setting up a new anti-corruption committee, sanctioned by the Lagerkommandant." Several of the men put their cards down. "I'm going to be heading up the committee. The Lagerkommandant asked me to take charge." They were all listening now. "I know that my findings won't affect any man here." Obersturmführer Seeler put down his glass of whisky. "If you have any doubts, any questions, come to me. If there's anyone you know who might have been engaged in anything that might look illegal, speak to them. Warn them. Tell them to lay off, for a few weeks at least, until the Anti-Corruption Committee has done its work." He put a hand on the shoulder of the man next to him. "I've no desire to put any of my mates behind bars, boys, quite the opposite. Tell your friends what's happening. Of course there's no need for me to tell any of you this. I just thought . . . in case you had friends around the camp . . ."

"Yes, we understand," Lahm said. There was no more talk about the Anti-Corruption Committee that night.

The first meeting of the Auschwitz-Birkenau Anti-Corruption Committee was held in the administration building the next morning, just a few doors down from Liebermann's office. The first tiny snows of the season were floating down outside the window. Christopher sat at the head of the table. Breitner sat directly to his left. He seemed to have pressed his uniform especially for the meeting. Flick and Müller were there, and opposite them sat the Kommandoführers Kuntz, Strunz, and Roehrig, the heads of the crematoria. At the opposite end of the table, away from the others, sat Jan Schultz, the head of the Sonderkommandos in Canada.

"Thank you for coming here today, gentlemen, for the first meeting of our committee," Christopher began. "I will keep this short, as I know you are all busy and there is a train arriving in less than an hour that we will all need to attend to. I want to particularly thank Kommandoführers Kuntz, Strunz, and Roehrig for taking time out of their busy schedules to attend. I have summoned you here today because you are men I know I can trust, and, in matters of this importance, trust is absolutely essential. Word is that we will have a new Lagerkommandant soon, as Herr Höss will be moving to Berlin to take a more direct role in the war effort. It is our job to prepare the camp for the new Kommandant, to show him that we are not prepared to put up with the insidious cancer of corruption that is slowly taking a hold of all corners of Auschwitz-Birkenau. A successful anti-corruption campaign will lead us all on to great personal glory, as well as securing the future of the camp in its current guise. Let's not forget, gentlemen, why we are all here, to further the ideals that our Führer himself has passed down to us, and to secure the future of our world and our civilization." Schultz's face was stoic, rendering absolutely no emotions. "I have asked the head of the Sonderkommando unit in the Economic District to attend today. I know that several of you were surprised at his inclusion in the committee, but I think in order for us to be successful, we need to work with the prisoners."

He spoke for another twenty minutes, about checks and procedures, about secrecy and punishment for transgressions. Each man had a dossier in front of him that he had compiled himself, with explicit instructions on each stage of their operations. Kuntz shifted uneasily in his seat as he read through the papers. The meeting was over in less than an hour. Each man left clear about, if not entirely happy with, the new regulations.

Christopher walked down the hallway after the others had gone. He didn't bother knocking on the door, just pushed straight inside.

"Liebermann. I trust you've heard who the new head of the anti-corruption task force in the camp is?"

"Yes, I did hear that. Congratulations on your new appointment. Who on earth saw fit to give you of all people such a role?"

"None other than the Lagerkommandant himself. He knows a good SS officer when he sees one."

"Perhaps it is best that he moves to Berlin after all."

"You know me too well, Herr Liebermann, but I know you too. Let's not forget that. Now that I'm head of the Anti-Corruption Committee . . . well?"

"Don't try to strong-arm me, Herr Obersturmführer. Don't forget who your superior officer is."

"Of course not, Herr Hauptsturmführer. I want what you want, to serve the Fatherland and the Führer."

"Indeed. Speaking of your service to the Fatherland and the Führer, I may have some news of your prisoner."

"Where is she?"

"You seem eager, Herr Obersturmführer."

"Are you going to tell me?"

"I've managed to find some prisoners from Jersey, in a camp in Baden-Württemberg. I don't know if your friend is there among them, not yet anyway."

"When will you find out?"

"I have written another letter. I should receive reply within a week or so, depending."

Christopher stood up, his legs wobbling under his own weight. "Very good then, I will check back with you in a few days. Keep up the good work, Herr Hauptsturmführer." He walked out without another word. The hope inside him made it impossible not to smile as he went.

The day passed like any other. Thousands of prisoners trudged through the snow to their deaths, many children among them. Where was the word from the Lagerkommandant about them? Should he go to the head of the factories himself? He knew he had to be patient, but the agony of watching them file into the changing rooms was becoming too much to bear. He made his excuses to go back to his office. He sat in his office for several hours, poring over reports and files, ledgers and records, anything to distract himself.

The end of the day was dark and cold. The snow was falling again when he left his office to see Schultz in Crematorium IV. He reached for his long coat and tucked the collar up to cover his ears as he made his way out into the darkness. Work was officially over for the day, but there were still Sonderkommandos tending to their own duties. They all saluted him as he walked past. The warehouses were empty, the ladies from Canada returned to their bunkhouses a few hundred yards away. The searchlights were on now and one came across him as he went. He waved up to the guard in the tower above and was just able to discern the wave back.

The yard outside Crematorium IV was deserted except for a couple of Sonderkommandos pushing carts of suitcases toward the warehouses in Canada. The Sonderkommandos' quarters were luxurious by the standards of the rest of the camp. The Sonderkommandos were given bunk beds, one each, with clean sheets in heated dorms. They ate their meals alone, and blind eyes were turned to allow them to steal as much booze as they could ever drink. These were their rewards for the work they did, as well as the right to live one more day themselves. Schultz was not there. Christopher asked a Sonderkommando, a young Polish boy, probably no more than nineteen years old, where he was and was told to check the haircutting room, downstairs near the ovens.

Schultz whirled around as Christopher found him. There were four other Sonderkommandos with him. They were all experienced in their jobs. Most of them had worked in the crematorium for two months or more. It was rare a Sonderkommando survived any longer. All five men stood in a line in front of a bench at the back wall.

"What's going on in here?"

"Herr Obersturmführer, what brings you down here?" Schultz began. "Have you come to check the progress of the Anti-Corrup—?"

"What's going on here?" Christopher repeated.

"Not a thing, Herr Seeler," Schultz again spoke. Christopher heard it, the faintest gasp, and wished he had never walked into that room. He drew his pistol.

"What was that?"

"I didn't hear anything, Herr Obersturmführer," one of the other Sonderkommandos, a Pole called Becker, replied.

*Shoot him. Run out to get help. Get the head of the crematorium.* "What do you have back there? Stand away, stand away or I will shoot all of you!" The men parted. The crumpled body of a little girl, perhaps eight years old, was lying on the bench, her chest expanding as she gasped for breath. Her long brown hair fell almost to the floor in straggly knots, half covering her filthy face. She was wearing a gray man's shirt. "Where did she come from?"

"She was in the last shipment," Schultz said. "We found her in the gas chamber, underneath her father's body." He was walking toward Christopher now. Christopher trained his gun on him, aiming right at his face. "She was alive. Still alive after the gas poured in." He was still approaching, now only a few feet away.

"Stop right there, Schultz. I will shoot you right in the face. I swear I will." Schultz stopped six feet short.

"She survived the gas. She's the first any of us have ever seen survive the gas chamber. She must have been trapped in a bubble of air. It's a miracle; there's no other explanation for it." Schultz stopped. "Are you going to shoot her?"

"I will shoot you, Schultz."

"Go ahead," he said, standing still, his hands out in front of him.

"Don't make me do this. All of you will be dead in minutes if I report this. I just have to . . ."

"We all know that, Herr Obersturmführer. All our lives are in your hands, even hers." He let his arms fall to his sides. The men at the back were standing still. The girl coughed again. One of them turned to her and knelt down to press his ear against her chest. He said something in Polish. Another man knelt down beside them and began compressing her chest and then blowing air into her mouth. Christopher didn't move. He was still aiming the pistol at Schultz's face. The prisoner drew his mouth away from the girl and she began to cough and splutter on her own.

"Is she going to live?" Christopher asked.

"Maybe, we don't know. Tomas is a doctor," Schultz said, gesturing toward one of the men. "Tomas, how is she doing?"

"Her lungs are damaged, but I think she's going to make it."

"It's all up to you now, Herr Obersturmführer. Do you kill her? Kill us? Or just walk out of here and pretend you never saw anything?" Schultz said.

He pressed his gun back into its holster. "What are you going to do with her? Have her work in the crematorium, burning stiffs? You know there's no place in this camp for children." He brushed past Schultz toward the girl, stopping about three feet short. "First thing we need to do is get her out of here. There are too many guards around." He moved past the others, knelt down beside her. Her heartbeat was faint to the touch and her chest heaved as her lungs scratched for air. "Let's get her over to my office."

"How are we going to get her over there?" one of the men asked.

"Get a cart," Schultz said. "Heap it up with whatever clothes you can find. We'll put her under there. Get some clothes for her too."

"But the changing rooms have been cleared," the man said.

"Well, then, improvise. Go, all four of you, and be quick," Schultz ordered.

Christopher had his hand on the girl's chest, feeling the rhythm of her breathing, in and out. Schultz was standing behind him, but Christopher didn't turn around. "Herr Obersturmführer, you should probably stand at the door in case . . ."

"Schultz, if you breathe a word about this . . ."

"Of course not, Herr Seeler, I would be just as culpable. . . ."

"Don't interrupt me, Schultz. If you tell anyone, I will have the entire Sonderkommando unit sent to the punishment block, where you will all be tortured to death."

"Yes, Herr Obersturmführer. This never happened."

Schultz tended to the girl as they waited. Christopher stayed by the door, watching for any guards that might have been walking past. None came. The only sound was that of the girl's fractured breathing. "Do you know what her name is? Where she's from? Was she in the last shipment from Prague?"

"She hasn't spoken; she's barely been conscious, but yes, she was in the last shipment."

"What the hell are we going to do with her once we get her back to my office?"

"Could you get her into the children's block in the family camp?"

"I don't know. I could try. I don't know if I want to subject her to that." The children's block was one of the worst in the entire camp. If the children somehow managed to survive, they were often picked off for medical experiments or even by sexual predators. Many of the Kapos had their own little boys or girls they kept for themselves. Christopher reached down to the little girl and ran his hand across her hair. Perhaps a quick death might be better than the children's block.

There was a knock on the door and the whispered voices of the other four Sonderkommandos filtered through. Christopher opened it. They were carrying sheets and clothes from their own quarters. One of the men said something in Czech and another spoke Polish. Schultz spoke in German. "Where is the cart?"

"Outside the main door," Becker said. "There's no one out there." It was past eight o'clock and most of the guards would be off duty. That didn't mean it would be easy. There were always guards around. The searchlights still swooped down on anything that moved.

The girl was covered over in blankets and coats within a few seconds. Two of the men picked her up with gentle hands, one holding her shoulders, the other her feet. Christopher opened the door and looked up and down the dull concrete hallway before he bade them to come through. They stepped outside, placed her on the cart, and then heaped more clothes over her.

"We don't need five men to push a cart full of clothes. Tomas, is she okay?" Christopher asked.

"She just needs to rest, needs liquids. But I think she'll be fine. It truly is a miracle."

"Save the religious exhortation. Schultz, push the cart; the rest of you back to your quarters." The cart wobbled through the slush and snow. It was several hundred yards to Christopher's office. A guard passed by. Schultz pressed his eyes to the ground. They kept going. The girl began to cough, the sound clearly discernible through the clothes. "Is she choking?" Christopher whispered to Schultz, walking beside him.

"I don't know." There was a group of guards standing underneath an awning by the first of the warehouses. They were pushing the cart directly toward them. There was no way around. The coughing from beneath the clothes was getting louder.

Christopher strode on toward the guards fifty yards ahead of Schultz and the cart. "Evening, boys," he said. "I see the snow is setting in. Do any of you have a cigarette?" One of the guards offered him one.

"You're working late, Herr Obersturmführer," another guard said.

"Yes, no rest for the wicked. Did you hear about the new Anti-Corruption Committee? Yeah, my advice would be to be careful for the next few weeks." The cart trundled past, the rasping sound from below still clearly audible. Schultz began coughing loudly. None of the SS men looked at him. Christopher waited until the cart had passed before throwing down the half-smoked cigarette.

"Just be careful, boys. With a new administration coming in, we all need to watch ourselves." The guards thanked him. He went to catch up with the cart. He walked five yards behind Schultz until he knew he was out of sight. They moved in silence. The coughing had stopped. Christopher knew she was dead. They reached the office and pushed the door open. They brought the pile of clothes inside, still no noise from within, and laid her out on the floor. The only light in the office was from the silver beams of the searchlights outside. Christopher put his ear to her chest.

"I can't believe it. She's alive." He slapped Schultz across the back.

The girl coughed again and her eyes opened. She was lying just in front of Breitner's desk.

# CHAPTER

## 29

Schultz put a cup of water to her mouth, the liquid dribbling down her chin as she coughed again. The office was dark. Both men were completely silent, the only sound that of the girl's breathing. Her bare legs were shaking. They found a pair of pants among the blankets, and Schultz helped her into them. Christopher motioned toward a blanket draped over Flick's chair, and Schultz covered her up. The adrenaline of earlier was clearing, and Christopher was thinking, trying to find some solution to a situation that seemed impossible. There was simply nowhere for her to go. Schultz certainly couldn't take her back to the Sonderkommandos' quarters. They had been lucky to get her out of the crematorium at all. Where would he keep her? How would he get her out of the camp? There was only one way out, the prisoners said, and that was through the chimneys of the crematoria. He put his hand on the girl's forehead; it was a little warmer than before. Her entire family was probably dead now, their bodies heaped in the crematoria or already crammed into the ovens. Was there any real mercy in saving her? He picked up the cup of water and dripped it into her mouth. Schultz began to speak, something in Czech.

"Does she hear you?"

"I don't know."

Her eyes flickered, opened, and looked up at Christopher through the dark. She was alive, truly alive. "She's awake. Ask her what her name is." He elbowed Schultz, decrying the half-second hesitation before responding. "Do it." Her eyes were now fully open. Schultz reached down and stroked her cheek before asking her name in Czech. She said nothing. "Ask her again," Christopher demanded.

"She's terrified. Her family is all dead, and now she's here all alone. . . ."

"Anka," she said. He took her hand, warm in his.

"You can leave now, Schultz."

"Are you sure? What are you going to do with her?"

"Well, you can hardly bring her to the crematorium with you, now can you? I'll take care of her. Go back to your quarters." Schultz reached down and touched her face once more and leaned down to her ear. Christopher could hardly make out the muffled whispers in the language he didn't understand, but he did hear his name. Schultz stood up. "What did you say to her?"

"I told her who you were. I told her that she would always be safe as long as she was with you."

She began to cough again, and he sat down beside her. He held her to him and felt her arms spread around his torso. He waited for her to take her arms away, but two minutes later they were still there stuck together. He brought his arms away. The tears on her cheeks were silver in the moonlight. She said something. Something low that, even if Christopher had spoken Czech, he would probably not have made out. He felt Rebecca, as if she were in the room with them.

"I'm sorry, I can't understand you." She spoke again, and he knew by the inflection in her voice and the look of bewilderment on her face that she was asking him something. It must have been about her parents. He was glad not to be able to answer. "Now you stay right here." He took one hand off her, pointed to her chest and then toward the floor. "You stay here. I'll be back in a few seconds." He stood up. Outside, the cart was gone, as he had hoped. He fumbled in his pocket for a cigarette before throwing it down without lighting it. There was no one around. He went back inside. Anka was still sitting, exactly as he had asked her to. She hadn't moved or made a sound. He picked up the blankets where Schultz had left them and opened the door to his office. He dumped the blankets on the floor and went back to her. "We're going in here now, into my office," he said, reaching out to take her hand. She curled her fingers around his and stood up. He laid out the blankets just in front of the desk. *I'm risking my life, Rebecca's life, for this little girl I hadn't even met an hour ago?* He flattened down the blankets and gestured for her to lie down, but she didn't move. "Come on." She was crying loudly now. He put his arm around her and she embraced him, her arms around his neck. "Shhh," he said, his finger to his lips. "You need to be quiet, Anka. It's okay, I'm here. I won't let anything happen to you." The words came easily. He hugged her again and got down on his side, his black jackboots sliding on the floor. He took off his SS jacket and put it across her as an extra blanket and lay down, taking her into his arms, and held her until she fell asleep.

He awoke with the dawn, his arms still around Anka. She was warm, still alive, the first thing he checked. It was just after seven. There was another meeting of the Anti-Corruption Committee in two hours, and he would be gone most of the day. There were two shipments coming in. Müller, Flick, and Breitner would be in and out of the office. Anka's eyes were still closed as she stirred in her sleep. *Is there any hope? Any point in this?* He pushed her dirty, matted hair away from her face. There had to be some way of hiding her until he could smuggle her out of the camp on his next trip to Berlin. His father could take her, could find somewhere for her. It was five days until his next trip to Berlin, five long days to hide her, but where? Perhaps Schultz could hide her during the day, or he could ask some of the ladies in Canada to hide her. His body ached from sleeping on the floor. Anka still slept. He sat in the seat in front of his desk and stared at her for twenty minutes or more. Then he heard a knock on the door. Anka opened her eyes at the noise, and Christopher shot out of his seat. Christopher tried to calm himself, to stay still, but knew the person must have heard him.

"Obersturmführer Seeler?" Friedrich's voice poured through. "Are you inside there?"

"Yes, Herr Rapportführer, just give me a second. I must have fallen asleep at my desk last night." Anka's eyes were wide open and she sat up. Christopher put a finger to his mouth and looked around the room, his eyes going from the overstuffed closet to the safe to the desk in less than a second. He raised a finger to his lips again. Anka stayed quiet.

"Herr Seeler, I only wish to speak with you briefly."

"Coming, Herr Rapportführer." Christopher lifted Anka off the blankets and threw them over his chair. She crawled under the desk, seemingly hidden. He walked to the door, smoothing back his hair before he unlocked it. He opened the door a few inches.

"What is the holdup, Seeler? Why is this door locked?"

"Nothing, Herr Rapportführer, I just wanted to be presentable," he replied as he tried to slip out through the door to the office. Friedrich blocked him. They were face-to-face, inches apart.

"I'd really rather talk in your office, Seeler."

"I'd rather we didn't if you don't mind; it's a mess in there."

"I am requesting we do not speak out here. What I have to discuss is of a sensitive nature."

"But, Herr Rapportführer . . ."

"Seeler, don't make me ask again. I won't speak about this out here." Friedrich pushed against the door. Christopher just had time to glance back at the front panel of his desk. Anka was completely hidden behind it. He moved backward and stood in front of the desk. Friedrich sat down, dragging the chair two or three feet from where Anka was hiding. Christopher walked around the desk and sat down. He pulled the seat out and brushed the blankets to the floor.

"I see you had a late night."

"There's . . . there's always so much work to do."

"And I hear you've volunteered to do more." His tone was sharp.

"I assume you're referring to my activities with the Anti-Corruption Committee?" He felt Anka moving, felt her brush against his trouser leg.

"I am surprised you would set up such a committee without referring to me, your direct superior."

"I apologize, Herr Rapportführer. I should have included you in any plans I made; it's just that I know how busy you are, how much responsibility you shoulder." He felt Anka clutching his leg underneath the desk. "There are some things that I would like to show you in the warehouses . . ." He stood up.

"Sit down, Obersturmführer," Friedrich growled. "Don't forget who the ranking officer is here, even if you've got your nose up the Lagerkommandant's backside."

"Herr Rapportführer, in no way does my position as a part of the Anti-Corruption Committee lead me to any false beliefs about my status in the camp. I am just an accountant, and that's what they needed. I do apologize for not involving you in the process further, but it's a process that has barely begun. There is plenty of room for your input." Anka was tight around his right shin now, and he could feel the shudders through her body as she tried not to cough. "If you want to join any of our meetings . . ."

"And what exactly will be the methods that the committee will be employing?"

"We will be tightening security at all points during the process of repatriation of goods to the Reich. The checks will begin from the . . . initial selection all the way to the final process of loading the goods to be sent back to Berlin. The system that my predecessor put in place is too . . . loose, there are too many holes." His hands were clammy with sweat.

Friedrich hesitated for a few seconds before he began again. "What of these checks? What can my guards expect?"

"We have been given full access to all personal property, lockers, closets, and all other spaces to carry out searches for any contraband. If the individual guard is not stealing, then he has no reason to worry."

"I see." Friedrich sat up straight in his chair. A cough came from beneath the desk. He looked across at Christopher, who felt a bead of sweat run down his back. "Did you . . ."

"If that's all, Herr Rapportführer . . ."

"What was that?" Friedrich stood up and darted to the window. Christopher jumped up, feeling Anka's grip fall away beneath the desk. "I'm sure I heard something."

"I didn't hear anything."

"No," he said, holding his hand in the air. Christopher could clearly discern Anka's breathing against the silence. "Do you hear that, coming from outside the window?"

"What? From outside? Do you think it's a prisoner?"

"There's only one way to find out." Friedrich bounced out of the office. Christopher followed him around the side of the building where the sun was casting a dull yellow onto the camp below.

"It must have just been a prisoner walking past. Believe me, Herr Rapportführer, this happens all the time. I get a lot of traffic outside my window." The chill of the morning almost froze the sweat against Christopher's skin. "I have a meeting at ten a.m. with Kommandoführer Strunz in Crematorium IV regarding the new procedures we wish to put in place. Would you like to sit in on it?"

"Yes, yes, I would," Friedrich said after a few seconds' hesitation. "In his office at ten?" Friedrich walked away.

Christopher burst into his office and reached under the desk. Anka said something as he pulled her out, and he held her in his arms, one hand underneath her and one on her head. "I can't take this," he said in English. "You did so well, darling. You did so well." Tears were welling in his eyes. He kissed her cheek and bounced her up and down in his arms in tiny movements. Her light brown eyes flickered in the morning light. He drew the blind down. Her skin was dirty and her lips were chapped and cut; yet she was so beautiful. "Now, Anka, you have to wait here, while I get you some food, and while I work out where you're going to be today." She seemed to have some idea of what he was trying to tell her and sat down in the seat Friedrich had just occupied.

He fumbled the key as he locked the door to his office from the outside. There was a shipment of prisoners due in about an hour. He scrawled a note telling Breitner and the others to go directly to the selection and oversee the processes there. They would understand, would think it was part of the anti-corruption activities. He hung it on the door. The bike he used to travel to Auschwitz was locked up under the awning outside. It was ten minutes to the canteen in Auschwitz, a long time to leave her alone. He thought better of it and jogged over toward Crematorium IV. The Crematorium yard was full of Sonderkommandos, pushing carts of clothes, suitcases, and dead bodies back and forth. There was no sign of Schultz, but Tomas, the doctor from the night before, was there, pushing a cart brimming over with open-mouthed naked corpses. Christopher stopped him, trying not to look at the contents of the cart. "Where is Schultz?"

"Inside, in the changing rooms." He felt a touch on his arm as he went to walk away. "How is that item, from last night?"

"Doing fine." The touch fell away, and he continued inside.

Schultz gathered what food he could find, more than enough for the girl's breakfast. They made their way to Christopher's office in silence. The office looked empty. Christopher's blood ran cold until he saw her hiding under the desk. The blind in the office was permanently down now. The semidark of the office made it harder to find her. Schultz spoke in Czech, and Anka poked her head out, almost smiling as she saw them. She stuffed the food into her mouth, chewing two or three times before swallowing each piece down. She murmured something back to Schultz, and they spoke again.

"What are you talking about?" Christopher asked.

"Her parents, her brothers. She was asking where they were."

"What did you tell her?"

"I told her I didn't know, that she had to stay close to you, to keep quiet, and we would try to find them."

"What?"

"What was I meant to say?"

"Forget it. Does she know the danger she's in?"

"I don't think she understands."

"I don't think any of us do," Christopher answered in English.

"What was that?"

"Never mind," Christopher continued. He took Anka in his arms, conscious of Schultz watching him. "Can you look after her during the day? I can't."

"Can I take her into the crematorium? No, I can't. Have you seen what I do in there?" Schultz said. "I apologize for my tone, Herr Obersturmführer."

"Never mind that, Schultz, we have more pressing concerns than your tone. I have meetings all day. I have to attend to the currencies coming in this afternoon. There will be men in and out of here all day. If she makes a sound . . ."

"Is there somewhere in the warehouses?"

"No, there are guards all over the place in there, and with the new Anti-Corruption Committee, they've been told to search through all warehouses twice daily."

"So what options do we have?"

"We have to leave her in here. I'll try to get her out of the camp next Thursday."

"Five days is a long time to survive here."

Schultz went first, leaving Christopher alone with her. Her coughing, the only sign that she had survived the gas chamber, was almost gone. He held her for a few seconds and kissed the top of her head. "Stay safe, Anka. I will be back as soon as I can."

# CHAPTER

## 30

He thought of Anka, Rebecca, and little else during the morning's meetings. The information was laid out in the dossiers, and most of the meetings consisted of his placating the various officers, convincing them that morale would not be destroyed among the troops, and reassuring them, without words, that they would not end up in jail themselves. A special unit would be arriving from another camp within hours to begin the first sweep. The first searches would be of the SS men's quarters and their personal lockers. After that the searches of the prisoners' quarters would begin. Schultz and the others had managed to spread the word among the prisoners themselves. Any guilty SS man would receive a court-martial; any guilty prisoner, an instant death. Friedrich stayed quiet during the meeting, and despite Kommandoführer Strunz's confident assertions and seeming relish for the process, Christopher knew that they were all as guilty as one another.

Christopher made it back to his office just after midday, carrying the remnants of his own lunch to share with Anka. He immediately locked the door behind him. The office outside was empty, Flick,

Müller, and Breitner having obeyed the orders he had left. She was asleep under the desk, just as he hoped she would be. She awoke with a jolt, but seemed to calm upon seeing him, and attacked the food he brought. He sat with her, holding her, his hand on her wrist. Her heartbeat was strong and even, the coughing less. The clock on the wall dragged him away from her. He began to work when she was hidden underneath the desk, where he had given her some ledgers and pencils to keep herself amused.

Two hours later the troops bustled into the SS men's living quarters. Flick stood beside him, overseeing the search. Breitner was up front giving needless orders as the SS men looked on. There were about fifty men tasked with searching the SS quarters. It took almost three hours. There were shouts every so often when one of them found contraband banknotes, jewelry, or even alcohol and came out of the room brandishing it like a trophy before it was boxed away as evidence. Christopher wondered who would skim the evidence boxes once the courts-martial were finished. There were twenty-seven arrests, no one that he knew, just SS men who had been too greedy. One had a box of watches in his locker. Another had eight gold teeth hidden in his clean socks. Most of the men had heeded the warnings. They had found jewelry in the trash, gold coins thrown under barracks, and banknotes strewn about the yard outside the SS men's quarters. Even so, the take was still big enough to impress any superior, and it was a triumphant first day for the Anti-Corruption Committee.

The checks on the prisoners were done during and after the day's work. Prisoners were forced to strip naked in front of the guards and deposit their clothes on a table while they were searched. The prisoners' quarters were almost destroyed in the searches, but nothing was found. There were no executions.

The overall take of valuables and currency from the shipments that day was enormous, out of all usual proportion to the amount of prisoners liquidated. It was obvious to anyone who looked closely what had happened, but no one was asking questions. All the officers in Berlin would see would be the enormous influx of wealth coming from Auschwitz. It would be Christopher's job to maintain that flow.

By five o'clock the anti-corruption troops had ravaged the entire living quarters of most of the SS men and prisoners stationed in Auschwitz. The piles of contraband were driven away in trucks to be stored as evidence in the trials that would follow. Most of the men could expect jail terms. Some might be shipped off to the Eastern Front. Christopher felt no satisfaction at this justice he had meted out. It was disturbing, but somehow he felt the opposite. Somehow he felt like a traitor. He lit a cigarette and walked away from the living quarters, his thoughts focused on Anka once more. He needed to get back to her. Breitner walked over to where he was standing.

"Are you happy with the work done today, Herr Obersturm-führer?"

"As happy as one can be, having fellow SS men arrested."

"Yes, no one likes a rat, do they?" Breitner moved away.

He arrived back at the office. It had been empty all day, but there was no way that he could keep the others away for the next four days. The smoke from the crematoria billowed into the darkening sky outside. There was no escaping the death that surrounded him like a cloak. Yet somehow Anka had survived. The others had spoken of a miracle, as if God had come down, touched her, kept her alive for some reason that only he knew about. But there was no God here. That was the one thing Christopher was sure about.

She was hidden under the blankets in the corner when he came in.

"Anka, come out. It's Christopher."

She pushed the blanket back to reveal herself.

The phone rang, piercing the silence. He was frozen, trying to listen for the sounds of the SS men coming to take them both away. But there was nothing, only the shrill sound of the telephone.

"Obersturmführer Seeler?" came the voice on the other end of the line. It was Liebermann.

"Hello, Herr Hauptsturmführer."

"I have news for you. Come immediately." He hung up.

Christopher felt the ice inside him and reached up to rub some nonexistent sweat from his face. "You stay there. Understand? That was a very important phone call. Very important. I'll be back as soon as I can. I'll bring food, and some water. We can wash you." She whispered some words in Czech. "I will come back," he said as he closed the door behind him. The key turned as he locked the door, and he was almost outside before he realized he had left it in the keyhole. He walked back and picked it out, trying to compose himself.

Darkness descended, the light of day faded into the blackness of night in the camp. The searchlights that ran along the wire flickered to life. He rubbed the condensation off the seat of his bicycle and climbed onto the saddle, almost tripping over his own feet in his haste. He was sweating as he reached the checkpoint to leave Birkenau. The guard made a comment, which he acknowledged with a smile, although he had not heard it. If Rebecca was arriving, he could get her and Anka out together somehow. There had to be some way of smuggling them out in the car, or, at worst, getting Rebecca into Canada where he knew she would be safe. Anka was small enough to fit in the trunk. The car was never checked. The guards all knew him. They all trusted him. Why couldn't he do this?

He threw down the bike outside the administration building in Auschwitz, his legs still burning from the ride. He took a few seconds to smooth over his hair and to set the bicycle against the wall.

"Hello, Obersturmführer Seeler," the guard at the door said.

He knocked on Liebermann's door, waiting for a reply before he pushed it open. Liebermann motioned for him to sit down.

"You're the talk of the camp today, Seeler. A young Obersturm-führer, only here two months and already heading up an anti-corruption committee? Your progress has been quite astounding."

"I'm just doing my best to serve the Reich and the Führer himself."

"Oh yes, I forgot about that, the Führer himself, of course, of course."

"So you have news for me?"

"Oh yes, the reason I called you down here. You'll forgive me, Seeler; I am an old man, not a young firebrand like yourself."

"Are you going to tell me?"

"Patience, young Herr Seeler. I received a phone call from an old colleague of mine, working in a camp called Ilag V-B Biberach. It seems he has your Ms. Cassin."

His heart was on fire. "So she's alive?"

"It does seem so."

"And when can we get her transferred here? That was the deal."

"I'm very much aware of what the deal was, Herr Obersturm-führer. She'll be arriving on the last train on Wednesday."

"This Wednesday? In three days' time?"

Liebermann nodded.

Christopher bit down on his lip, trying to hold in the smile. "Where's she coming in from?"

"Does it matter?"

"No, I don't suppose it does. She's getting here on Wednesday evening, not Thursday, because I am going to Berlin on Thursday morning, first thing. I'll be gone all day."

"What is it? You need to be here, to welcome her?"

"Just stick to the details please, Herr Liebermann."

"I'd watch my tone if I were you, young man." Liebermann pointed at Christopher across the table. "How would it look if the new golden boy, the head of the new Anti-Corruption Committee, was seen to be giving bribes to a senior officer?"

"How would it look for a senior officer to be seen taking bribes? Listen, I've already told you, I don't give bribes. What time is that train getting in on Wednesday, Herr Hauptsturmführer?"

"Five thirty. I've had Ms. Cassin put onto the list to be transferred directly to the facility in the Economic District for sorting through the goods to be repatriated to the Reich."

"Excellent. That concludes our business here, Herr Liebermann. Let me commend you on the good work you've done here. If you ever need anything from me . . ."

"Oh, don't you worry, Seeler. I won't be shy about asking."

He sped back to his office. "Come here, Anka," he whispered. "I've had the most marvelous news, my darling." He was speaking in English for some reason. She seemed puzzled and murmured something back. "I'm sorry, Anka, I don't speak Czech," he said, switching to German again. "But I heard today that Rebecca is alive and being transferred here." He reached down and picked her up, taking her in his arms. "Maybe there will be some reward at the end of all this misery, for us both." He brought her head back to look at her face, still dirty and unkempt, her hair falling over her face. "I'm going to get you out of here, Anka. I'm going to get you away from this. I swear I will."

# CHAPTER

31

He washed her hair the best he could and used a cloth to wipe the dirt from her face. When she settled down to sleep, he finished his work, totting and checking the numbers from the day, numbers that were sure to please Höss. The numbers were up more than ten percent from what they would usually have been. His superiors would be happy that the goods and monies they were stealing were not being stolen. He and Anka slept on the floor of his office again, this time with pillows and blankets appropriated from the stores to ward off the winter cold clawing at the window. The searchlights passed by the window, illuminating the room so that he could fully see her face as she slept, his arm around her.

He imagined that she was from a small village outside Prague, and saw her playing with her friends, her brothers and sisters. He imagined her coming home to her parents, her father lifting her high into the air and hugging her before planting a kiss on her cheek. Her family was all dead now, her home taken over by settlers brought in from the Reich or by jealous neighbors. What life was there for her now? Perhaps he could get her out of here, get her to his father. His father could hide her; keep her safe until all of this was over. Once he and Rebecca got out, they could take her, raise her as their own, and give her the life that was stolen away from her. There were still places like the beaches of his youth in the world. There was still happiness to be found.

The chill of dawn woke him. Anka was still asleep. She seemed to sleep all the time. He drew his arm away from her and stood up, the only sound the cracking of his joints. The irrationality of hope consumed him. He felt Rebecca with them again.

More snow had come during the night, tingeing the warehouses and crematoria with a beauty undeserved of a place like this. Christopher wiped the snow from his bicycle seat and set off toward his living quarters in Auschwitz. Lahm was awake when he arrived. He was standing in front of the mirror, shaving.

"Where were you last night?" he asked.

"There's so much work to be done at the moment. I suppose I fell asleep at my desk again."

Lahm did not reply, just kept shaving. Christopher went to his locker and laid out fresh clothes. The two men were silent for a minute or more before Lahm spoke again.

"Yes, it must be very tiring work, turning in your fellow SS men." He was still facing the mirror.

"I have a job to do, just like you have yours. Like your job, mine isn't always the most pleasant. I mean, you can hardly enjoy working in the punishment block, can you?"

"I do. I enjoy giving these vermin what they deserve. There is no such thing as an innocent Jew."

"Well, many people would not enjoy that work, but it is important for the security and future of the Reich," he countered. "My job is the same. I did everything I could to protect my SS brothers. If some of them were too stupid to heed my warnings, well, I can't be held responsible for that. I didn't ask for this job, Lahm, I'm just trying to serve the Führer in the best way that I can."

"By locking up men with wives and families?"

"The orders on corruption come directly from Himmler himself. Are you going to question him? Who is next? Are you going to question the Führer?" The words tasted sour coming out of his mouth. He said them as someone else, as if he were stranger in his own skin.

Lahm put down the razor and wiped off his face. He rested his arms on the side of the sink and glared at Christopher in the mirror. He turned around and put on his shirt, and when Christopher looked at him again, his expression had changed. "I knew some of the men arrested, Seeler."

Christopher felt good about the arrests now, for the first time, as if there was finally some justice. "Were they guards in the punishment blocks?"

"Some of them, yes."

"Why didn't you warn them? I told you to warn them." He was enjoying the words as they came.

"I thought I did. I couldn't see everyone. I thought I told most of the guys."

"They probably heard but didn't believe you. You tried, Lahm. We both did. That's all we can do." He picked up his clothes and walked out of the room to the showers. He was trying not to smile.

Rebecca was a constant in his mind now. He could feel her breath on him, the softness of her hair against his neck. The thought of seeing her brought him a happiness alien to this place. Once she arrived, everything would change for him. He would have to shield her from death every day that she was here.

Christopher had the remnants of his breakfast in his pocket as he trudged past the warehouses in Canada toward his office and Anka. He heard the noise from a hundred feet away. It was Frankl, the Kapo. He dragged one of the ladies out by her long, straggly brown hair and threw her down in the snow. He shouted something and pulled out his baton. Christopher had witnessed this too many times. Frankl drew the baton up and brought it down on the woman's head. The sound of baton on skull came as a crunch. The urge to run forward to grab Frankl's arm and throw him back on the snow was like a dog snapping inside his chest, but he knew better than to cede to it. Christopher quickened his pace but barely enough that anyone watching him could notice. Frankl brought the baton down again. Blood spattered onto the white snow. Two prisoners walked past, pushing a cart full of pots and pans. They were oblivious to the spectacle in front of them, forcing themselves to completely ignore the screams of the woman as he hit her again and again. Frankl connected with the palm of her hand as she tried to protect herself. She screamed again. The seconds it took for him to reach them seemed like hours.

"Frankl?" Christopher said when he had finally reached them. "What's going on here?" He was completely calm, his voice absolutely smooth, absolutely even.

Frankl whirled around, his arm still raised to strike the woman, who lay prone at his feet. "This wretch, thinks," his breathing was heavy, the words struggling to get out. "This wretch thinks she can fall asleep at the table while she's working." He looked to Christopher for the permission to continue, to beat her to death, or however close to her death his whim would lead him.

"And you respond to problems by disabling my workers, Frankl?" Christopher shook his head. "If she falls asleep, by all means slap her to wake her up. March her outside in the snow with no shoes on, but don't disable her. For every worker you kill, I have to find another, and that means more work for me. Do you know how busy I am, Frankl?"

"Of course, Herr Obersturmführer, it's just that . . ."

"Frankl, I appreciate the . . . thorough nature of the work you do here, but you need to think things through." The woman on the ground was whimpering. Christopher didn't look at her once. Two prisoners moved past pushing an empty cart. Christopher motioned them across. "Pick up this prisoner, bring her down to the hospital." Although the woman was bleeding heavily from her head, her eyes were open. There might still be hope. The prisoners picked her up and placed her on the cart. "Just remember that this operation depends on the workers, Frankl, and so do our jobs." It took all the will Christopher had to pat Frankl on the shoulder. "Go back to the warehouse."

Breitner, Müller, and Flick were at their desks as Christopher arrived at the office. "There's a shipment coming in an hour or so. I want you three out there, watching everyone and everything." He moved toward the door. Anka was under the desk when he walked inside. He moved to her, putting his finger to his lips. She put her own finger to her lips. She came out from underneath the desk and knelt down beside him as he sat down. He worked and she drew, in absolute silence. An hour passed. It was time for the next shipment. He wanted to see the others off, to make sure they left. He walked out into the main office. Only Müller was still there, and he was walking out the door.

"I saw what happened earlier with Frankl. I was passing by," Müller said.

"Oh, did you? I can't have my workers being . . ."

"Frankl is an animal. The word is that he hates you, because he can't exact his bloodlust anymore."

"I'm certainly not threatened by him. I am an SS officer. He's just a Kapo."

"He has killed more prisoners in here than any other Kapo I've ever heard of. The previous Obersturmführer let him run wild. He must have killed four, five, ten prisoners a week. I've seen him beat prisoners to death with a shovel for the gold fillings in their teeth. Anyway, I just thought you should know."

"Thank you."

Müller put on his hat. "Oh, and there was one more thing. I think you might have mice in your office. I could have sworn I heard some noise coming from inside there earlier, before you arrived."

The blood drained from Christopher's face, his body cold as a corpse. "I'll check into that. Thank you again, Müller."

Christopher put his hand on Anka's head as he sat down in the chair behind his desk. He picked her up and put her into his lap.

"What's wrong with these people, Anka? Thursday morning will come. We can start to live again, because this isn't life, Anka. This is just the absence of death." He held her to him and kissed the softness of her cheek. "Oh, why didn't I do this sooner? Why did I let so many die?" Anka leaned back in his arms and took the lapels of his SS jacket. She looked happy, as if sitting on her father's knee on a visit to his office. She whispered something to him in Czech.

# CHAPTER

## 32

It was Wednesday morning, Anka's last day in the camp, Rebecca's first. Every minute was a minute closer, to both Rebecca's arrival and Anka's liberation. The minutes drew out like razor blades. He had prepared the way for Rebecca the next day. She would be immediately placed into one of the work groups in Canada. He had prepared a suitcase for Anka, just big enough to fit her tiny body inside. He had cut air holes, but would leave it until the last minute to pad it out, just in case. The assignments for that day had already come through. The shipment that Rebecca would be in was coming in at five thirty, around an hour after the setting sun extinguished the gray light of winter in the camp. The thought of seeing her filled him with a joy he had scarcely believed existed anymore, and he hugged Anka close to him as she awoke.

He pulled on his jacket as he stood up. Anka knew not to make any noise. She would be safe here for just one more day. This would work. He bent down to hug her before he left. As he put his hand on the doorknob, he heard her call to him. She waved and he walked out with a deep smile on his face. He ran a finger across his unshaven chin. He had a meeting in Auschwitz with the other members of the Anti-Corruption Committee at ten. They were to collate the results from the first week to present to the Lagerkommandant. The committee had proven a great success. No one had asked why there had been so few arrests and such a massive increase in revenues coming into Canada. No one seemed to care.

He went back to his dorm to shower and shave. He hadn't seen Lahm since their conversation the other morning, and he wasn't there as Christopher arrived in the room. He wasted little time getting showered and changed and went straight to the mess hall to wolf down his breakfast, making sure to pocket some food for Anka. He made his way back to Canada and the office, which was always empty at that time of the morning. He gave Anka her breakfast. It was a routine, one he would miss. But tomorrow there would be a new routine, with Rebecca.

All the members of the committee were at the meeting, along with Friedrich, who was officially there as an observer. Christopher stood up to address them. His hands were shaking. He put them behind his back. The tension within him eased as he spoke about the numbers, the figures behind the activities of the committee. Schultz came late, and sat alone in the corner. Christopher saw them all in the room, Anka, Rebecca, and even his father and his sister. His thoughts were independent of his words as he addressed the committee seated before him. His thoughts were for the people in the room only he could see.

The meeting ended with handshakes and backs being slapped, but Friedrich seemed less happy. He left without a word. No one shook Schultz's hand, and he went back to the crematorium to assist in burning the bodies of the freshly murdered. The report was ready, and Christopher would be the one to present it to the Lagerkommandant. There was talk of a promotion for him, and that the committee might be installed on a permanent basis, but Christopher didn't care about any of it. Müller, Flick, and Breitner made their way down to the train station to oversee the first selection of the day. Christopher went back to the office for no other reason than he wanted to see Anka, to tell her about the meeting and what had happened. She was under his desk, drawing on the pieces of paper he had left for her. He emptied her pot outside and came back to her, taking her on his lap as he sat down behind his desk.

"We're nearly there, my darling," he whispered in English. "This time tomorrow we'll be on the road together. Don't worry. I won't keep you in that suitcase the whole journey. We can hide you in the backseat. Won't my father be surprised?" He hugged her, pressing her head into his chest. He kissed the top of her head and felt her arms spread around him.

There was a rap on the door, and Schultz's voice bled through. "Herr Obersturmführer?"

He opened the door just wide enough to see the Sonderkommando's face. "What is it?"

"Can I speak to the child?" Christopher let him past. Schultz knelt down to the girl and put his hand behind her head, stroking her hair. "How is she?"

"She's doing very well under the circumstances. She cries sometimes."

"Don't we all?" Schultz answered. He began to speak to her in Czech. Christopher tried to make out what he could, but there was nothing there for him. Schultz pointed at Christopher and Anka smiled. He spoke for a minute, or maybe more. Anka said something back to him. Schultz stood up. "I told her. She knows."

"What does she know?"

"She knows you're taking her away from here tomorrow. I told her she had to be quiet when you brought her out. I told her that we would always be there for her and that you were going to keep her safe."

"What was that she said?"

"She is excited. She is looking forward to seeing her family again."

Schultz took her in his arms and hugged her and then was gone. Christopher stayed in the room, watching her eating the lunch that he had brought her. It was after one o'clock. Rebecca would be nearing the end of her journey from Biberach. There would be a lot of explaining to do. She would not be expecting to find him. He would have to keep his distance, so there could be no emotional reunion. His mask couldn't slip, not now.

He wiped Anka's face with the handkerchief from his pocket as she finished up the bread and milk he'd brought for her. He hugged her for the last time and walked out into the snow.

A crowd of new arrivals had gathered in the yard outside Crematorium IV, but he was long past the stage where he could even watch this. The false hopes the SS officers instilled in the people tore at his soul. Breitner was milling about in the yard, ledger in hand. He walked over to Christopher.

"There was a call for you earlier, Herr Obersturmführer. Rapportführer Friedrich wanted you to meet him down in the administration building, right away."

"All the way over in Auschwitz?"

"That's what he said to me. I believe he's down there waiting for you now."

What could Friedrich want with him? Was this something to do with Liebermann? Surely he couldn't have said something? He would be just as guilty as Christopher. There was snow on the ground, and the roads were still being cleared off. It would be difficult to get all the way down to Auschwitz on his bike. He would have to borrow Strunz's car. He went to Kommandoführer

Strunz's office in Crematorium IV. Strunz was at his desk, poring over papers. He agreed to lend Christopher the keys. As Christopher left the crematorium, the people were filing in. He didn't make eye contact with any of them. Looking at them was too much.

He ran to the car and cursed as the engine failed to start. He was just about to get out and look for a mechanic when the engine finally revved into life. It was less than five minutes to the main gate at Auschwitz and, although Christopher knew the guard on duty, he still flashed his credentials as he passed through. A light snow was beginning as he pulled up outside the administrative building. He leaped out, barely remembering to shut the door behind him, and ran up toward the door.

"Obersturmführer Seeler?" Liebermann looked annoyed to see him. "What are you doing here?"

"I got a message to meet Rapportführer Friedrich down here. . . ."

"What? I know nothing about that. I haven't seen the Rapportführer at all today."

Christopher felt the palms of his hands wet with sweat. "Thank you, Herr Hauptsturmführer, I'll check with the secretary." Aumeier was sitting at his desk with his feet up as Christopher walked in. He didn't take them down. "Aumeier, is Rapportführer Friedrich here?"

"No. Should he be? Frankly, I'm surprised that you're down here yourself with what's going on this afternoon."

"What?"

"The searches going on in Canada today. They were due to start at, well, about ten minutes ago. I would have thought that you would have wanted to have been there to oversee them, particularly when they go through your offices." Aumeier smiled.

"Oh yes." Christopher managed a smile somehow. "I didn't want to get in their way. I'd better be going now." Christopher was gone. He was dead. They would find Anka, and he was dead. He realized why he had been sent to the other side of the camp. This was Friedrich's revenge, together with Breitner. But what did that matter? The last office was empty, the phone sitting on the desk, and Christopher stole inside, closing the door behind him. There was only one tiny chance. He called Crematorium IV, the phone seeming to take hours to connect. Kommandoführer Strunz's assistant answered.

"Hello, this is Obersturmführer Seeler, is Schultz there? I need to speak to him most urgently." Thirty seconds passed before Schultz's voice came on. The Kommandoführer's office was right beside the incineration room. "Have the searches begun?"

"Searches?"

"Canada is being searched, as we speak. Friedrich is behind it. I'm down here in Auschwitz; I was drawn away on purpose. You've got to get to Anka."

The line was silent for two excruciating seconds. "I hear the troops. The searches are beginning. I . . . I'm going to get her."

"The door is locked," Christopher said, and then there was nothing. Schultz was gone. Christopher cranked the phone, and then again, but there was no response. He ran out of the office, almost losing his balance in the slip of the snow.

"Careful, Herr Seeler," the guard on duty called after him.

He threw the car door open and slammed down on the steering wheel as the car failed to start again. The curse he roared was raw, painful in his throat. He turned the key again. The car started. The wheels skidded on the snow before they found the traction of the road, and all he could think of was Anka. He slowed to go out the gate and then accelerated as much as he dared back toward the gate at Birkenau. His entire body was shaking as the warehouses of Canada came into view. The soldiers were tossing them. Heaps of clothes, blankets, and suitcases littered the snow outside. Christopher pulled up fifty yards from his office just as the troops were entering the main door. He was too late. There was no chance to stop them now. There would be no escape. Flick, Müller, and Breitner were marched out and the troops poured inside. He felt the hope draining from inside him, and the deep pool of mourning and rage that instantly replaced it.

There was one chance. He had to be officious. He approached the door of the office and looked for the commanding officer; it was Friedrich himself. "What's going on here? I wasn't informed of this," Christopher said.

"Standard searches that happened everywhere else in the camp. No one is immune, not even the head of the Anti-Corruption Committee."

Christopher pushed past him and inside. The troops were tearing the office apart. Several were in the process of breaking down his door.

"I have the key!" Christopher shouted, but the SS men ignored him and kicked the door in. Several of them burst inside, and he rushed in behind them. Nothing. Where was she? The window in the office had been broken and shards of glass covered the floor. The soldiers turned over his desk. There was nothing. There was a gunshot outside, then shouting. Christopher ran out.

Friedrich was standing outside. "What is going on?" he roared.

Schultz appeared from around the corner, his arms above his head. An SS man was behind him, prodding him forward with his pistol. Frankl followed behind them, dragging Anka by the arm. *No! No!* "We found these two behind the offices. It seems the head of our Sonderkommandos was trying to hide this one," Frankl said. Anka was crying, trying to pull away. Frankl held her in place. Friedrich drew his pistol. He held it to Anka's head and pulled the trigger. Her head jerked backward and her body crumpled. He brought the gun to Schultz's forehead. Schultz said something in Czech, the tears rolling down his face. Friedrich fired. Schultz's body collapsed in the snow beside Anka. His eyes were still open, and her hair was saturated in black blood. Friedrich replaced the gun in his holster and walked away. He used a sleeve to wipe away the blood spattering his uniform.

Christopher turned his body away, desperately aware of where he was, of being watched. He threw his head downward, resting an arm against the side of the warehouse in front of him, fighting back the grief that was threatening to overcome him. He couldn't cry for her. He couldn't even make a sound.

"Are you all right, Herr Obersturmführer? You don't look well."

Christopher realized that the SS man wasn't going to shoot him. He managed to raise his head to look at him. "Yes, it's just, you know, seeing the blood from the little girl." The soldier shook his head and mumbled something under his breath about desk jockeys and joined the rest of the SS men milling around outside the warehouses.

# CHAPTER

---

## 33

The searches took less than fifteen minutes. The troops moved on to search the crematoria before the final light of day faded. Christopher stumbled into what remained of his office. A tear broke out and slid down his cheek, but he wiped it away as quickly as it had come. His desk had been cleared, the papers all over the floor, and the shelves opposite torn down. The suitcase that he was to pad for Anka was opened and turned upside down, and the glass was still all over the floor from where Schultz had broken in to try to save her. The safe behind his desk, packed with suitcases full of money, remained unopened. He closed the door behind him. The cold of winter seeped in through the broken window. He turned over his seat and placed it behind his desk. The door opened. Friedrich turned the other chair over and sat down opposite him.

"I have some questions for you, Herr Obersturmführer," Friedrich said, looking at the broken window and then around the room. "My men tell me that the window was already broken when they came into the office."

Christopher felt the pistol at his side, had his hand on it. *Rebecca coming today is saving your life, Friedrich.* "I have no idea about the window. Were any of your men checking the outside?" "No, they were all at the front of the building. It was only due to the Kapo, Frankl, that we found Schultz and that child he had been hiding. How on earth does that happen?"

"Once more, I have no idea. Perhaps you should be having this conversation with Kommandoführer Strunz. Schultz must have smuggled her out of the children's camp and kept her in Crematorium IV."

"She was not from the children's camp. She wasn't tattooed."

"I wish I could help you, Herr Rapportführer, but I have no idea what happened with Schultz and that girl." A childish drawing lay on the floor underneath the window, covered in broken glass. "I received a message to meet you down in Auschwitz, Herr Friedrich, just before the searches began."

"So sorry about the mess, Seeler, but no one is above the law here. I realized that the only place that hadn't been searched properly was here. Now, that's hardly fair, is it?"

"No, Herr Rapportführer, I don't suppose that it is."

"So let's go back to the window. It seems that Sonderkommando Schultz broke it. I spoke to the guard in the tower nearby, but he didn't see anything. Why would Schultz do such a thing, Herr Obersturmführer?"

"I can only imagine he wanted to take advantage of the confusion in the camp and break into my office to steal some of the valuables that he thought might have been inside."

"With a young girl in tow?"

"Who knows how the Jewish mind thinks, Herr Rapportführer?"

Five seconds passed before Friedrich finally spoke. "Well, soon we won't have to worry about that anymore, will we?" Friedrich said, raising himself to his feet. His boots crunched on the broken glass and

Anka's picture below. "I will oversee the rest of the searches today. You have quite enough to do here." He left. Christopher walked around his desk to the window and reached down for the picture, picking it up by the corner before blowing tiny specks of glass off it. It was a new one. She had drawn it that morning: a farmhouse with the sun high in the sky above it, cows in the fields, and stick figures outside. His tears fell onto the page.

He forced himself upright. He was an officer, and had to be seen to be taking charge. He walked out into the main office where Müller and Flick were picking papers off the floor. Breitner was nowhere to be seen, presumably still at Friedrich's side, helping to direct the searches. He called for someone to replace the window-pane in his office and had several of the Sonderkommandos come in to help with the cleanup. In less than an hour it was just like it had been before, except that everything was different now.

The time was approaching. It was five o'clock, the train due in half an hour. He went to the bathroom, looked at himself in the mirror, but saw only Anka's bloody hair on the snow. He wondered if Rebecca would recognize him. He hardly recognized himself now. His time in the camp had changed him. He was so many people now. Were the scars too deep? Could she still love the person he had become? It didn't seem like the places where he had known her could possibly exist anymore, not in a world that could create somewhere like Auschwitz-Birkenau. And what of her, how had her own experiences changed her? There had always been an uncommon strength in her. She would need every bit of it here. He looked at his watch, and it was time to leave.

He made his way down to the train station with Müller. Breitner was already down there when they arrived. He didn't speak to him; he didn't want him to sully this moment. The doctors arrived, conspicuous by their white coats. They were the ultimate power, the ones who decided who should live or die. It was important that there should be no mix-ups, so Christopher made his way down to where they were standing, waiting for the train to arrive. Some of the Sonderkommandos from Canada were there. Could he ever be as truly noble, as truly brave as Schultz had been? He pictured Schultz running through the snow toward his office, seeing the troops already there, knowing what little chance he had of succeeding and still refusing to give up on the girl trapped inside.

The smoke of the train came into his sight, gray against the black of the night. The engine pierced into view, pulling into the train station. She was on this train. The Sonderkommandos threw back the heavy doors on the boxcars, and the shouting began. The bewildered prisoners dropped down onto the gravel, and he began walking back and forth, scanning for her. There weren't many women on the train, mostly middle-aged men and children. They formed into lines, separated by sex, the doctors at the front of each, choosing who looked fit to work and those only fit to die. He saw one of the administrative staff, pacing back and forth with a clipboard, ready to call out the names, and he heard him shout, "Rebecca Cassin, Rebecca Cassin." The comfort in hearing her name quenched the horror inside him, if only for a few seconds. There was no answer. The SS man moved between the two lines of people, calling her last name this time. "Cassin, Cassin." An arm flew up. Christopher couldn't see any more of her through the crowd and ran around, trying to catch a glimpse. He pushed through the crowd of people, toward the arm, barely able to make it out in the dark of the night. He ran around and bustled through the crowd around where she was standing. All of this would be worth it. He had her now. Finally he had her back. He pushed around the last person, trying to keep the smile off his face; it melted. Pierre Cassin stood in front of him, his arm aloft.

Cassin looked older; his face even more lined than before, as if every drink he'd ever taken was finally exacting revenge. His facial hair was gone, and he looked thinner, but he looked as healthy as Christopher remembered him being. Cassin stepped out of line. Christopher stopped. *How can this be? Where is she?* Cassin shrugged as the administrator spoke to him. Christopher walked over. Cassin still hadn't looked at him.

"Yes, this one is with me," Christopher said, gesturing to Cassin, whose eyes bulged as he recognized him. Christopher took him by the shoulder and walked him away from the line, past the doctors and the guards with their dogs. Cassin didn't speak. They were far enough away when Christopher turned to him, speaking in English. "Where is Rebecca? Is she on this train?"

"No. I . . . I don't know what you're talking about . . . why would Rebecca be on this train?"

"She was meant to be transferred here, on this train. What the hell are you doing here?" he shouted. One of the SS guards looked across at him, holding his stare for a second.

"I got orders to transfer. I wasn't in a position to refuse," Cassin said. "Please don't kill me. I know that . . ."

"But you're not meant to be here! Where is Rebecca?"

"I . . . I . . ."

"Answer the question. Where is she? Where is Rebecca?"

"Rebecca is gone."

"What?" The pain was like a red-hot dagger plunged into his chest. "What are you talking about?" The SS guard was looking again. Christopher didn't care.

Cassin cringed as if Christopher was about to hit him. "They killed her. I'm sorry. They transferred me here."

The officer in charge of the site walked over. "Who is this prisoner, Obersturmführer?"

Christopher immediately stood firm and straight. He saluted. "He is a transfer going into my section in Canada, Herr Hauptsturmführer."

"So he is your responsibility, then?" Christopher nodded in reply. "Well, then, get him out of here before I lump him in with the others. He looks old, not of much use in this camp."

"He is highly skilled, Herr Hauptsturmführer. Thank you." He took Cassin by the shoulder and led him back toward the car. Walking was difficult, the pain inside for Rebecca, for Anka, almost debilitating. Still he trudged on, each step a triumph of will. Pierre Cassin was all there was left of her, the only other person in this godforsaken place who knew what it was to have their life touched by her.

# CHAPTER

## 34

The shared car ride with Breitner and Flick offered no chance to speak with Cassin. Christopher opened the door before the car had come to a stop and dragged Cassin by the arm toward his office. Cassin saw the smoke from the crematoria, the barbed wire, and the guards. He looked into the last warehouse where the ladies were sorting through a mass of shoes. The main office was empty. Christopher flicked on the light switch. There were no words between them as Christopher unlocked the door to his office. There was nothing left of Anka. Her drawing in his pocket was the only sign that she had ever existed. Christopher directed Cassin to sit in the chair opposite him and he took his seat behind his desk. Every move Cassin made was guarded. He sat in the chair as if he were made entirely of stone.

"What happened to Rebecca?" Cassin stared back at him, seemingly unable to get the words out. "Tell me." His voice was lethargic, his throat and eyes sore and tired.

"They killed her."

"Who? Who killed her?" The force of the tears behind his eyes burst and they flowed down his face. He tried to think of her, but the picture of her as an adult was somehow blurred, and when he saw her, it was as a child. The six-year-old girl he had found. He stood up. This uniform, everything he'd become, everything he was trying to do here; it was all for her. He reached into the drawer in his desk. Somehow the bottle of whisky had remained unbroken. There were unbroken glasses sitting on the men's desks. He took two. He laid them out on the desk and took the half-full bottle in his hand. He poured each of them a generous glass. He then took out his pistol and placed it beside the bottle on the desk. Cassin held the glass in front of him as if scanning it for what it might contain. "Go on, drink," Christopher said, the tears still thick in his eyes.

Cassin raised the glass to his lips, knocking half of it back in one swig. "The camp guards took her away." It had been more than five minutes since Christopher asked the question.

"What happened? When?"

"What am I doing here? Is this your revenge? Why don't you just get it over with?"

"I'm asking the questions! What happened to her?" He took a sip of the whisky. It hit his empty stomach like a fireball.

Cassin drank from his glass. "It was in the late summer. We had been at the camp for a few months. It wasn't that bad there, not compared to some of the stories of places that we'd heard about."

"Had you heard about this camp?"

"Only in whispers from prisoners who had been transferred out. This is the hub of the murder that you Boche perpetrate. I always knew . . ."

Christopher sat back down. "What happened?" he interrupted.

"The conditions in the camp were nothing I couldn't handle. We were fed and were forced to work but nothing too strenuous.

Nothing I couldn't take." Christopher wondered what work a man who had never worked a day in his life could take. "But then a new Kommandant came in and things changed. Food rations worsened and the beatings began. Rebecca never was one to abide by what she saw as . . . unjust behavior." Cassin finished the glass of whisky, and Christopher poured him some more. "There was a prisoner, also from Jersey. She was from one of the families that had been deported to be interned there, not Jews, just those that had fought in the first war; Sergeant Higgins's daughter, Anna. She wasn't strong like Rebecca. One of the guards took a liking to her. He began to harass her, all the time. With her father ill, Anna had no one to stand for her. No one except my Rebecca of course."

"Your Rebecca?" Christopher said, and then stopped himself. "Keep going."

"One morning, at the end of August, the guard tried to force himself upon her. Rebecca was on her way to work when she found them. We heard the screams of the guard from the other side of the camp. It was only a small place with less than a thousand prisoners. The guard stumbled out from behind the barrack, holding his head, blood pouring through his fingers from where Rebecca had struck him with the spade she was carrying. Then we saw Anna limping out from behind the hut with her arm over Rebecca's shoulders. That was it."

"What do you mean, that was it?"

"They took her away. She was executed."

Christopher was frozen, the tears gone. Pain, failure, and pride in her filled him. He couldn't feel his body, as if he were sitting there as someone else. The only thing he could hear was the sound of Cassin reaching forward for the bottle of whisky. The effort of raising his eyes the three inches or so until they rested on the gun on the desk was almost too much for him. He could kill him here and now. No one would ever question him. In fact, it would help his cause, deflecting suspicion. Killing Cassin here and now could help him save others. He placed his hand on the cold metal of the pistol. Their eyes met. Cassin stopped, the glass in midair.

"Did you see this happen? Did you see her die?"

"I was hardly in the position to make such requests."

"Were you close to her in the camp? Did she speak of me often?"

"We were close. Our hatred of everything you people stand for united us. Everyone in the camp, all the people from Jersey drew strength from her. I don't know where she got it, certainly not from her mother. God only knows where she is now. . . ."

"I don't want to hear about that. Tell me about Rebecca." Christopher raised the gun and was pointing it at Cassin. He had the whisky glass in his other hand and brought it to his lips.

Cassin let the almost-empty whisky glass fall to his side. "I didn't speak to her much about you. I never wanted to hear it and she knew that. I could lie to you . . ."

"Why not? You've done it so many times before."

"I did hear her speak to the other prisoners about you." Cassin was sweating. "They would say things about you, because you were German . . . but she always spoke up for you and told them your nationality didn't matter, even in times like these."

He felt the urge to tell him why he was sitting here in an SS uniform, imagined how good it would feel if someone else here knew his real intentions, his real self. "I am an SS officer," he said, his voice cracking as he spoke. "That's who I am now."

"Why did you bring me here?"

"I never wanted *you* here," he snarled. "Why would I ever want *you* here? I tried to have Rebecca transferred here, and they sent you. Some sick joke that is. With the story I told them, I suppose they thought that you were the consolation prize. They must have thought I'd ransom you back instead."

"A ransom? Back to whom? The Durrells? I don't understand."

"Shut up, just shut up."

Cassin finished the whisky. "What are you going to do with me? Is this your revenge?"

Christopher saw Anka's head jerking backward as the bullet burrowed into her skull, the tears on Schultz's face as Friedrich murdered him. He tried to picture Rebecca as she died, but it was too painful. His hands were sweating in the cold room. This would prove to the other SS men that he was committed to the cause. This would give him the freedom to help people who deserved life. He felt his finger squeeze around the trigger. Cassin pushed back in his seat. Christopher placed the gun back down on the desk. "You will be assigned to the work group I oversee, here in the Economic District. Life in the camp is hard, but I will protect you. As long as you work, you will be safe, and I will do my best to keep you alive." Christopher stood up. "What can you do?"

"I can do anything you want."

"Just do your best. If anyone ever finds out the reason you're here, then I will have my revenge. In fact if you ever tell anyone that we knew each other or that I knew Rebecca, you will die. Do you understand?"

"Yes, of course."

"There is no law here. Not for the prisoners anyway. Respect me and I will protect you, as much as I can anyway."

Christopher poured one last glass for himself and passed the bottle to Cassin.

# CHAPTER

---

## 35

A sleepless night ended with the dawn. Christopher's movements were slow and labored as he climbed out of the bed and placed bare feet on the cold floor. The emptiness inside him had spread throughout his entire body. He felt like an old man. He left the light off as he got dressed. His eyes were used to the darkness by now. He trudged through gray slush to the car he had the privilege of using on his trips to Berlin. The searchlights and lamps lit the way enough for him to see the faces of the prisoners, roused from their sleep to begin work, lining up for roll call, each person a walking corpse. He stopped the car and got out to look for the spot where Anka had been shot, along with the man who died trying to save her. The blood was still there, a darker pool of black against the brown-gray slush around it.

The car was packed and ready to go in ten minutes. There were six cases, each so full of banknotes that they were hard to carry. He strained as he piled them one on top of another in the car. There was no mission left now. He was just an SS man, trying to do his job, trying to stay alive. There was no purpose left for him, no reason for him to ably assist in the murder of innocent people. He could take the car and keep driving, drop off most of the money in Berlin and desert. He could try to pick up Alexandra and his father and make for the Swiss border with all the bribe money he could ever need. That didn't seem enough.

He drove past the gates into the dead landscape beyond. He thought about the pistol on his belt and what he could do with it. Would killing Friedrich end the pain? He pulled off to the side of the road perhaps fifteen miles outside the limits of the camp. He was completely alone. It would only take them a day or so to find his body in the woods. They would certainly search for him once the money had not been turned in. The pistol was heavy, cold in his hand, and the barrel was ice against the soft of his temple. The weight of it felt right against his skin. How could he be a part of this now? It was better to end it this way rather than to assist in the horror of the camp. He closed his eyes. He let the pistol fall into his lap. For the first time since he was a child, he saw his mother, as the woman she might have been now, gray-haired and wrinkled, like an older version of Alexandra, and he put the pistol back into its holster. The road was empty. The key to the trunk slid in easily, and the cases opened just the same. He took a little from each, reminding himself to adjust the ledgers. When he had finished, he had three large wads of American and British currency, about the equivalent of three thousand American dollars.

———

He went to Cousin Harald's house to see his father and sister. They cried when he told them about Rebecca. Christopher sat back and watched them, his emotions dulled and shocked to the point where he couldn't share in their grief. Alex went to him and put her arms around his shoulders to hug him, but he barely felt her touch.

"There is something else I need to tell you about." A feeling of lethargy overtook him once more, whereby it became an effort even to speak. He told them about Anka, about Schultz, about their murders.

It was Alexandra who spoke first. "Christopher, what you did was very brave, but if you had been caught . . ."

"If I had been caught instead of Schultz, I would be in jail right now, or possibly executed, but he is dead, murdered in the blink of an eye. He knew the risks. He still tried to save her. He still did it."

"Christopher, I don't want you to risk your life," she said.

"These men you told us about, Friedrich, Breitner, Frankl, Lahm, they seem like monsters. They wouldn't have a second's hesitation in turning you in," his father said.

"I know that, but why did I join the SS, Father? Was it to further the cause of the Third Reich, to serve the Führer?"

"Of course not, Christopher, but . . ."

"I've already made my decision. I'm going to need your help. I won't be able to do this without both of you."

"What about the security system in the camp? You're an accountant for God's sake, not a commando," Alex asked.

"Security system? You're looking at it as far as the funds are concerned. Diamonds, gold, that's a different story. They're transported separately. But cash is my job. It's my job to gather, count, document, and transport cash. There's no one else, at least not right now. I have the ear of the Lagerkommandant. I am head of the Anti-Corruption Committee, and I hear the model I introduced is being adopted in other camps. I can't do nothing. I can't just be an SS officer. Especially now. I owe Rebecca that much. I owe Anka and Schultz that much."

"There is one thing that I insist upon," his father interjected.

"What would that be?"

"That you wait. There seems to be too much consternation in the camp at the moment. Wait until the new Lagerkommandant comes in, until you get to know him, until he trusts you the way Höss did. Just do your job like everyone else, for a month or so, and then when the New Year comes, we'll see about your plan. That will give me time to prepare the way."

# CHAPTER

## 36

It was January 5, 1944, when Christopher met with Rudolf Herz, the head of the metalworks at the Krupp factory in Auschwitz III, the industrial complex set up around Auschwitz to feed off the slave labor of the inmates. Herz shook Christopher's hand as he opened the door and offered that his secretary take the leather briefcase Christopher was carrying.

"Thank you, but no," he replied.

The briefcase came down with a light thud on the thinly carpeted floor. Herz was a balding, fat man in his late fifties. There was an almost-empty whisky tumbler on his desk. He immediately offered Christopher a drink, which he accepted. Christopher held the glass to his lips. A massive portrait of Hitler hung on the wall above the desk.

"So, business is good these days, I trust?"

"Oh yes, even though the costs are going up. Never down, always up. First they charge us seven reichsmarks for a Jew, then nine, now twelve. I mean how much is one Jew worth really?"

"That depends on the Jew, I suppose."

Herz's face turned an unhealthy-looking puce as he laughed. "Yes, but I can't complain, I suppose. At least we have a goodly supply of Jews. They wear out quickly, don't you know?"

"I suppose they'd last longer if you fed them a bit more." Christopher smiled.

"We all have our orders, Herr Obersturmführer. I can't contravene the rulings of the SS. You should know that better than most."

"Believe me, I do. I tried to convince my commanding officer otherwise once. It wasn't a pretty sight, let me tell you. But seriously, we're all just trying to make our way the best we can, and all the while serving the Führer, awaiting that final victory."

"Of course, which brings us back to the business at hand today; to what do I owe the pleasure, Herr Seeler?"

"Yes, to the business at hand. Do you mind if I smoke?" Herz gestured for him to continue and pushed an ashtray across. Christopher took out a silver-plated cigarette case.

"Very nice," Herz commented.

"Thank you," Christopher said, shaking the match out. He took a deep drag and puffed the smoke out above Herz's head. "We were talking about labor earlier—such a delicate issue for employers. My grandfather was an industrialist himself, made furniture. I remember the stories from when I was growing up, complaining about workers, unions, and rights. But, of course, that's not something we have to worry about anymore, is it?"

"Not as such, no."

"Anyway, with the turnover of workers here, you're in constant need of able-bodied prisoners, correct?"

"Well, I wouldn't say the need is constant, but some of the guards here can be quite brutal. There's very little one can do to stop that."

"Yes, indeed, I understand that. Is there ever a need for child workers in the factory? I heard they're required from time to time."

"Sometimes, yes. We spent some time cleaning out the machines last year. They're smaller, so obviously good for getting into those little spaces."

He thought to ask where those children were now. "So, if you were to request a consignment of children, it wouldn't be completely out of the ordinary?"

"As I said, we do require some from time to time. Where are you going with this, Herr Seeler?"

"Well, what if I was to tell you that I needed a consignment of children myself for a business venture on the outside?"

"Your grandfather wants to use child labor from the camps?"

"No, my grandfather is long since retired. This is a lovely office you have here. What is this carpet, Persian?"

"Yes, I had it brought in from my home."

"Yes, most tasteful. You do seem like a man who enjoys the finer things in life. Yes, you're very astute, Herr Herz, very astute indeed. But for those not directly associated with the SS, coming across Jewish child labor is difficult."

"You can't just . . ."

"Oh, that's all taken care of. My contact has friends everywhere, friends who have assured him that they won't stand in the way of commerce." The cigarette was twitching in Christopher's hand, so he brought it down below eye level. "So what my contact needs are some workers, workers that you could, indirectly, provide."

"And how might I do this?" Herz leaned forward, clasping his hands together over the desk.

"Well, as we discussed earlier, it wouldn't be entirely out of the ordinary for you, as a businessman, to place an order for a consignment of Jewish children, perhaps forty or forty-five, who would otherwise be liquidated, to be transferred over here directly from the ramp in the main camp."

"No, not entirely."

"What if that truck, carrying those children, or workers, were to be redirected to an outside location without the knowledge of the camp authorities?"

Herz leaned back, feigning outrage. "This is outrageous! What kind of a businessman do you think I am?" He wasn't doing a very good job.

"One who knows a good opportunity where everyone is a winner." Christopher stubbed the cigarette out. "You would only have to sign the papers and lodge the order. We would take care of everything else, including paying the fee for the workers, of course. There would be no costs incurred to the factory itself whatsoever. I know you're the man to come to, a man who can make a decision that's going to stick, a man who makes his own mind up." Christopher stood up. "I'll leave you for now, as I'm sure you'll want time to decide. But I'll need an answer within a day or two. I don't mean to rush you; it's just that my contact's need is great, and we've a few other offers to consider." Christopher left the briefcase on the chair where he was sitting.

Herz called after him as he walked to the door. "You're head of the Anti-Corruption Committee, aren't you?"

"Not anymore," he said, and continued out the door.

Meetings of the Anti-Corruption Committee had become shorter but more regular since Friedrich had installed himself as chairman. Friedrich took his seat at the head of the table with Breitner at his side. The heads of the crematoria no longer attended, and there was no prisoners' representative. Friedrich went through the order of the day. There had been no arrests the previous day. There had been no arrests for weeks. The meeting progressed as they always did now, with lists of numbers. There were few confiscations now, the meetings more concerned with glorifying the achievements of the Economic District. Christopher read the numbers from the ledger, which, even with the money he was constantly skimming now, were prodigious. The killing was gaining pace. More and more trains were arriving, and there was more and more booty to be stolen and counted. Times had never been busier.

The meeting ended and each man stood up. Friedrich motioned for Christopher to come over. Friedrich waited until the last man had left before he began to speak.

"A few months ago, when you first arrived, you put in place a new system in Canada whereby on-the-spot executions were barred."

"Yes, it's been very successful. The numbers are there to prove it."

"Yes, well, I was thinking about that. The lack of discipline is frustrating some of the men. This is the only section of the entire camp where such rules exist."

"This is also the only section of the camp where it is our prisoners' jobs to handle valuables all day long. If we start killing off our own workers, production will undoubtedly suffer. The turnaround since I've taken charge is evident in . . ."

"I spoke to the guards and the Kapos earlier this morning. The decision on the guilt or innocence of a prisoner will be taken by them, and they will carry out whatever punishment they see fit."

"I have to insist that this doesn't happen. My workers are some of the most skilled in the camp. If I were to lose some of them, the entire system would break down. Now, what is the new Lagerkommandant going to say if the numbers in the Economic District suddenly begin to fall?"

"The decision has already been made, Seeler."

"I don't mean any disrespect, Herr Rapportführer. It's just that things are working so well at the moment, why change?"

"These are not workers. These people, if you can even refer to them as that, are vermin, enemies of the state, who want to destroy everything decent. If you can't see that, Herr Seeler, perhaps you would be of more use to the Reich elsewhere."

"Thank you for letting me know, Herr Rapportführer." He walked away.

He returned to Canada, saw the pool of blood in the middle of the warehouse. The body had been removed. He knew the women who worked in here, knew who had been killed, and knew that it had been because she had rejected the guard's sexual advances. The women in the warehouse didn't look up as he walked back and forth. He wanted to beg their forgiveness. There were two guards on duty. He took out a pack of cigarettes as he ambled toward them. He smiled as he caught their eyes and motioned them both toward him. A scream from another warehouse pierced the cold gray air.

"Hey, boys, how are we doing today?" He proffered the cigarettes to them and each accepted. "Great, good to hear it, just a quick question for you," he looked at each of them as he spoke, clouds of smoke swirling into the air above them. "What happened here?"

"We caught one of these bitches with her hand in the box," the first guard, Schlesinger said. Christopher knew him; he was from Hamburg. The other guard, Hauser, was his cousin.

"Oh, okay. It seems funny, though."

"What seems funny, Herr Obersturmführer?" Hauser asked.

"It just seems funny that they'd want to steal used eyeglasses, because that's all they sort in this room." There were eight women in the warehouse, one less than that morning, sorting through a mountain of eyeglasses. The pool of crimson was coagulating in the filth of the floor. Neither of the guards spoke, but their eyes did not move from his. "You like working in the Economic District, don't you?"

"Of course, Herr Seeler," Hauser replied.

"Of course you do, boys, now get this blood cleaned up; it's disgusting."

The freezing air stung his skin as he walked outside. The adrenaline in his blood threw each foot forward faster than usual so that he almost burst into a jog. The atmosphere in the warehouses had changed. No one looked back at him as he peered into the warehouses. There was fear everywhere. He threw down the cigarette and heard a scream and the thud of Frankl's baton against a young girl's skull. He twitched as he watched her crawl out of the warehouse into the snow, her hands desperately reaching out to Christopher for help he could no longer give. Frankl hit her again and she went down. He hit her again and again, her head collapsing under the pressure of the blows. There was nothing to do but walk away.

His hands were shaking as he reached into the safe for the bottles he had been hoarding. He took out a bottle of vodka and poured himself a stiff glass. The telephone receiver was cold in his hand as he picked it up.

Lagerführer Fritz Ekhoff was second only to the new Lagerkommandant of the entire camp complex. And since Arthur Liebehenschel, the new Lagerkommandant, had proven impossible to meet with since his arrival in November, Ekhoff was the only man above Friedrich's head that Christopher could meet. Ekhoff ushered him into his office. They had met only on brief occasions before. Ekhoff was a tall, muscular man with dark stubble and a firm handshake. He did not return the smile Christopher flashed at him.

"What is it, Seeler, things not going well down in the Economic District?"

"No, Herr Lagerführer, things are going wonderfully well. We seem to set new records every month just so we can break them the month after."

"Glad to hear it. If production slips, you will certainly be hearing from me. Now what is it that you want?"

"I can see you're a busy man, so I'll get to the point. I want to change a Kapo in the Economic District."

"How many Kapos do you have down there?"

"Well, we have several, but there is one with more power than the rest, far too much power if you ask me. It would be an excellent lesson to the others if he were demoted. He is abusing the power that we have given him. He's become a threat to production."

"Who is this man?"

"Ralf Frankl, Herr Lagerführer."

"Why did you come to me and not Rapportführer Friedrich?"

"Rapportführer Friedrich is an excellent leader, and the figures in the Economic District speak for themselves, but he isn't close enough on the ground to see what I see. He has so much responsibility, so much pressure, almost as much as you do yourself. I feel that he is too attached to this Kapo, and it's up to me to cut away the deadwood."

"Uwe Friedrich attached to a Kapo, eh? Now I've truly heard it all. What do you propose to do?"

"Just demote him back to the general population, and have someone else installed in his place."

"Fine, do what you need to."

"Thank you, Herr Lagerführer. This is long overdue." Christopher stood up and shook Ekhoff's hand again. Christopher turned to leave before the Lagerführer interrupted him.

"You do know what will happen to this Frankl when he is put back into the general population, don't you? He won't last an hour."

"Oh, is that right?" Christopher said, and walked out.

# CHAPTER

## 37

The knock on the door came the next day. Christopher was at his desk. The door opened before he could answer. Friedrich returned his salute with a look of contempt. He sat down before Christopher could offer him a seat.

"What seems to be the matter, Herr Rapportführer?"

"The orders for the transfers came through this morning, Herr Seeler."

"Oh, I was looking to speak to you about that, but, with your extra responsibilities, I couldn't find a time when you would be available."

"Why did you have Frankl removed? Is it from some misplaced affection for the prisoners? If it is, I'll have you shipped off to a punishment division on the Eastern Front so quickly that you'll be hauling bodies by the end of the week."

"It was a simple case of him being here too long." Christopher paused and reached back into his mind for the lines he had been practicing. "Why do you care what happens to Frankl?"

"He was good for discipline."

"We don't have discipline problems in Canada. Since the Anti-Corruption Committee put the new system in place, we've hardly had any losses. There is no need to execute workers here, and the more experienced they are, the better they do their jobs and the better that we all look, especially you."

"Why did you go to Ekhoff? He has no interest in this section so long as the money keeps flowing."

"That's exactly why I went to him." He held up an empty glass. "Would you like a drink, Herr Rapportführer?" Christopher poured out two glasses of vodka. Friedrich took the glass and swirled the clear liquid around a few times before knocking it back in one.

"No matter what the reason, those decisions are mine."

"I agree, but I wasn't sure you could see how lazy Frankl had become."

"I wasn't aware of any laziness on his part."

"I saw it, many times. Again, you can't be everywhere at once. That's why the lower ranks exist, to help out the decision makers such as yourself."

"Very convincing, Seeler." He placed the glass down on the desk. "You always have a story, don't you? You'd make a wonderful actor, I think. Let's see how your acting abilities help you out on the Eastern Front."

"Herr Rapportführer, what use would an accountant be on the Eastern Front?"

"I'm sure they'll find some use for you, Herr Obersturmführer. Just like the two guards you had transferred there this morning, Schlesinger and Hauser I believe were their names? I'm sure they'll be just thrilled to see you again."

It couldn't end like this. There was too much still to do. The orders still hadn't come back from Herz for the truckload of children. There was too much to do to have this man's ego stand in his way. "I'm sure there's something we can do to work this out, Herr Rapportführer. The Lagerkommandant thinks I'm doing a wonderful job here."

"No, Seeler, the old Lagerkommandant thought you did a great job here. I will admit I did too, at one time, but you've gone over my head for the last time." It was hard to tell if Friedrich was doing this for personal pleasure or not. Either way, the smirk on his face was fixed now.

"I can assure you, Herr Rapportführer, I have nothing but the utmost respect for you and for every decision that you make. . . ." There was nothing he could do on the Eastern Front, no reason for him to even be alive there.

"I have a ready-made replacement for you, someone who will obey my orders, someone who has the inside knowledge of the organization of this section of the camp."

"So, it seems the decision has already been made." Christopher heard his voice harden and poured himself a shot of vodka. He thought of the money in the safe. How much would it take to buy this man?

"Yes, I can assure you that it already has. I will be lodging the order tomorrow morning. The transfer should take a few days to process, and then you'll be on the front lines, serving the Reich. You know, if I were a little younger, I'd be out there myself. I am almost jealous of you, Seeler."

"What can I say to make you change your mind, Herr Friedrich? Let me assure you that I am best off serving the Reich right here, right from this chair. There are two types of men in this war: fighting men like you and pencil pushers like me. I can't shoot a gun, but I have organized this section better than anyone before me and certainly better than Herr Breitner ever could."

Friedrich was clearly enjoying this. He rocked back in his seat, the anger from earlier now dispersed. He didn't speak, but did motion to Christopher to fill his glass once more. Christopher felt the heat in his head. It felt as if it was going to implode. The thought of actually fighting to propagate this was more than he could bear.

"Thank you, Herr Seeler. You will certainly be missed around here."

"A day or two is simply not long enough for the handover. I need longer, at least a week. I have a trip to Berlin in two days. The contact there knows me. I will have to go through all the systems with Breitner, introduce him to the Kommandoführers, the Blockführers, and the new Kapo. There is just too much work to do. Don't do this. Don't kick me out of here and have the whole section suffer because of it."

"I suppose that might be counterproductive. You were a good accountant after all, and I wouldn't want to fall behind."

"The one thing that Lagerführer Ekhoff said was that if production slowed here, for any reason, he would be very displeased."

"Don't you think I know that?" Friedrich snapped. He took a sip of vodka again and swirled it around in his mouth. "Okay, Seeler, I'll give you a week, but if you're not organized by then, I'll shoot you myself just to save the Russians from having to do it."

A week would give him time to think. "That's the right decision for the camp, Herr Rapportführer."

Friedrich stood up, holding his hand out to Christopher. "Thank you for the valuable work you've done here, Herr Obersturmführer. You've got a glittering future ahead of you, just not here."

"Give me a few days until you put that order in, until after I travel to Berlin on Thursday."

"You've got until Friday morning; that's when the order goes in."

He waited until Friedrich had left to pour another glass of vodka. He thought of Uli, who had been on the Eastern Front for more than two years. Perhaps they were to share the same fate and die in some nameless marshland in Belorussia. There was no more time to waste. He picked up the phone.

"Herz? It's me, Christopher Seeler."

"Herr Seeler, it's so good to hear from you." It was hard to tell if he'd been drinking yet today or not.

"Have you made a decision?"

"Yes, I have. I don't see any reason we can't do business together."

*The contents of the suitcase must have helped.* "Good, I'm glad you've seen sense. There has been a change of circumstance, however."

"And what might that be?"

"It needs to happen this week."

"This week? Why the rush?"

"Circumstances beyond my control. Can you do it this week, perhaps on Friday?" Only silence answered him. "Herz, are you still there? Can you do it or not?"

"Yes, we should be able to do that."

"I will see you in your office at ten a.m. tomorrow to go through the final details." He hung up the phone.

There wasn't time for a letter to his father. The next phone call would be riskier, but what were they going to do to him now? Execute him? A trip to the Eastern Front was tantamount to the same thing. He picked up the receiver again and spoke to the camp operator, explaining it was an emergency—that his father was dying. Lying had become so easy. The operator patched him through and the phone rang. Cousin Harald picked up. The surprise mingled with a genuine affection in Harald's voice. Christopher asked to speak to his father as politely as he could. He heard the echo in the background and he knew that the Political Department was listening in.

"Not in work today?" Christopher said as his father came on the line.

"No, I'm very busy with the arrangements we were trying to organize together."

"How is your health, Father?"

"The same. I'm still hanging on."

"I wanted to call you about our arrangements. Things have changed. I've been offered a wonderful opportunity to serve the Reich directly on the Eastern Front." He paused. "I'll most likely be shipping out next week."

"So, is our arrangement off?"

"No, but it's going to have to be pushed forward to Friday of this week."

"Friday? Today is Tuesday."

"Yes, I know what day it is. This is the way it has to be. Can you do it?"

"Well, I suppose that I'll just have to, won't I?"

"Yes. It's the only way. The same thing we discussed, but just this Friday."

"I understand. Stay safe, my son, we're thinking about you all the time."

"Good luck, Father." He hung up the phone.

The handover would not be easy, in so many ways. There had to be some way to stop it. Without him to protect the ladies in Canada . . . there was so much to do. There were three shipments coming in that day and he had still not caught up with the work from yesterday. He stood up and opened the door to the main office. Breitner and Flick were at their desks.

"Herr Breitner, can I see you for a moment?"

Breitner raised his head, his skin a paler gray than usual. He stood up and walked into the office.

"Sit down, Wolfgang," Christopher said as Breitner closed the door behind him. "We've never really gotten to know one another too well, have we?"

"How do you mean, Herr Obersturmführer?"

"Socially, I mean. You're never around after dark to play cards with us. Where do you go? What do you do?"

He picked a pen off the desk and began to pass it from one hand to the other. "I am in a different part of the barracks, quite far from you."

"Quite far, yes, one could certainly say that much." Breitner's thin features contorted with discomfort that Christopher was enjoying. "Do you enjoy working here, Breitner?"

"Yes."

"But not especially, no? Do you feel you might be happier getting closer to the action, as it were? What I'm trying to get at is— would you be more contented to be on the front, with the rest of our brave lads? It's not everyone who's cut out for that. Perhaps you're not."

"What makes you think I'm not able for that?"

"I never said that. It's just that you're not really that good of an accountant and I have to submit a report to the Lagerkommandant saying as much. There are just too many mistakes, too much shoddy work, Wolfgang, I'm sure you understand."

"Well, that's your opinion. No one around here works harder than I do. Perhaps I'm not the politician that . . . some people are, but I'm a hard worker."

"Yes, but sometimes there's more to work than just putting the hours in. This work requires skill and patience. I just had a meeting with Rapportführer Friedrich. He said very much the same thing and, unfortunately, we are in agreement over what needs to happen to you." Christopher kept the invective from his voice, though it was bubbling over inside him.

"Is that right? Herr Friedrich said that, did he?"

"Do you know something that I don't, Wolfgang?"

"No, of course not."

"That will be all, Breitner," Christopher said, and Breitner left. The conspiracy against him was going to have to be broken before Friday morning. But how? What of Pierre Cassin? He was working in Crematorium IV with the other men, shaving hair off dead bodies to be turned into blankets and nylons. What could he do? Even if Christopher could somehow convince him, or another prisoner, to kill Friedrich and somehow got away with it, a feat that seemed impossible, there would be horrible retributions. There had to be another way.

# CHAPTER

## 38

Friday morning came with dreams of Rebecca, or was it Anka? They ran together like separate streams into the same river, mingling in his mind to become one. They were with him as he dressed, shaved, in everything he did. Lahm shifted in his sleep and cast an eye toward Christopher before closing it again. There was nothing to be done about Lahm now, but that day would come. This war would end someday, and the power yielded by Lahm and those like him would be broken. All of this would end, all of this. And who would know that he, Christopher Seeler, was any different from Lahm and the others? Who would know what he had tried to do here? He took Anka's drawing out of his pocket, the folds deep in the flimsy white paper. He ran his eyes over it again, the lemon sun high in the sky over the rectangular farmhouse, and in the field, three brown cows. Perhaps it was her home, drawn from memory, or perhaps not. He would never know. He wished he had been able to bring a photograph of Rebecca, a record of her beauty to keep for himself. Instead he looked into the mirror and saw her in his own eyes.

The snow was thick on the ground as he made his way out to the bicycle shed. The roads had been cleared already. The SS enjoyed the snow, enjoyed making the prisoners shovel it. Christopher had seen Blockführers and Kapos force prisoners to cover the road with the snow that they had just shoveled off it, just so that they would have to dig it out again. He cycled past skeleton people, standing barefoot in snowdrifts as they struggled to lift shovels to plunge into the snow. He heard the screams of a Kapo as one man seemed too slow, and more screams as an SS man came across. He accelerated away, trying to escape the sound of what he knew was to come, but he couldn't. The shot rang out. He wiped it from his mind, as he always did, as he had to. He looked at his watch. It would not be long now. The first shipment of the day, the children were from the same part of Czechoslovakia as Schultz, Christopher's tribute to him.

He arrived at the office first, as always. He picked up the envelope lying on his desk, opened it, and read the letter inside again. It would be enough. He placed it back into the envelope, put it into his pocket, and walked outside. He wandered into one of the warehouses, where fifteen ladies were rummaging through winter coats, scarves, and hats. He looked over toward the guard on duty, who was having a cigarette in the corner. The room was cold, barely any warmer than the air outside, and each of the workers was huddled in coats and scarves of their own, their breath plumes of icy white in front of them. Petra Kocianova was working at the table nearest the door, her sister, Martina, by her side. He felt himself drawn to where she was sitting, and, without knowing he had moved, was standing directly beside her. She looked up at him. He wanted to apologize to her, for not being able to save her children, for letting her live when they died. He turned his body away, his hand resting on the table. He felt fingers wrap around his. Petra was looking up at him, her hand on his. Martina was smiling through her tears, looking directly into his eyes.

He was there as the train arrived and the prisoners spilled off the cattle carts and onto the gravel below. The shouting, the dogs, and the selections began. He waited for the administrator to call out the orders. Finally he did. The Krupp factory needed forty-five children, young children under the age of seven, and they began to step forward. SS men walked up and down the lines picking out the children Christopher had bought. They gathered together in a shivering mass. Many of them cried, reaching out for their mothers. Some stood silently as if somehow they knew what was going on. Then they crowded into the truck that would take them away. There was barely space for them, but the SS men packed them in, some on top of others. They had no idea of the long journey they had ahead of them, first to the factory and then to the meeting point with Christopher's father and Alexandra in Leipzig. From there they would be taken to an orphanage in a convent. Christopher's father had organized the purchase and furnishing of an old unused wing for them to live in. They would have food and a place to sleep somewhere the war would never find them. They would be kept as war orphans, complete with papers. The children waved, shouted goodbye to the parents they were leaving behind. Then they were gone.

The snow began again, tiny specks of white trickling down onto the shoulders of the prisoners as they lined up for selection. Christopher was close enough to hear the doctors proclaiming the sentence of death, or life as a slave, each decision made in five seconds or less. Friedrich was talking with Breitner. He walked toward them.

"Good morning, Rapportführer, good morning, Herr Breitner."

"Good morning to you, Seeler, did you enjoy your last trip to Berlin yesterday? I think I will take that particular role myself upon your departure. This time next week, you'll be one more of our brave boys on the front line. Exciting times, eh?"

"You must be barely able to contain the excitement," Breitner chimed in.

"That's what I wanted to talk to you about," Christopher began. "Have you put in the orders for the transfer yet?"

"No, not quite yet, don't you worry, though, Seeler; it's only a matter of a few hours. . . ."

"Good, I'm glad you won't have to waste your time. I do know how valuable your time is."

"What are you talking about?" Friedrich asked, still sneering.

Christopher reached into his pocket and passed the envelope to Friedrich, who looked at Breitner before he opened it. Christopher watched his eyes, waiting for them to move down the page, before he spoke.

"As you can see, the rumors of my transfer out of the camp have been greatly exaggerated. It seems like I'll be staying here after all."

"This isn't real," Friedrich said, holding the letter out in front of him as Breitner struggled to push his head across to read it. "This can't be real."

"Check the signature, and the seal. You'll find that it's completely genuine. Breitner, the transfer we spoke about previously will be going through later on today." He turned to Friedrich. "I will expect a countersignature from you, Herr Rapportführer; we really don't want to bother the Lagerführer with the likes of this. I will, however, be reinstituting the rules in Canada regarding the execution of prisoners, and resuming my role as head of the Anti-Corruption Committee." Friedrich didn't speak, just handed the letter back. Christopher looked at SS Reichsführer Heinrich Himmler's signature and seal at the bottom of the letter before folding it back into the envelope. *Not bad. It's amazing what you can buy for three thousand reichsmarks.* Himmler's secretary should have charged more, particularly as he had guaranteed to cover the letter if anyone called to check on it. Christopher would have paid double that. He turned and saluted, and then walked away.

Christopher finished up the paperwork for Breitner's transfer to the front and sat back in his seat. Friedrich would have to wait, but the Rapportführer wouldn't bother him anymore, not after this. It had taken him ten minutes to persuade Himmler's secretary to write the letter. How many times had he done it for other officers with money to throw at their problems? It would all be over soon. The secretary knew that. Christopher picked up the phone. Herz's secretary pretended not to know him, even after he had sent her flowers the previous week. She was good. Herz answered with a cough.

"I trust everything went well this morning," Christopher started.

"Yes, yes, the truck arrived on time. The driver took them to their new quarters."

"Excellent, I'm glad that everything went so smoothly."

"Will that be all?"

"For now, Herr Herz, but you can expect to hear from me again, and soon." Christopher hung up the phone.

He came at the end of the day. He was a tall man, bigger than Schultz, with broad shoulders that still bore the shadows of faded muscle. His name was Markus Klaczko. He was the head of the Sonderkommando unit, Schultz's replacement. Klaczko sat down opposite Christopher.

"You called for me, Herr Obersturmführer?" he began.

"Yes, I did." Christopher sat back in his chair and looked out the window at the snow and the wire, the trees beyond. "Tell the other prisoners the summary executions are going to stop. If there are any problems with Kapos, guards, or even officers, I want you to come to me." Klaczko nodded, slowly and deliberately. "I will do my best to protect you as much as I can. I will warn you of anything that I hear, but there is only so much I can do for you. I wish I could do more."

"I know."

# CHAPTER

---

### 39

*New York, September 1954*

"Next, I'd like to talk to you about that remarkable day in Dachau, the day the ladies from Canada saved *your* life." Christopher adjusted the headphones and pressed his face closer into the microphone. "What are your thoughts on what the US soldiers did that day in Dachau—executing an estimated fifty to one hundred SS troops on the liberation of the concentration camp in April 1945?"

The interviewer motioned for him to talk. "Perhaps if they'd seen all the killing done in the years before, the soldiers might not have been so quick to presume that more killing was the answer. I can see why they did it. It was the only justice those prisoners had seen in years of torture, starvation, and death. I think I might have done the same thing in their place. But I wasn't in their place." Christopher looked around for Hannah, even though he knew she wasn't there.

"Why didn't you speak up for yourself when the soldiers rounded up the SS men? Why didn't you tell them you were different from the others?"

"I think I was the only guard who didn't try to speak up." He smiled.

"But there were no other guards there who did what you did, who saved three hundred and forty-two children from certain death in the gas chamber, who protected the lives of more than six hundred women under their care."

"How do you know that? I didn't know their stories, and they didn't know mine. The truth of it is I was tired. Rebecca was dead. Even after her father told me that she was executed I still looked, but there was never any sign of her. And who's to say I didn't deserve to die along with the other guards for what I did? I delivered hundreds of thousands of dollars, pounds, marks, and any other currency you can name to the SS."

"The prisoners who saved you didn't seem to think you deserved to die."

"No, they didn't." He shifted back in his seat, thinking back to that day. He saw the young American soldier, his brown eyes reddened at the sides, his lips tight as a scar on his face, coming to him and lifting his rifle with shaking hands. The soldier aimed at Christopher's chest. He closed his eyes, never expecting to open them again. The rifle sounded. It was a funny feeling, to accept death and have life given back to you. Martina Kocianova saved him. When he opened his eyes again, she was clawing at the soldier's face, bashing on his shoulders. The shot meant for him flew into the air above his head. Some of the other ladies from Canada pulled him away, protecting him with their bodies. There was the sound of more rifle shots, and as he looked back, all the other SS men were dead.

"And why was it that you and the ladies under your care ended up at Dachau when the rest of the camp at Auschwitz was taken to Bergen-Belsen?"

"I had heard about the typhus outbreaks in Bergen-Belsen. The sheer numbers of prisoners arriving from the eastern camps meant that it had become a death trap. I used the last of the monies I had appropriated from the safe to bribe the proper officials, and I had the ladies in Canada, along with the few remaining Sonderkommandos, transferred, via train, to Dachau."

"These were the same monies that you used to bribe the officials to have the children taken off the trains and diverted to the factory where your father met them?"

"From the same source, yes." Christopher felt cold and alone. He thought of Hannah again.

"And what happened to this money?"

"It's all gone, long ago. If you're trying to suggest that I squirreled any of it away for myself, you're wrong. That money was only ever for one purpose."

"How do you reconcile the fact that the money you gave to these officials, these Nazi war criminals, may have helped them to escape, as many have?"

"That was a choice I had to make at the time. I had to deal with the situation I saw in front of me on a daily basis. If I had done nothing, there is a good chance that the people I oversaw would have died, certainly the children we took off the trains anyway. It is unfortunate that some of these men have escaped."

"Let's move on to your own trial for war crimes, which took place in Poland in 1946. You had twenty former inmates testify on your behalf, and your defense lawyer stated that there were over two hundred others who wished to be given the chance to speak for you. Some wanted to travel from France, the United States, and even Israel."

"You've done your research."

"Then, in 1947, you testified against several of your former superior officers in the Auschwitz trials in Poland, where you gave evidence against the former head of the camp, Arthur Liebehenschel, and your own direct superior officer, Uwe Friedrich, both of whom received the death penalty for their part in the war crimes that occurred there. How did it feel testifying against your former colleagues?"

Once again the interviewer waved his hands at him, motioning to him about the dead air they had mentioned before the interview had started. "It was easier for some of the officers than others. I thought that certain things, certain visions and dreams, would be put to rest after that." Christopher looked up and around the gray interviewing room. The producer was in the corner, headphones on, and Christopher saw the tape recording his every word. It felt like he was on trial again. He thought of his family, and Jersey, and wondered why he had ever agreed to this. "It was my duty to those who died to do what I could on their behalf." David Adler from the American Jewish Committee was smoking a cigarette at the studio window. "The things that went on in those camps, the things that I saw myself, were monstrous, and I was . . . happy to bring even some of the perpetrators to justice."

"Are there any guards you worked with who have yet to be brought to justice?"

"There are thousands of guards who worked in Auschwitz still walking free today. But people I worked with? Yes, I believe that my roommate, Franz Lahm, is still at large, although I never saw any of the acts that he himself perpetrated." There was a woman at the window talking to David. She motioned toward Christopher. She was looking directly at him and his whole body went cold. It couldn't be. He had dreamed this so many times. She was standing beside David, her hand to her mouth, laughing. It was impossible. How could this be? David was talking to her. Her long blond-brown hair fell beyond her shoulders to her floral dress. Her beauty stunned him, rendering all his senses useless. He was standing now, although he couldn't remember getting to his feet, and he ripped off the headphones. He drew his finger to his throat and brought it back and forth. He felt clammy and cold, yet his heart was burning inside him. He ran for the door.

"All right, ladies and gentlemen, we're here with Christopher Seeler, former SS guard, and the man some are now describing as the 'Angel of Auschwitz,' but right now we have to take a commercial break. We'll be right back." The interviewer glared across at Christopher. "What the hell is wrong with you?"

Christopher ran to the door and was in the hallway. She turned to face him.

"Rebecca?" Christopher said.

"Christopher?" A tear broke down her cheek. He had her in his arms. She drew back more quickly than he wanted. She was older; but he hadn't seen her in eleven years. "I can't believe it's you! It's been so long," she said, crying now.

"It's been eleven years, Rebecca, almost eleven and a half," he gasped, almost spitting out the words. Her face was thin, almost as thin as when he had last seen her back in Jersey, but still perfect, utterly perfect. "You look wonderful. Where have you been for the last nine years? I thought you were dead."

"I thought you were a Nazi. I heard you were a guard in Auschwitz. I went back to Jersey to find you, but the house was empty. No one knew where you were. I only found out who you really were when I read about you in the newspaper."

"But your father said you were dead."

"He thought I was dead, but I was transferred to another camp." She wiped the tears away with her wrist and Christopher saw the wedding ring.

"Do you want to go somewhere? I don't know the city too well. I've never been here before." He turned around to David. "David, this is Rebecca, the woman I told you about."

"It's a pleasure, a real pleasure."

"I have to leave now, David. Rebecca, do you live here?"

"No, I'm flying back to Israel tomorrow morning." Her mannerisms were memories in themselves.

"David, you heard her. I have to go." It was just after six. "We don't have much time." The host was glaring at him through the window, pointing to his watch.

"Christopher, I understand, but this interview is the main reason we brought you here. It's nearly finished; we've barely half an hour left. This is important. You can spend the rest of your time here with this young lady after we finish. You can have the whole night after we wrap this up. This is a live broadcast."

"I can wait," Rebecca said. "I mean, I have to leave early tomorrow morning, but I can wait around tonight. Do what you need to do."

"I don't know."

"Please, Christopher, finish the interview. We can be together afterward. We can spend time together after the interview."

"All right, I'll finish the interview, but can we at least have a few minutes together? An hour and then I'll finish the interview."

"I'll see what I can do," David said, and walked into the studio.

"So, how are you?" Rebecca asked. She turned toward him and he moved to her but was suddenly too close, and she stepped back.

"I'm doing really well. I can't believe you're here. You look great, just great."

"Thank you. You look wonderful too."

David popped his head out of the studio. "They managed to find an old show to broadcast. You've got an hour, but then back here to finish the interview."

"Thanks, David," Christopher said, and turned to Rebecca. He gestured toward the elevator. "Shall we?"

# CHAPTER

---

## 40

"It's been so long since I've seen you, I feel like everything I say should be brilliant or important," Christopher said.

"Life doesn't really work like that, does it?"

"No, not usually." He pressed the button for the elevator again. "How did you find me here today, and what are you doing in New York?"

"I'm over here on business."

"Oh, what do you do for a living now?"

"I'm in marketing. I work for a firm in Tel Aviv, where I live. I read about you in the paper on Monday. I called the newspaper and spoke to the journalist who interviewed you, and he told me that you were doing this radio interview today, and here I am." She shrugged. "I can't believe that I'd never heard of you, after all you did."

"I was never interviewed before. I've never been in the newspaper before this week. I wouldn't have been except for the American Jewish Committee bringing me over here."

"How did they find out about you?"

"One of the children I brought out of the camps wrote to them." Christopher paused and looked at her, drinking her in with greedy eyes. "I'm so glad that you made it." The elevator arrived. "I'm so glad you're alive; I thought you were dead. I can't believe this."

The elevator attendant asked what floor they were going to.

"The lobby, please," Christopher said. "The park is only a few blocks away. We could walk up there."

"Okay." Her face seemed to sour.

"What's wrong?"

She shook her head. "I've hated you all these years, ever since the war. And then I find out what you did, and the whole reason that I hid myself from you all these years was a lie."

"How were you to know? You could only believe what you were told, or what the evidence told you. How did you find out that I was in the SS?" Christopher asked. The elevator attendant lifted an eyebrow and glanced sideward.

"I met my father in the displaced persons camp after I got out of Buchenwald. He told me about you. He said that you worked in Auschwitz."

"Of course." He afforded himself a wry grin. "I should have known. Where is your father now?"

"He lives in Surrey now, as far as I know, but I haven't seen him since '51. He tried to look for my mother after the war, but she was killed in the Blitz in London."

"I'm sorry to hear that." Christopher extended his hand toward her.

Rebecca smiled at him, but did not take his hand. "Thank you, you're very kind. He found another woman after he found out that she was . . . gone."

"He never did like me, did he? I suppose he got his wish in the end."

"I still remember the moment he told me about you. I couldn't believe it and I didn't at first. I cried for days. I was weak. I weighed around seventy pounds. I thought I was going to die after I found out." She stopped. "It's hard to talk about this, even to you, especially to you."

"You don't need to tell me anything. . . ."

"No, I do. I really do."

"Okay. I'm listening."

"The camps were hard, more difficult than I could ever have imagined."

"I know how hard they must have been."

"You didn't experience what we went through, as prisoners."

"No. I absolutely did not."

"You were all that kept me going through the camps, the thought that one day we would be together again. And when I got out, it didn't tally in my mind that you could have gone from being the man you were just a few months before to being one of them. I went back to Jersey to look for you. I went back in April '46, but the house was empty."

"I was in the internment camp then. My family was still in Germany. Even Tom had come over to Germany to be with Alexandra then. I can't believe you went back, and I wasn't there."

"No one knew where you were. I should have kept looking, but I had no money, and staying in Jersey was too painful without you. I did try. I asked around. Some said that you were collaborators. It took me a long time to accept something that I now know wasn't the truth. I had to. It was the only way for me to go on."

"My father was the first to go back, but that wasn't until months after you were there." Christopher leaned up against the wall, the frustration draining him. "You know who I am now. It took you nine years, but you know who I am now."

The elevator arrived at the lobby and Christopher stood back to let Rebecca out. The elevator attendant stared after them as they walked out of the building and onto Broadway.

"I think it's up this way," Rebecca said as they turned up toward the park. It was a warm evening, the streets thick with people.

"So what happened, Rebecca? Where were you? Your father told me that you had been killed, that you had struck a guard."

"The part about hitting the guard was true. We've spoken about my family now, but how are yours? I've thought about them so much over the years."

"They're fine, Rebecca, we'll get to all that. Please, the questions about you have been burning a hole in my mind for as long as I can remember."

"Are you sure you wouldn't rather talk about this lovely weather we've been having?" He turned his head sideways to look at her, almost bumping into a large middle-aged woman, who glared at him as he edged around her. Rebecca reached across to him, taking his elbow before she began to speak again. "After I hit the guard, I was brought before the Kommandant of the camp. I had dealt with him before, speaking on behalf of some of the female prisoners. I was sure he was going to execute me, but he didn't. He liked me for some reason and decided to transfer me rather than have me killed."

"I can guess why he liked you." Christopher felt his voice thick, tried to disguise the feelings behind it, to understand. But she didn't even look at him, just kept talking, and he was glad.

"I was transferred to Westerbork in Holland. Westerbork was an assembly point, a place for Jews, gypsies, and political prisoners to gather before being sent off to the concentration camps to be killed. Many of the people that I oversaw in Westerbork would have been sent to Auschwitz." Christopher remembered the Dutch Jews coming through. Two of his ladies had been Dutch. "I stayed there for a few months before I was shipped out to Buchenwald. I arrived just after the winter ended, in February 1944. I was there until March of '45 when I was shipped out with several thousand others. We were put on a train. They were taking us to be gassed, trying to kill us while they still could, but I managed to escape after a few days, between stations. I hid out in the woods until some British troops found me. That was in April 1945."

He thought of where he was then, being arrested in Dachau despite the protests of the prisoners, who sent a delegation to speak to the American officers on his behalf. The sign for Fifty-Eighth Street came into view. Columbus Circle and the park were directly ahead. "What was it like in Buchenwald? How bad was it?" They were crossing the street as he asked.

"It's hard to talk about it here on the street. I want to tell you, Christopher, I want to tell you everything. But it's hard."

"I understand." They walked across Columbus Circle to the entrance to the park and continued through in silence. "Why didn't I find you? I'm sure the people I had searching for you would have checked the camps you were in."

"The Kommandant of Biberach made me change my name so that I couldn't be traced by his superiors."

"So he really did like you?" He had seen when officers took a liking to female prisoners enough times in the camp himself.

"I suppose he did."

"What did you change your name to?"

"Rebecca Klein. I chose it at random. That was my name for the remainder of my time in the camps, not that a prisoner's name mattered."

"So when I had your father transferred to Auschwitz, he really did think you were dead?"

"Yes, I suppose at that time he did think so. The Kommandant at Biberach had me transferred that night. He wanted the guards to think that I had been executed too. I never saw any of the prisoners there again, not until after the war anyway." They were slowing now, their steps languid and faint against the flow of people around them. "Christopher, all that you did in Auschwitz, organizing the release of the children, bribing officials, smuggling out children yourself, were you ever scared?"

"I was terrified, all the time, constantly afraid from the moment I woke up in the morning to when I fell asleep at night." The trees were enveloping them overhead. "The worst part was not having an ally, someone to talk to, to be able to tell someone the real reason that I was there. After a while the Sonderkommandos and the ladies in Canada realized who I was, but I could never truly let them in. It was just too dangerous. I had to keep them at a distance. But was I scared? Yes, I was. The fact that I got to see my family every two weeks was what saved me. I don't think I could have gotten through without their support."

"Yes, how is your family? I think about them all the time."

"Not me, no?"

"The SS officer?" She smiled. "No, I tried to put you out of my mind. I didn't know what to think."

"But you know now. You know who I am now. I can't believe my plan, all that I did to find you was what kept us apart."

"How could you have known? You did what you thought was right at the time."

"You know who I am now, don't you? I need to hear you say it again."

"Yes, I do, but answer the question about your family." The old mischief was in her eyes, or at least a version of what was once there.

"It's good to see that age hasn't changed you, that . . . everything that happened hasn't changed you."

"I never said that my experience hadn't changed me." They were silent for a few seconds. "Anyway, anyway, anyway, how is your family?"

"Yes, my family. They're splendid. They're all back in Jersey."

"All of them?"

"Yes, they eventually all made it back, some later than others. Yes, well, they're all back there now. Alexandra went back to Tom after the war. They live just outside Saint Helier. They have six kids now."

"Six kids?"

"Yes, six. You could say they're making up for lost time. It seems every time Alex turns around these days, she's pregnant again. I think Tom only has to look at her to impregnate her. They deserve it, though, for everything they went through."

"They're great people. I'd love to see them again. What about your father? I've missed him so much all these years. Breaking up with you was so much harder because of him. The thought of never seeing him again made it even more painful."

"I never realized we broke up. I thought we were still together after all these years." He turned to her, waiting for the reaction. "I know. You thought I was a Nazi," he said. Her smile was the signal for him to continue. "My father is doing very well. I saw him last week. We live together with my daughter and my cousin Stefan."

"Wait, you have a daughter? The newspaper article never mentioned that."

"I wanted to keep her out of the newspaper. I didn't want to get her involved in this."

"What age is she? What's her name?"

"Her name is Hannah. She's eleven. She's back in Jersey with my father and her cousins. I spoke to her last night, long-distance." He heard Hannah's voice in his mind again. It warmed him.

"She's eleven?"

"Yes, she's adopted. She was one of the children I took out of the camp. Klaczko, the head of the Sonderkommandos at the time, brought her to me, one night before I was due to go to Berlin. He smuggled her out of the crematorium, hidden in an old coat." He grimaced at the memory of the baby in the coat, something he had never sanctioned at the time. Klaczko just brought her to him. He shook his head at the impossible bravery of that. "The next morning I took her out of the camp in the car, brought her to my father in Berlin."

"How did she stay quiet when you were driving out?"

"Hannah was only a baby, maybe around a year old at the time. I gave her some vodka, some of the really good stuff. She never made a sound."

"Good thinking."

"She was too young to go to the safe houses or the orphanage we had organized, so my family took her in. They raised her for those first few months. That was in October '44. Hannah was the last child I got out of Birkenau. The whole camp fell apart after that."

"What do you know about her? Do you even know where she's from?"

"She's Hungarian. We searched for any family she might have had left, after the war, but it was impossible. I don't know much." He pictured his daughter as a baby, with the family that should have raised her. "There were no records of who her family was or even of what her name was. Alex used to bring her to visit me when I was in the internment camp, after Dachau. And when I got out, when Alex went back to Jersey, she left Hannah with me. I adopted her as my daughter. She was absolutely everything to me, my savior. I don't think I would have made it through if it wasn't for her."

"What happened to the prisoner, Klaczko?"

"He died. He was murdered by the SS." He and the Sonderkommandos he had worked with were all dead. The mention of Klaczko still caused a stab of pain.

"I would love to meet Hannah someday."

"I'm sure she would love to meet you too. She's heard all about you. I'd say she'd probably think you were a ghost."

"Who says I'm not?"

Christopher poked her in the shoulder with a rigid finger. "You're no ghost."

Rebecca stopped a young man in a blue suit. "Excuse me, sir, do you have the time?" It was 6:45. Rebecca thanked him and turned to Christopher again. "We should turn back. You have an interview to get to."

"Do we have to?"

"Yes, we do." She turned around to walk back. He stood still, watching her from behind as she went and the swish of her dress in the warm air. They were walking through a tunnel of trees, the branches intertwining overhead, and the light of the evening sun sprinkling shards of light down through layers of leaves. She turned around. "Am I going to have to drag you back there?"

"I think so, yes." But he started walking after her. She stood still to wait for him.

"I can't believe you've got a daughter."

"Have you any kids yourself? I noticed the wedding ring."

"No, we've no children." She was walking more quickly now toward the end of the pathway and the exit out of the park. "I miss Jersey. I think about it all the time. Tel Aviv is wonderful, right on the Mediterranean, the beaches, the sea, just like Jersey, but there's something missing, you know?"

"Me?"

"The Nazi war criminal, you mean? No, I don't think so."

"I did it for you, Rebecca."

"I know that, I know that now," she said, and reached across to take his hand. It felt wonderful. She squeezed his palm and released, leaving his hand dangling by his side. "So the years have been good to you, Christopher, a few grays at the side," she said, brushing her knuckles to the side of his head, "but you look good. How do I look?"

"Wonderful."

"I used to think about that day you found me in the hedge down by my parents' house, when I was in the camps. Funny, isn't it? I really didn't think about much when I was in the camps. The only thing I ever thought about other than you and Jersey was food. Not the war, not what I was going to do afterward, not how I was going to bring the monsters running the camps to justice, just those three things. But even then, I never thought about you as much as I would about getting a piece of bread, or a potato."

"My experience was nothing compared to what you went through."

"It's a strange, horrible thing to be always hungry, always cold. A friend of mine, Emily Rosenfield, died and left me her spoon. She said it would save my life. I used to carry that spoon with me everywhere I went so that I would be ready." He wanted to say something but didn't feel worthy. "I ate it all, wood, leaves, grass. I learned to look for the juiciest pieces of grass, the ones with the most 'meat' on them. It hardly seems real now."

Her voice seemed hollow as she spoke, as if it wasn't her talking, but some pale reflection of the person he knew. "It's funny, but I don't think I would have made it through if I'd had what people think of as 'normal' parents. Their bad parenting gave me the best possible training for life in the camps." Rebecca moved close to him, interlocking her arms with his, and whispered, "I never thanked you for what you tried to do, what you did, for me. Thank you, Christopher."

Christopher felt her warmth against him. "I never had a choice. How could I leave you there? I had to do what I did. I never had a choice in any of it."

# CHAPTER

## 41

The light of the evening sun reflected off the windows of the cars, and Christopher felt a drop of cold sweat down the center of his back. He undid the top button of his shirt, lit a cigarette, and offered one to Rebecca. She shook her head and they walked on, crisscrossing through the traffic until they were back on Broadway. They had not spoken for a minute or longer. There was almost too much to ask and far too much to say.

"So, you're married? Whatever happened to Jonathan Durrell?"

"He died in '47, in a motorcycle crash on the island. I never saw him after I left. Let's not talk about him. That's ancient history now." She ran a hand through her hair, letting it fall down to the side. Christopher felt his heart turn inside him. "You never got married? What happened, Christopher? There must have been a line of eligible ladies all the way from the house in Saint Martin down to Saint Helier. None of them ever managed to snare you, no?"

"No. They had a tough act to follow, you know?" He took another drag on the cigarette. The weight of the silence between them was suddenly huge, and he broke it. "There were women, of course, but there was never anyone truly special. I was raising a young daughter, and, with little Stefan in the house, I was practically raising two kids with my father. I wanted a mother for Hannah; I still do, but I didn't want to fake it. I couldn't." He wished that she would redirect the conversation. "It took me a long time to get over you and to accept the fact that you were dead. I don't suppose I ever really did."

"I'm not dead, Christopher."

"I can see that, but we still haven't fully ascertained whether you're a ghost or not." The interview was starting again in less than ten minutes. He threw down the cigarette.

"I shouldn't have come here today."

"What are you talking about?"

"I'd been doing so much better lately; I thought I'd made a breakthrough in my life. I was so much happier until I read about you again. Everything I've based my life on these past nine years has been a mistake. I survived the camps, but I left a massive part of me behind. When I finally began to believe that you were SS, the last part of my innocence died. The memory of you was the only evidence I had that love really existed in the world, and that there was a life to be lived afterward that would be worthwhile, that could be a real tribute to all the people I saw die." The tears were coming down in great swathes now. They stopped on the street. He put his arm across her shoulder and kissed the top of her head. "I've tried to live my life as a tribute to those people. That's why I've lived the way I have since. It's all been for them. Now I come to meet you here, and all this is revealed. I knew I should never have come. I should have left things the way they were."

"No, Rebecca, you're wrong. Finding out that you're alive is the greatest joy I could ever have."

"Finding out that I'm alive and married? I'm married, Christopher."

"I know you are, but just the thought that you're happy and alive is enough for me."

"Is it? The thought that I'm lavishing in my perfect marriage, that's enough to keep you happy until you die of old age, wondering how the girl you became an SS officer in Auschwitz for is doing over in Tel Aviv with her husband?"

"No, of course not, but it's up to me to construct my own happiness. I can't rely on you for that, not anymore. Maybe I could come over to Israel, some of the kids live over there now. They write to me all the time, inviting me over . . ."

"Yes, that sounds just perfect. You could watch Ari and I play happy families together. If you're lucky, he may even be around long enough for you to have a proper conversation with."

"Does he know who I am?"

"No, if Ari ever found out that I was with an SS officer . . . I don't even know. Maybe he wouldn't even care," she said, turning away. "We need to get you back to your interview."

"I don't care about that."

"I do. You're going back." She strode away, back toward the studio.

Christopher stood still, feeling her words course through him, and just for a brief second, he contemplated letting her go and never seeing her again. *I know she's alive. Is that enough?* He walked after her. He had to jog to catch up. "I'm not saying that what I went through was anything compared to what you did, I never would, but after the war I had to build a new life for myself too. Everything had been focused on finding you, and the wonderful life that we were going to have together. But when I found out you were dead, everything else died too. I did the things I did because I thought they were what you would have wanted me to do."

"It's not my fault. What happened after the war isn't my fault."

"I know that. I never thought that it was. I'm not looking for anything from you. How could I be? An hour ago I thought you were dead. I don't know that I'm not going to wake up from this in a cold sweat and realize that this was all some dream."

"It's no dream, believe me, it's very real."

"So tell me about your husband. When did you get married?" The husband was his buffer, the limit to what he could hope to achieve. It was best to establish boundaries.

"We were married on April 9, 1950. I really don't want to talk about that, though."

"Talking to me about your husband isn't being unfaithful."

"Okay, what do you want to know? That he was a survivor too?" He knew her mannerisms so well. It was like being back in the apartment in Saint Helier with her again.

"That would be a start. Where did you meet him?"

"We worked together. I met him in '47."

"What happened to you after the war? How did you end up in Israel?" The words were coming quickly now. Somehow that made it easier.

"We don't have time to talk about this. Your interview is starting again in five minutes."

"I don't care about that. This is more important."

"No, this is no good. I shouldn't have come here today. All this is doing is opening up old wounds." They were outside the studio building. "You were fine without me, and I was fine without you. We've survived."

"Rebecca, just knowing that you made it through, that you survived the camps, makes me so happy. I had thought all these years that I was a failure, and that the one thing that I'd gone there to do was the one thing that I couldn't."

"You, a failure? All those people are alive today thanks to you."

"That didn't make the pain of losing you any easier. It didn't ease the guilt I felt."

"Oh, Christopher, no."

"You never would have been deported if it wasn't for me. You would have been safe in England. The only reason you stayed in Jersey was to be with me."

"If there's one thing in the world I'm sure of, if there is only one thing, and God knows these days it's hard to be sure about anything, it's that I do not regret staying in Jersey with you. That was the most wonderful time I've ever had. You gave me everything. I was never happier. You've got to go back upstairs now," she said. The tears were in her eyes again.

"I will if you stay. I'm not going back inside there without you."

"No, Christopher. I can't." She shook her head. "I'm married."

"I'm not trying to get you. Just come inside. I won't go if you're not with me. I'm not letting you go this time."

"All right, I'll come upstairs, but only because you joined the SS to find me." She smiled.

"That'll do for me." They walked inside. The elevator came within a few seconds and the same operator looked at them as they got inside. "You have to stay where I can see you. I want you standing at the glass."

"Yes, sir."

David met them as the elevator arrived. "I knew you'd make it back. The others here weren't so confident, but I had faith in you."

"Thanks, David. When am I on?"

David looked at his watch. "Oh, in about fifteen seconds or so." The interviewer was waving his arms at Christopher, who jogged inside and put the headphones on again. He leaned into the microphone and looked up at Rebecca by the window as he waited for the next question.

# CHAPTER

---

## 42

The thrill of seeing her face was almost giddying to him. No photo he had could capture the sparkle in her blue eyes or the energy he felt when he was around her. She dragged her hair back in her hands, tying it up as she watched him. The minutes spent in the studio were an agony. He was looking at his watch all the time, begging for the end, but he did what he was there to do, what the American Jewish Committee had brought him over to do. There were five minutes left when he looked up to her again, but she was no longer there. David was still standing at the glass, and he looked calm. He tried to draw comfort from the look on David's face, but as the seconds built into minutes, she had still not returned. The interview ended, and somehow the interviewer seemed happy.

"That was a hell of a thing you did." He reached out to shake Christopher's hand.

"Yes, thank you," he said, and looked up at the window into the studio again. David was looking worried. He walked out. "Where is she, David?"

"I don't know, she said she was going to the bathroom. That was about five minutes ago."

Christopher knew that she was gone. They searched the bathroom, but she wasn't there. They ran to the elevator and onto the street. David apologized again.

"It's not your fault, David, really, it's okay." Christopher looked up the street into the sea of people. David reached up and put a hand on his shoulder. Christopher lit up a cigarette. The sun was setting over the city, and the buildings of Times Square were bathed in orange, red, and gold, each window a separate reflection, like gold bars piled on top of one another. The process of mourning her loss was beginning again. David went back inside. Christopher looked at the faces of the people as they walked past, but none looked back, as if he wasn't there at all. The cigarette was finished and he threw it down and stood there, motionless.

"I'm so sorry, Christopher. I didn't think I could stand to see you anymore. I thought it was best for both of us, for your family, for your daughter . . ." Her voice came from behind him.

He turned around and took her in his arms. "I thought I'd lost you—again." She moved her mouth to say something but instead just shook her head and leaned in against him. They went back into the building together, to say goodbye to David and the others in the radio station.

A few minutes later they were back on the street together. "The sun's going down, where shall we go?" she began.

"Have you eaten?"

"No, but I'd love a drink. I'd say we both deserve that," she said.

"We can do both. I think I know where we need to go. Come on."

They crossed the street and began to make their way across town, east along Fifty-Second Street. "There's something we haven't touched on yet, something I wanted to ask you," she said. "I'm not sure I want to hear the answer."

The cross street was almost quiet in comparison with the avenues, and they didn't have to swerve to avoid the crowds as they had earlier. "What? You can ask me anything you want."

"It's about Uli. What happened to Uli?"

"Uli died in June 1944. He was killed in some field in Russia."

"We don't have to talk about that."

"No, it's fine, it's ten years ago now. I've had time to deal with it. I mean, if I haven't gotten over it by now, when will I? The last time I saw him was in late January of '44, on one of my trips to Berlin."

"Did he know what you were doing?"

"Yes, he knew, and he delighted in it. He had seen too much killing. I only spoke to him for an hour that day, but it was obvious he was changed. I suppose we all were." Uli had been a shadow of the man he had known. It didn't seem fitting to remember the emaciated version of Uli he met in '44, his gray beard covering sunken cheeks, his eyes lifeless and dull. "The light had gone out inside him. He didn't care about the war or winning it. He didn't care about Hitler or any of his objectives. He just wanted to get back to his wife and son, just wanted to get his men back safely. But he never did. I wish I'd known that was the last time I'd ever see him. Perhaps I would have said more."

"There was so much death, so few proper goodbyes."

Christopher paused and stepped around a homeless man whose feet were jutting out across their path. The man looked up at them with filthy brown eyes, sucking from the bottle in his hand, murmuring gibberish. Just for a second Christopher thought to reach into his pocket, but changed his mind and walked on. "The last few months in Germany were chaos, everyone was fleeing west. I managed to get the kids, the kids I had smuggled out of Auschwitz, to a number of safe houses in Frankfurt, away from the Soviets. Alexandra went with them, along with some of the nuns from the convent. My father stayed in Berlin with Karolina and Stefan, as he had already been drafted into the Volkssturm."

"What?"

"The Volkssturm—the militia the Nazis set up to protect themselves. Kids and old men were called up. My father was in command of a squadron of sixteen-year-olds."

"Was he there when the Soviets came?"

"Yes, he was in Berlin, age fifty, fighting against the Soviet tanks as they rolled into the streets. He knew that if he tried to desert, they would hang him. Karolina tried to take Stefan and leave, tried to run when the Soviet tanks arrived. The Gestapo caught her and hung her from a lamppost on the street." They passed onto Fifth Avenue and began to walk upward, toward the park. "The Gestapo brought little Stefan back to Cousin Harald's house. They hanged his mother, but made sure little Stefan got safely home."

"I'm so sorry. That's horrible."

"Somehow my father survived and got back to the house, back to little Stefan. After the battle was over, after Berlin had fallen, he used the last of the money that I'd given him, to bribe some Soviet troops to let them out of the city into the countryside. He made his way toward Frankfurt, behind the American lines. After that he brought Stefan back to Jersey. They were there by the end of October '46, a few months after you came looking for us. I'll never know how the old man survived; most of the Volkssturm were wiped out."

"I'm sorry about Uli, Christopher, and Karolina and everything."

The day was fading, the streetlights coming to life. "Stefan is a wonderful boy. He's fourteen now, so much like his father. He's a character."

A young couple brushed past them, their arms linked. The woman whispered something into her lover's ear. Rebecca was silent for a few seconds. "It's so hard for me to think of Uli as a German soldier."

"He wasn't SS. I was SS. We were the ones who committed the atrocities."

"You didn't commit any atrocities. You weren't one of them, Christopher."

"I was an SS man. I can show you the tattoo they gave us. It's still with me, it always will be."

She grabbed his arm. They stopped. They were outside a bakery. Fresh cakes in the window adorned by colored lights reflected in her eyes as she spoke, and the smell of bread through the open door filled their nostrils. "You were not one of them, Christopher. I know that. You were there for me. You joined the SS for me."

"We're nearly there. You said you were hungry, didn't you?"

He tried to move away, but her grip was tight on his arm. "You weren't one of them. You wore the uniform and you got the tattoo, but you weren't one of them."

He remembered Anka; saw her in his office and her tiny body beside Schultz in the snow. "I knew you weren't dead," he said. "It's hard to say how, even after I couldn't find you, even after all the signs pointed to the fact that you were. Somehow, I knew we'd meet again. I would see you everywhere. I was in London only a few months ago and I thought I saw you, walking along under a black umbrella, holding hands with a little girl, and I ran after you. I put my hand on that woman's shoulder. When she turned to me, and after I'd apologized, I felt sick, a deep nausea passed through my whole body. I see you every day. I think about you most days. I feel like I'm going crazy sometimes. I feel like telling the kids about you all the time, and sometimes I do talk to Hannah about you. She feels as if she knows you. But now what do I tell her? That I met you in New York, that we had dinner together, and you're alive and married and happy and you're living in Israel?" Rebecca didn't speak. "I feel we shouldn't be doing this, as if somehow this isn't right, as if we're starting something now that shouldn't have an ending."

"Is there ever really any ending other than death? We both fought so hard to be alive, for this. And if I never see you again, if you walk away now and don't let me back into your life, that wouldn't be the end. That wouldn't be the end of anything. I'd still go on and so would you, but that's not what I want. I didn't come back to you today for that."

"What did you come back to me for?"

"I don't know. I really don't know. All I can tell you is that when I heard about who you were, who you really were, and why you joined the SS, I had to come. It was all I wanted to do."

"You don't owe me anything. You don't need to feel any obligation to do anything. . . ."

"I know that, and believe me, I don't. You were the center of my life, the fulcrum of the happiest times I've ever had. I had to come back. There was no other choice."

"You said you were hungry, didn't you? Well, we can talk about all of this over dinner. This is all going be so much easier with some food in our stomachs."

"Yes, let's go." They turned to walk back up the street toward the Plaza Hotel where David and the other members of the American Jewish Committee had brought him on his first night in the city. There was a bar ahead. Christopher peered inside as they went. It was almost full, the smooth sound of live jazz music inside sliding out onto the street and following them as they walked past.

"So, what's it like being married? You haven't really mentioned your husband much."

"What do you want to know? Ari is a good man." Her words were sharp, as if he had ventured onto private property.

"I think I should like to meet him someday," he replied, trying to form a picture of him in his head.

"Would you really?" Her exasperated tone didn't encourage further questions, and Christopher didn't really want to talk about him anyway.

"Do you still think about our time in Jersey?"

"It seems like a dream from a previous life, as if I saw it happening to me but never participated directly in it myself." They crossed the street as she began again. "I think everyone changes as they get older; you don't have to be a survivor of the camps to realize that our experiences change us as we get older."

"And are you different now?"

"Because of the camps?"

"Or otherwise."

"We all are. We're not the same people we were when we lived together in Jersey for those years. The camps accentuated that. I felt scarred for many years, as if I'd never be able to love again. Perhaps I was right about that, I still don't know. I felt indebted to those who died there, as if when I met them again when I died, they'd ask me what I did for them, and what they died for. I have a duty to them, for the rest of my life."

"I thought the dreams, the visions I have, would fade over time, but they haven't. The kids are used to it now, almost expecting to hear the screams from my room in the night. Hannah comes in when she hears me, gets into bed beside me, and holds me until I fall back to sleep. But I wouldn't change it. Even if I knew that I wouldn't find you, I would still go to Birkenau. Hannah wouldn't be alive today if I hadn't been there, and that's enough." He felt her hand in his. "And the other kids, and the ladies from Canada, I get five, six, sometimes fifteen letters a month. They're all over the world now; there are even some of them in Tel Aviv. I've spent my days here in New York seeing some of them and their families.

So I can't regret what I've done, the choices I've made. But, still, it seems like so little."

"It doesn't seem fair that they knew who you were and I didn't, and they were right there in Tel Aviv, right in the city I live in."

They walked on in silence for a minute or more. "You still haven't answered the question," he said.

"What question?"

"The question I asked you about married life."

"Why, are you engaged? Looking for advice from an old pro maybe?" Christopher didn't pander to her. "Ari is a good man, very dedicated to what he fights for. He is what the state of Israel needs. He is righteous and true, determined." Her voice was like a candle flickering in the breeze.

"Are you happy with him?"

"You mean would I be happier with you?"

"No, I don't mean that at all." *Don't I?*

"In my mind I've always compared him to you. It was as if I only had so much love in me and because I had given it so completely to you, I could never have it back. I felt like I'd already given to you. I thought the camps changed me. I felt that I had lost the ability to love, like the experiences in the camps had somehow eroded that away."

"That's not true, Rebecca, you're still the warm, loving person you were. Of course you've changed. Everyone has, and everyone would have even if the camps had never existed. You can't live your life holding back. You have to give all of yourself."

"I did give all of myself. I gave myself to you."

"And that's it then, is it? You just give up on your whole life? Because of me and what we had?"

They crossed the street at Fifty-Eighth and made their way across toward the Plaza. Christopher didn't speak, still waiting for an answer to his question, but Rebecca stayed silent as they walked inside.

# CHAPTER

## 43

The maître d' seemed to recognize Christopher from the previous night and led them across the restaurant to a table in the corner. Christopher thanked him as they sat down. They had barely spoken in several minutes. They were directly opposite each other. She didn't look across at him as she sat down. He ordered the wine.

"This is amazing." Just for a moment, she sounded like a little girl again.

There were perhaps forty tables in the packed dining room, each covered in a white tablecloth with sparkling silver cutlery. The drapes were brown, as was the carpet beneath their feet. Many of the diners were in evening dress. He had buttoned his top button as they moved to their table, but she had not even mentioned the notion of their being underdressed.

"I did always bring you to the best places."

"I think that this is a cut above the Red Lion in Saint Helier. I wouldn't say they get too many fishermen in here."

"No, I wouldn't have thought so." He paused, waiting for the right moment before he began speaking again. "What happened to you after the war, Rebecca? You still haven't told me. There's still so much I don't know."

"Do you have to know everything? Aren't some things better left unsaid?"

"I've been thinking about you almost every day for all these years, and you were out there. What were you doing?"

"Trying to piece my life back together."

"How? Where were you?" Christopher brought the glass to his mouth and felt the red wine sliding down his throat. There was an elderly couple at the table next to them. The man had a large white mustache and was glancing over between bites of the generous steak on his pristine china plate.

Rebecca took a sip of wine. "I was in the hospital for a while. I was probably days away from death when those British soldiers found me. They tried to feed me from the rations they had, but I couldn't keep them down. The food they gave me made me even sicker. They nearly killed me." Rebecca was looking into her wine as it rolled against the sides of the glass. "After I got out of the hospital, I was put into the displaced persons camp. There were thousands of us, all with nowhere to go, and no way to get anywhere. I met my father there. Some of the other prisoners had spoken to him and remembered that he was from Jersey and they brought me to him."

"What did he tell you about me?"

"He said that you were SS. He said that he had always been right about you. I didn't believe him at first, not until I saw the lists of names. And even then . . . it took me a long time to accept it. He never told me what you did for the prisoners or even if you did anything for him," Rebecca continued. Her eyes locked on to his. "Did you help him?"

"I had him transferred to the camp by mistake. I asked for a Cassin and they sent him. Some joke, eh?"

"You might say that."

"Yes, I helped him, as much as I could anyway. I gave him extra food and organized a job for him where he could stay alive." They were both silent for seconds, which dragged into minutes, as they looked at the menus laid on the table in front of them. The waiter came back just as Christopher was about to speak. He was young, perhaps twenty-two, and very tall, well over six foot, with a full beard.

The waiter left and Rebecca began again. "We stayed in the displaced persons camp for weeks. The authorities had no idea what to do with us, and I didn't know what to do with myself. Without you, I had nothing left to live for." The words cut through him. "I went to the British authorities in the camp to offer my services as a go-between for them and the rest of the refugees there. I met with some of the officers charged with collecting testimonies on war crimes, and I began to help them. I wrote a list of all the SS officers I had ever encountered and began to quiz the others in the camp about what they remembered. Somehow I gained strength from that. I shrugged off everything else. It wasn't revenge. It was never about that. It was justice, only that."

"Did you speak to many prisoners from Auschwitz?"

"No, I never did. I just dealt with the camps that I knew, that I was in. I suppose our lives would have been quite different if I had."

"I suppose they would have been."

"I collected lists and testimonies and handed them over to the authorities. But that still wasn't enough. I got in touch with some other former prisoners I still knew. I moved to Vienna to continue my work."

"Why Vienna?" Christopher thought of the city and imagined himself meeting her there at some random place in a city he'd never been to. But the image faded as Rebecca spoke.

"That was where Ari was from. He was a survivor too. I met him through some of the other former prisoners." The waiter came to the table, asked if they needed anything. He immediately seemed to regret it and began to back away. "We had successes, and we met Simon Wiesenthal and soon started working with him. Do you know who he is?"

"The Nazi hunter? As a former member of the SS, it pays to know of people like Mr. Wiesenthal. They might still come for me one day."

"We joined with him for a while before we moved to Israel."

"And you were married there?"

"Yes."

"You never seem to want to talk about him." Christopher was trying to picture him. He almost asked her for a photograph.

"Ari?"

"Yes, your husband. Every time I ask about him, you deflect the question."

"Do you really want to hear about him?" She raised the wine-glass to her mouth, holding it by the stem. A pianist began playing, and the sounds of the music drifted through the restaurant like confetti on the wind. "Earlier on, you spoke about not wanting to fake it and realize that you were married to the wrong person." She took a sip of wine. "The fact that Ari and I are married is . . . not as important as it once might have been."

"What do you mean?"

"Ari is an excellent person, very good at his job and very effective in what he does for his country. But I feel like we're business partners more than a married couple. He's dedicated and kind . . ." Her voice trailed off. "He had a difficult act to follow, you know? I think now that it was a reaction to you. Maybe I didn't have the strength to be alone, and Ari and I had the same determination, the same mission. Marriage seemed the logical step, but you never left me. Even if I didn't think about you during the day, I'd have these dreams where you'd come to me and we would be on the beach

299

in Jersey. I'd reach out to touch you, but you'd disappear, and Ari would ask me why I'd wake up sweating."

"I had almost the same dream."

"But the dedication I feel to my country and my people is more important than anything else to me. I have to be where I am right now. There's still so much work to do, still so much healing to go through, for so many of us. I couldn't walk out on my country now, not when it needs me most, and being married to Ari is a way of serving my country and my people. It seems to me that you have the perfect life now. You have your daughter, your father, and Uli's son. Alexandra and Tom are right there with their children, and you have this network of love around the world in the people you saved."

"Perfect? That's a big word, Rebecca. It's true what you say. I've been very lucky that my father and sister survived the war, and little Stefan is a joy, but sometimes I feel sorry for Hannah. She has so much responsibility for someone her age. I thought that the nights where she would have to come in and sleep with me would become less as time went on, but they haven't. I woke up last night in my hotel room, on the floor, screaming. I was begging that she would be there but she wasn't, so I just got back into bed and shivered alone until the alarm call came this morning." The restaurant was full, but no one was paying them any attention. "I have dreams where I'm shooting the prisoners, where it's me feeding the crematoria, it's me conducting the experiments and making the selections."

"No, Christopher, that wasn't you. You didn't do any of those monstrous things. You are the only reason that hundreds of people are alive today." The words felt good, but only as a spattering of water on a massive fire.

"That's what everyone tells me. I still see Anka all the time. She was the first little girl I tried to save in the camp, and I saw her shot in front of me. I still see her body collapse in the snow. And she comes to me, as a teenager, as the young woman she should have been today, and I couldn't save her, I tried to, but I couldn't. . . ." He tried to hold back the tears. He didn't want to be crying here, with her, but it was too much. Rebecca stood up, walked around the table, and held his head against her.

"Oh, Christopher, you did so, so much. You couldn't save everyone, you just couldn't."

He put his arms around her waist but then suddenly became conscious of where they were and stood up. He kissed her on the cheek and walked toward the bathroom. He thought of Hannah and his family in Jersey and felt the calm spread back through him, his heart rate falling as he reached the bathroom. The water from the faucet splashed down, and he cooled his hands under it and then brought them up to wipe his face. He thought of what Rebecca had said about Ari. He looked at his reflection in the mirror and judged himself fit to return to the table. The food was on the table as he arrived.

"Are you feeling better, Christopher?" she asked. "What you did was important. You should never feel like any kind of a failure. Your actions have been recognized, in Israel too. You have no reason for guilt or shame. You should be as proud of yourself as I am of you." She reached across the table and put her hand on his. It should have felt wonderful.

He took a deep breath and then opened his mouth to speak, but the words didn't come. He stared at her for a few seconds. "What are you really doing in New York? Why are you all the way over here alone, without your husband?"

"I told you already. I'm over here on business."

"You're in marketing, is that right? When did you stop hunting Nazis? How would you know what the Israelis are thinking about me?"

"What are you talking about?" she whispered.

"Is it me? Did you come here to investigate me? How long have you known about me, about what I really did?"

"I don't know what you're talking about, but I'd really appreciate it if you stopped now."

"What did Israeli intelligence tell you about me? Why didn't you contact me if you knew?" He felt his voice shudder in his throat. "You don't work in marketing, do you?"

"Stop this at once."

"Answer the question."

"It's not like that, Christopher, it's not. I only found out about you a few days ago. I wanted to come here, to see you." She reached across the table to take his hand. "I'm not here . . . in that capacity. I'm here because I want to be. . . . The Israelis . . ."

"The Mossad," he corrected her.

"I'm not here as an agent of the Mossad. I'm here as me, for you. I've wanted to see you, wanted to talk to you for as long as I can remember. There hardly seems a time in my life now when I wasn't pining for you and what seems like a dream that we had together."

"What could the Mossad want with me?"

"They thought I might be able to get information from you, that you might have information about others. With your background, you were deemed a valuable person, someone who could help the cause. But my superiors weren't convinced that you weren't a war criminal yourself, so someone had to come to investigate you. I didn't know either. I'm sorry. When I found out that you were in the SS, I didn't know what to think."

"So you came here to spy on me. To get close to me, to see if I was someone the Mossad could use?"

"They knew we were both from Jersey, and that I could get close to you."

"What about you? What did you know?"

"I knew that I loved you, that you were the person in life who was most important to me, but that you had been an SS man. I saw your file, and what it said rang true. You were cleared of all crimes.

I knew that if I met you, I could find out the truth for myself. I had to find out myself."

"So I suppose that's it, then." He threw his napkin down on the table. *How can I just walk out? This is Rebecca.*

"No, no. I see who you were and who you are. I know what you did in that camp and since. You're a wonderful, beautiful person. I know that you did it all for me, even after you thought I'd died." There were tears in her eyes. They looked genuine. "You've got to believe me. Any suspicions I had died hours ago, probably before we even met. The things you did were extraordinary."

"How did you find out about the mission? Did you research it yourself?"

"Ari handed me the file on you because he found out you were from Jersey."

"You never told him about me?"

"Tell Ari that the love of my life was an SS guard in Auschwitz? No, I never told him." Her voice was dry as she spoke, and she looked away to the side.

"How could you have not known about me all these years? You were investigating Nazi war criminals. How did my name never come up? More than twenty people testified on my behalf at my trial."

"I only dealt with the camps I was in. I never gathered or shared information about anyone from Auschwitz. We have other operatives who were there. I'd never heard of you until last week. There are thousands of SS men, and thousands of files. I never saw yours. I wish I had. I wish I had heard about you, and I'm sure this would all be different."

The words warmed and hacked at his heart equally. Rebecca sipped the red wine from the glass in her hand. She stood up and excused herself and walked toward the bathroom. Was she calling her husband, or even her commanding officer? What was the point in this, and who knew if anything she said was the truth now? But what would the Mossad have to gain from him? There wasn't anything he could tell them that he hadn't already said at the trials of his superiors all those years ago, and the files they must have had on him would show the testimonies of the people who spoke on his behalf at his trial. There couldn't be any other reason that she would be here, in the Plaza Hotel in New York, with him. He had to trust her. This would probably be the last time he would ever see her. He picked up the knife and fork, forced himself to eat. He thought of Hannah, and little Stefan, and his father, and he thought of Rebecca. *Is she the same girl I met on the beach in Jersey?*

The pianist in the corner of the room was young, perhaps not even twenty years of age. The music lilted and swam through the massive dining room. There was a small dance floor in front of the long grand piano. Several couples were dancing. Rebecca was coming toward him, a half smile on her face. She reached a hand out to him. "Can I have this dance, sir?"

"I'm meant to be the one asking you, you know."

"Are you going to dance with me or not?"

He held up his hand and she took it, leading him past the tables and onto the dance floor. It felt so good to hold her, as if a warmth was flowing through her into him. "So you're a spy?"

"Not a very good one it seems," she replied. "No, I'm not a spy. I just continued my work finding Nazis with the Israeli government." There were several tables of people looking at them, but he was sure they couldn't hear what they were saying.

"And here you are, dancing in plain sight, with an admitted former member of the SS."

The song ended and the other couples on the dance floor parted to applaud the pianist, but he held her tight to him. He was staring at her, into her blue eyes, as the music began again, and they began to dance once more. His hand on her hip tracked every slight movement of her torso and his eyes, hers. The confusion of earlier cleared within him and everything felt right again.

They danced for ten minutes or more in total silence before they returned to the table, where Rebecca found her now-cold food. She ate it nonetheless. "I can't turn down a meal now, ever," she said as she put the fork into her mouth. It was after nine o'clock.

"When are you flying out?" he asked.

"The first flight is tomorrow morning, at six a.m." She put her knife and fork down. "I don't care about that. I just want to be here now."

"Where are you staying?"

"With friends in Brooklyn. What about you?"

"I'm in a hotel here in Manhattan." The longing for her was already there. The feeling of loss was with him already, even though he could reach out and touch her across the table.

Once they finished the meal, he watched her eat dessert. He lit up a cigarette. It was almost eleven o'clock now. It seemed like their time together was already over, as if he was observing all this as a memory rather than partaking in the moment. He leaned forward to her as she began to speak.

"I've been doing much better lately with things, with the memories and the feelings I have inside."

"What feelings?"

"I used to hurt like you do now," she said. "I had those dreams that you have. I was in Paris a year or two ago and I heard some people speaking German. I immediately went cold. I couldn't move. The terror I felt, just at hearing them speak. I was back in the camps again, hearing the guards. I had to get off the street and be sick in an alleyway." She pushed her now-empty plate out in front of her. "I know the terror, the guilt that you're feeling. That's not why I started doing what I do now. I thought that bringing these animals to justice would make me feel better, so that I could at least sleep at night."

"Did it?"

"No, not really. I still had the same mood swings, the same phobias of dogs and the German language. It was satisfying to see the murderers jailed or executed, but there will always be more. There are so many still out there. I think that I'm ready to leave it behind now. I can't do this anymore. I can't constantly be reminded of the worst times in my life." Her voice lifted. "I see you here now and I know that the times we had weren't some dream and that there is real happiness still to be had, even in a world that can create Buchenwald and Belsen and Auschwitz."

"Yes, perhaps there is."

"It's so easy to hate. That's what they did. I tried to clear the hatred out of my heart to forgive the Nazis for what they did to me."

"You're forgiving them?"

"I wasn't going to be a victim anymore, not one more day of my life. I was powerless as a victim. The SS guards and their dogs and the doctors in their white coats still had power over me, even though I was the one putting them in jail now. I found that by forgiving them, I held the ultimate power, and the pain stopped. Now I know that what they did to me and the people I knew is no longer going to hurt me, and that my life, my happy life, will be the ultimate tribute to all the people I saw die." He felt the warmth in his heart again. "To forget what happened to them, now that is something to be guilty about, but living your life, truly living your life, is not."

"So you're thinking about leaving the Mossad?"

"I've been thinking about it for a long time. I mentioned it to Ari, but . . . He is a wonderful person and he deserves better." She took another sip of wine. "There's still so much pain left. I know that you feel it. The only thing to counter pain is healing, and the only way to heal is to let go of the hatred and to forgive. I felt an incredible weight of suffering lifted from my shoulders when I let go of the hatred that was still burning inside me. I can honestly say now that I feel pity for those people who killed us in those camps. But not hatred, not anymore, that's gone."

"I am so proud of you." He paused before he whispered, "Can you forgive me?"

"I have nothing to forgive you for. I see that same pain in you that I felt, and the same guilt over those we were forced to leave behind. You have to let it go. We all deserve to live the most wonderful lives we can."

The light of midnight in the city was all around them as they stepped out of the hotel into the street. Neither had spoken since they left the table, as if they were both afraid to mention what had to happen next. He looked across at her, drinking in the sight of her, for he knew this was a scene he would play and replay in his own mind for years to come. The city lights shimmered on her tanned skin and flickered in her eyes. They talked about Jersey and their families again for a few minutes as they wandered the city streets, neither having mentioned any kind of a destination or the fact that her flight was in less than six hours. He craned his neck to look up the length of the buildings surrounding them as they went. They walked, four, five, six, and seven blocks before he asked her.

"So how were you going to get home, or at least back to where you're staying?"

"You know what? I hadn't even thought about it."

"Maybe if we don't talk about leaving, we won't have to, and this night can last the rest of our lives. Maybe this doesn't ever have to end."

"Maybe." They crossed the street onto the next block. "Is this going to be any easier if I leave now, or wait a few more hours?"

"Ask me that in a few hours' time." They walked on. The questions were burning his tongue and finally he broke. "So will you come to Jersey to see me? Maybe you could stay a while, a few years at least anyway." He knew she could see the rueful smile on his face. "Last time we saw each other, on that jetty in Jersey eleven years ago, you said that next time we met, the next time we saw each other would be to get married."

"That does sound wonderful, but you know I'm married to someone else now."

"Why should that stop you?"

"I . . . I don't know, Christopher. Who knows if we're even meant to be together anymore?"

"Meant to be? What does that mean? I thought you didn't believe in fate. I asked you that years ago."

"I remember. That seems like five lifetimes ago."

"I'm not going to push this. You know who I am now. You know what you want. Only you can choose what you're going to do. I can't force you, and I certainly wouldn't want to."

"I can't just go back to Jersey tonight and be a wife to you, a mother to your daughter."

"Marriage is your thing, Rebecca, not mine. We don't have to get married." He smiled and saw her smiling too, but it faded quickly.

They walked on in silence for the longest minute he could remember.

"I should leave now. It must be getting late," she said as a taxi whirled past.

He looked at his watch. It was almost one a.m., but he put his hand into his pocket without saying anything. She raised her arm to flag down a taxi, and he knew that they had only seconds together now.

She turned to him. "Leaving you again is the last thing in the world I want to do, but I have to do it. I have to go." He went to her and took her in his arms. He felt her against him as if he could take an imprint of her on his body. "I love you, Christopher, I always have. I never stopped and I never will." He had his hands on either side of her neck. She broke away and held out her arm for a taxi and it pulled up.

She hugged him again, and he resisted the feelings inside him driving him to kiss her. She was staring at him, the door to the taxi open now. They held each other's gazes for a few seconds. She took his hand, then let it go and got into the taxi. He was holding the door. He reached down and kissed her on the cheek. "I'll be waiting for you, Rebecca," he said, and closed the door. The taxi pulled away, her face in the back window fading into the night.

---

The sky was silver, the dull November light leaking through the gap in the curtains as Christopher awoke alone in his bed. The sound of Hannah and the two Stefans downstairs at breakfast filtered through the wooden floorboards, mingling with the whistle of the wind through the trees outside. It was nine o'clock on a Saturday morning, and he was the last one up. He drew himself out of bed. It had been better in the months since he'd seen Rebecca. The nightmares had lessened. He made his way into the bathroom and looked at himself. The flecks of gray were coming through in his stubble. He laughed and shook his head. He was looking more like his father every day. Ten minutes later he was downstairs in the kitchen with his father, his cousin, and his daughter, and it was she who spoke up as he walked in.

"Something arrived for you this morning, hand delivered." The letter was sitting in the middle of the kitchen table. "I wanted to open it up for you, but Grandfather told me not to."

Christopher tore the letter open and took out a single sheet folded in half. There were only seven words written on it.

"Who is it from?" Hannah asked. Christopher's father was in the corner, making tea. Little Stefan was seated at the table, eating his breakfast. Christopher looked through the back window at the old tree house. His heart was a raging sea.

"Who's the letter from?" his father asked.

He handed the piece of paper to his father. "I want you all to come with me. I want all of us to be there." His father read the letter, letting it drop to the table as he finished it. Hannah picked it up.

"What does this mean?" she asked. *"Gunde de viznay bin Butterfly's Table nuen?* What language is that? Does that even mean anything?"

"It means that she's here, that she's come home," Christopher said.

As they rounded the corner to the beach where the iron sea was boiling back and forth, where the sand turned to pebbles, the rocks of the Butterfly's Table came into view, and she was standing there, silhouetted against the sky, and turned to him, a deep smile on her face and the wind in her hair.

# ACKNOWLEDGMENTS

Writing *Finding Rebecca* was a fascinating, often sobering experience. It was an amazing journey that began when I was a new immigrant to the United States and still continues to this day with the wonderful e-mails, reviews, and other correspondence I get from readers all over the world. I have a few people to thank, people who helped me along the way by believing in me, encouraging me, or just putting up with me. First is my wife, Jill, who gave me all the love and support I ever needed. I want to thank my wonderful in-laws, Carol and Ed McDuell, whose constant support was invaluable, particularly when I was unemployed and living with them during the first draft of the book. Huge thanks to Dan Gallagher, Kevin Strunk, Susan Robbins, Brett Carty, Chet Czulada, Floyd Johnson, and Jason Fischer of the writers group in Ambler, Pennsylvania, who journeyed with me through Christopher and Rebecca's story weekly for almost eighteen months. Thanks to my agent, Byrd Leavell, for all the work that he put in and to William Callahan who discovered me. Massive thanks to Jodi Warshaw, my wonderful editor at Lake Union, for finding me and being so fantastic to work with, as well to Thom Kephart, who helped me get this book to you. People like Chelsea and Brian Barrish, Betsy and DJ Frimmer, Jackie Kosbob, and Kate Brandon were always a massive support and helped me get through any hard times I might have had. A huge thank you to Emmy Sponseller and the members of the St. Croix book club who had the courage to read one of my earliest drafts. My love and gratitude go out to Orla and Anne Dempsey, to Eileen and Brendan Balfe, Mick Dunphy, Nicola Hogan, Shane Mitchell, Jack Layden, Yvonne Cullen, Yvonne Cassidy, Gerry Mitchell, and everyone else in Dublin who have been reading my books since 1999. Your support over the years has been invaluable and has helped me massively on my own journey toward becoming the writer I one day hope to be.

# ABOUT *the* AUTHOR

Eoin Dempsey was born and raised in Dublin, Ireland. He moved to Philadelphia in 2008, where he works as a teacher and lives with his wonderful wife. *Finding Rebecca* is his first novel.